TALLOW

Rosemary

MJ Howson

ENGINE ❶❸

THE **TALLOW** SERIES

Published by Engine Thirteen

ISBN-13: 978-0-9996166-5-9

Cover design by MJ Howson

Other books by MJ Howson

The Tallow Series:

Tallow – An Urban Legend (Book 1)

for Mom

PROLOGUE

Blood runs warm through the bonds of love and family. Blood runs tepid when faced with loss and neglect. Blood runs cold when it clings to the sins of hate and betrayal. Blood runs. Blood runs. Blood runs.

Urban Legends of Cape Cod

Author – Unknown

ONE

Innocence

The body of the child formed a near perfect arch. It was perched midair, suspended in front of an old wooden ladder. The pitchfork, locked in place between the weathered rungs, held the young girl up almost as a sacrifice. Each of the six rusted prongs had pierced her back, with one of the spikes tearing through her thoracic spine at the T6 vertebrae. Had the inquisitive four-year-old somehow survived the fall, she would have spent her life as a paraplegic. Her body twitched as she hopelessly tried to pull herself up. An impossible task, given that she was almost six feet off the floor, impaled on a pitchfork. With her head hanging upside down, she fixed her gaze on her father, wondering why he was holding a long knife. She attempted to call out "Daddy," but all that could be exhaled were coughs of blood. Her shuddering stopped. Slowly her eyes rolled back in her head. Her breathing slowed. Her heart pounded once ... twice ... and she was gone.

Her father stood in stunned silence. His eyes inspected his daughter's tortured body. A trail of blood had slowly worked its way down the young child's right arm and dripped onto the floor of the barn. The hay beneath her began to change from a soft auburn glow to a bright shade of burgundy. The stain

2

expanded with each small drop of blood that fell.

His hand gripped a 12" long knife like a vice clamp. He managed to pry his eyes from his dead daughter to inspect his hands. Much like hers, they too were dripping in blood. He opened his hand slightly to study the handle of the nickel and turquoise inlaid knife he had recently made. *How could this have happened?*

"It was an accident," he finally muttered. "They must all know this was an accident."

These words were spoken to no one, as he was now the only person alive in the family barn. Suddenly the silence was broken by the sound of feet scuffing across the yard outside the barn. His heart pounded harder and harder in his chest until the side door finally opened.

"Jennifer went to the pond to get the girls," Laura Johnson said as she entered the barn. "The food is ready. What's ..."

Laura stopped roughly three feet into the barn. The site of the young girl with the white and yellow dress speared through the pitchfork shocked her. At first, she thought it was some kind of trick. Perhaps a game. Then she saw the blood and realized what had happened. The scream that came from her was shrill, deafening, and filled with despair.

Laura collapsed to her knees, covering her eyes as the tears fell mercilessly and without hesitation. She quickly regained her focus and directed it toward the man holding the deadly blood-soaked knife. She glared at him in anger.

"What have you done, Fred?" Laura screamed. "What on earth have you done?"

TWO

Haunted

Julie Perez could not escape the chill that was surrounding her. She pulled her knees up toward her chest as she slid her head under the white woven cotton blanket draped across her bed. Beads of sweat formed on her brow, just below the knit hat that covered her head. She descended further under the layers of shelter until all that remained exposed was the bright purple pom-pom on the top of her hat.

My hands are so cold, Julie thought to herself. She looked at her hands. They were wrapped in tight leather purple gloves. She held them to her mouth and blew hard against them to try and warm them. It was useless. Even her breath was ice cold.

Hiding beneath the covers did nothing to ease the panic that had started to consume her. Although she was alone in her bed, she knew she was not alone in the room. Julie's heart began to pound in her chest. She knew it was only a matter of time before she heard ... A loud creak broke the silence in the room. The creak came from the floorboards. After a brief pause, there was another creak. The sound that had started at her bedroom door was slowly getting closer to her.

Julie went to breathe into her hands again and was surprised to see they were now holding a book. Suddenly a warm yellow flickering glow appeared under the bed covers.

Julie looked around in a panic as her heart pounded harder and harder in her chest. The light was everywhere, but she could not tell where it was coming from. She turned her attention back to the book in her hands and looked at the cover – "Urban Legends of Cape Cod."

How is this here?

Another creak from the floorboards, this time from the far corner of her bed.

As she ran her hands across the corners of the book, she realized it had a large gash in the binding.

Another creak. This one was right next to her side of the bed.

Julie realized she was no longer wearing her gloves. The light that was glowing under her covers began to fluctuate rapidly, going from total darkness to a bright white. The flashing increased in speed, taking on a strobe effect. She ran her fingernail across the gash in the binding. Blood started to pour from the slit.

Without warning, the covers flew off the bed. The bedroom was filled with dozens of candles. They were scattered everywhere, from the floor to the window sills and on top of all of the furniture. Each candle was the same flip top glass jar design. Stickers on each candle read "FlickerWood Candles." The scent of sesame wafting from the candles was intense. Julie gasped for fresh air, as the aroma became suffocating.

Julie looked around, shocked at how many candles surrounded her. As she shifted her gaze across the four walls, she suddenly realized she was no longer alone.

Standing next to her was the woman that had attacked her in the townhome in Provincetown four months ago. She was wearing the exact same clothes from that dreadful night. Julie tried to scream for help, but she was in shock, unable to utter a single sound.

The woman slowly removed her hand from her pocket, revealing a shiny sharp dagger. She held it in the palm of her hand so that Julie could inspect the nickel and turquoise inlay of the wood handle. The shimmer from the candles reflected off the blade as she let it roll across the palm of her hand. The woman snatched the dagger with her other hand and held it high above her head. She looked at Julie and smiled. Her face began to melt as if it was made of wax.

"Time to pay!" whispered the disfigured woman as she plunged the dagger down toward Julie.

Julie immediately held her hands up to block the knife. She still had the book to use to defend herself. The book was now dry. The blood that had been dripping from it was gone. Her purple leather gloves were back on her hands. Julie thrust both arms out with all of her might, holding the book up as a shield.

The blade from the dagger came down hard and fast, tearing through the book and splitting it in half. The steel tip continued its descent until it plunged directly into Julie's throat.

"No!" Julie screamed as she flung her covers away and sat bolt upright in her bed.

Julie looked around her bedroom in a panic. Her entire body was drenched in an icy cold sweat. It took a moment for reality to set in. No candles were burning. No woman standing over her bed. There was only her cat – Mr. Fluffy – laying across her ankles looking very upset that she had woken him up.

"Fuck!" Julie cried out.

Julie looked at the clock on her nightstand. It was 4:18 a.m. She flicked on the lamp next to her bed and rubbed her eyes. There was no way she was going to get back to sleep after that nightmare.

"This is going to be a long workday," Julie said. "At least it's Friday."

Mr. Fluffy rolled over and began to lick his feet.

Julie pulled her legs out from under her cat and swung them onto the floor. She was wearing pink and white striped flannel pajama bottoms and a white T-shirt with a collection of various sized pink and red hearts scattered across the front. There was a thick cotton red sweater hanging from her bedpost. Julie sluggishly put it on. She then pulled her mangled Zombunny slippers onto her feet and made her way to the kitchen. Mr. Fluffy stayed behind.

It was a crisp April morning. Julie cranked the thermostat

up to 70 before heading to the kitchen. She pressed her face against the window and looked out at the darkness. The cold glass only contributed to her discomfort. A cup of hot cocoa was called for. It felt like the comfort she needed after that horrible dream. A dream that, unfortunately, had been haunting her for many months.

Mr. Fluffy casually made his way into the kitchen and watched as Julie put a mug filled with water into the microwave. She set the timer for two minutes. The cat jumped up onto a small square maple table in the open kitchen. He quietly observed Julie retrieve a packet of instant cocoa mix from her pantry.

"It was four months ago," Julie said to her cat. "Four months!"

Julie shook her head and grabbed a spoon from several utensils that were sitting in the drying rack next to her sink. The beep of the microwave brought the faintest of smiles to her face. She pulled the mug out and set it on the counter.

The mug was from a trip her and Tom had taken in the summer of 2015. It was one of those last minute four-day weekend escapes. It was a white mug adorned "Orlando" in blue letters.

Julie mixed the cocoa powder into the mug and carried it over to the kitchen table. She pushed her laptop aside and set the cup down a couple of feet from Mr. Fluffy. He gave it a curious look but did not approach it. The heat felt great in her hands.

"Why can't I shake this?" she said as she stared at Mr. Fluffy. "Why can't I move on? Why do these nightmares keep coming back?"

Mr. Fluffy extended his front legs and laid down flat across the table. He began to purr.

"And why the fuck am I asking *you*?" Julie asked with frustration.

Mr. Fluffy rolled to his side and stretched. Julie reached over and slowly ran her fingers across the back of his neck. It was his favorite. She took a small sip of cocoa.

"It's too early to call Tom," Julie said. "Although I wouldn't be surprised if he's awake as well. Who is up at this hour?"

Mr. Fluffy did not respond. Julie looked over at the coat hook rail next to the front door of her apartment. Her winter hat dangled from the hanger on the left end. The multi-colored hand knit hat was upside down, with its purple pom-pom pointing toward the ground.

A huge grin spread across Julie's face. She flipped open her laptop and waited for it to wake up.

"We're calling Yaya," Julie said.

Her grandmother, or yiayiá, lived in a small town on the island of Santorini, Greece. It would be mid-morning there. Julie and her grandmother had started video chatting a few years ago. Julie was very impressed that her grandmother was so high tech. They typically connected once a month, usually on a Sunday morning. Ever since the incident in Provincetown last December, however, Julie had only reached out to her twice.

Julie waited patiently as the word "Connecting" flashed across her screen. She glanced over at the dangling hat and wondered if she would have time to put it on. It might make for a cute surprise to be wearing it when the call connected. The screen cleared and a pixelated image of her smiling grandmother came into view.

"Tzoúli!" Helen Perez cried out through the laptop.

Julie quickly reached for the volume control to lower it. Mr. Fluffy squinted his eyes and stared at the back of the screen.

"Hi, Yaya," replied Julie. "Am I disturbing you?"

"You are never a disturbance. Never! I'm cooking. See?"

Helen spun her phone around, aiming the camera at her kitchen. The countertops were covered with a variety of vegetables, including different colored peppers and mounds of fresh herbs.

"It looks great. What are you making?"

Helen maneuvered her way into the kitchen. She did her best to keep the phone angled so that Julie could see all the food she had out. Once at the stove her grandmother opened up a covered pot filled with ice and shoved her hand in. Helen smiled as she pulled out a long purple tentacle.

"Grilled calamari!" Helen said as she dropped it back into the crock. "There is a big family gathering this weekend. You have so much family here. So many that you don't even know."

"I know, Yaya."

Helen walked over to the door next to the kitchen and stepped out onto her patio. The views of the ocean from her hillside villa were stunning. She propped the phone up against a potted plant on a mosaic tile table and took a seat across from the camera.

"You need to meet Adrian," Helen said with a wide smile. "Handsome. Wealthy. He's single you know."

"I can't date a cousin! Or is that allowed in Greece?"

"Oh no, no, no," Helen said as she laughed. "Adrian is family, but ..." She paused to think through how to explain it. "We are a big family. I am not sure how to describe it to you. He comes from my sister's husband side of the family. So, he is not ... not ... not a blood cousin. Is that right? Did I say that right? Did I mention he is wealthy?"

"You did," Julie said with a chuckle. She took a long sip of cocoa. Her grandmother always made her smile. "It's sweet of you to think of me, but right now dating is the last thing on my mind. And Greece would be a bit of a commute."

"Nonsense, he has a plane. And ..." Helen paused as she studied her granddaughter's face. "What time is it there? It must be early. Is everything alright?"

"It's fine. I just couldn't sleep."

"Tzoúli, I know all about what happened in December. Your father told me. All of it."

Julie clenched her grip around her mug as she lowered it to the table. She had explicitly told her parents not to talk about the events that had occurred.

"Yaya, you weren't supposed to know."

"You are just like him. You both think I can't handle bad news. If either of you knew half the adventures that I had in my youth, you would be shocked. But don't be mad at your father. I made him tell me. You have been so distant these past few months. So secretive. I had to find out what was going on. So, tell me, how are you?"

Julie was sort of relieved to know that she had another person she could now confide in. Every time she reached out to her parents for emotional support, their reaction was to insist she seek professional counseling to deal with her pain and grief. Julie refused to talk to anyone at work about it. Tom had been her only shoulder to lean on.

"It's been harder than I thought it would be," Julie said. "So, what did dad tell you? I know you said he told you everything, but …"

"He told me you and three friends went out to Cape Cod in early December. A vacation weekend away. Two of them – I forgot their names – went missing. A woman showed up at the place you were staying and tried to kill you. Kill you! I still can't … Your good friend Tom saved you, but the woman got away. They still haven't found the bodies of your friends or the woman."

"Wow. That … that pretty much says it all."

"I told you I made him tell me all of it. Everything. I don't like secrets."

"Well, dad doesn't know everything. I never told him about my dreams."

"Dreams?"

Julie took another long sip of her cocoa.

"I have this recurring nightmare, Yaya. It's that woman attacking me all over again. Last December I used a book to block the dagger. It sort of saved me before Tom could tackle her. In my dream, the book fails to protect me. Instead, the dagger goes right through it. And then it … it goes …"

Julie lowered her head, trying to hold back the tears. Helen watched from almost 5,000 miles away. She felt so helpless seeing her granddaughter so sad and broken.

"And then I wake up," Julie finally said. "Usually screaming. The dreams don't happen all of the time. I … I just want them to go away."

Helen tapped her fingers on the blue and white mosaic table as she searched for some sort of advice to give.

"I think you need some closure," Helen said. "That's why you feel so haunted. In your mind, it really hasn't ended. Maybe when they find your missing friends? Or the woman that attacked you?"

"I really don't know. To be honest, I don't think the cops will ever find the bodies. Or the killer. Not if the urban legend is true."

"Urban legend?"

"Dad didn't tell you that part?"

"No. I don't remember him saying anything about a legend."

Mr. Fluffy jumped down to the floor and sauntered over to Julie. With one quick thrust, he was up and on her lap. He curled up beneath The Girls as she began to stroke his neck.

"Dad bought me this book about urban legends in Cape Cod. I brought it on the trip. Just for laughs. But one of the legends, Yaya, it was ... it was so similar to what happened to all of us. The candles. The attack. Even what the woman said. It was so odd. So disturbing. In the legend, the killers always escape."

"Your father should know better than to give you a crazy book like that. Do you still have it? The book."

"It's gone. The woman that tried to kill me took it."

"How strange."

"There was no evidence of anything. We never even got her name. Tom and I call her Mrs. Closed."

"Urban legends are dreadful tales. Greece is filled with ancient myths. Trust me, some stories are best left lost and forgotten. Buried."

Julie took another long sip of her cocoa. It was almost empty.

"You know what you need, Tzoúli?" Helen continued. "You know what will rid you of these nightmares? A vacation to spend time with family."

Helen picked up her phone and turned it outward. She slowly panned it across the horizon. Julie stared in awe at the breathtaking view that scrolled across her screen. Her grandmother's home was on a hillside that looked out across the Aegean Sea. Its deep azure waters sparkled under the brilliant sun shining down from above.

"It's wonderful," Julie said with a smile.

Helen turned the phone around and propped it back up against the potted plant.

"You need to be far away," Helen said. "Far away from all of those horrors. Bring your friend Tom as well. You have so

11

much family here. So much love. And Adrian. Don't forget about him. You need to be elsewhere, my dearest kósmima."

Julie loved that her grandmother called her a jewel.

"I promise we will, Yaya. Someday."

"Not just someday. Soon!"

"Yes, soon. It looks like you have a lot of cooking to do. That squid isn't about to grill itself. Thank you so much for listening."

"I'm always here for you. Sending you much love across the ocean."

Helen leaned forward and kissed her phone before disconnecting the call. Julie looked down at her cat.

"She's right about one thing, Mr. Fluffy. We definitely need to be elsewhere."

Julie's phone chimed. The text message brought a smile to her face.

You up, Jewels? Still on for dinner tonight?

She quickly responded.

Totally! TGIF!!! So glad the weekend is here.

Tom replied.

Ditto on that, Jewels.

THREE

Clues

The deadbolt on Tom Leblanc's condo snapped open. Max pushed the door away with his nose and leaped into the hallway, finally free from his leash. The dog spun around two times and then sat down waiting for Tom to come in. Tom smiled as he stepped inside and put Max's leash onto the small table next to his front door. It was the same routine every night after their evening walk. Max's long tail was wagging back and forth across the rug in the front hallway. His ears were standing straight up as he waited for his master to speak.

"Is it dinner time?" Tom asked.

Max jumped up onto Tom, landing his paws right below his chest. Tom grabbed them and pushed his dog away. The German Shepherd mix took off down the hallway and came to a halt next to the pantry in the corner of the kitchen. Tom kicked his shoes off and quickly followed his dog, pausing next to him to give his ears a quick rub. Max tilted his head back and used his snout to push Tom's hand away.

"Alright already," Tom said.

He opened the pantry and pulled out Max's chrome dog bowl. Max began to lick his lips as Tom took a scoop of kibble from a plastic container in the pantry and poured it into the dish. Tom dropped the bowl onto the floor and Max immediately dove in and began to devour his meal.

"You should try chewing it," Tom said. "Instead of just inhaling it. I swear they should have named you 'Hoover' instead."

Tom pulled his phone from his pocket to see if he had any updates. Julie was due at his place any minute now. The screen on his phone showed no notifications. He stared at the image he had set as his lock screen. The photo was taken last December in Provincetown. The picture was of he, Julie, Chris, and Marc. He looked at Marc's brown eyes and contemplated what might have been.

The sound of Max gulping down his water broke Tom's trance. Tom figured it had taken Max all of 30 seconds to suck down his meal. After drinking half the bowl of water, Max took off down the hallway to the living room. A basket filled with dog toys sat in the far corner of the room. He began sorting through them, tossing some aside as he searched for tonight's toy of choice. Tom quickly refilled the dog's water dish with fresh water.

Max returned to the kitchen with a short six-inch long rope with a canvas ball attached to the end. He dropped it at Tom's feet. Tom whipped it down the hallway to the front door. Max ran to get it and quickly brought it back. It was the same routine each evening. Walk. Dinner. Water. Toys.

Tom's phone rang. The ringtone was the *Imperial March* from Star Wars. He frowned as he answered it.

"Hi Mom," Tom said.

"How's my baby doing tonight?" asked Mrs. Leblanc.

Tom winced. Even after twenty-nine years she still called him "her baby."

"I'm fine, Mom," Tom replied. He attempted to sound interested, but his tone was flat and detached. "The same as last night and the night before that. You don't need to worry."

"I do need to worry! I can hear it in your voice."

"I'm just tired, Mom."

"That's because you're still obsessed with everything that happened out on the Cape. You need to let it go and move forward. You keep contacting that police detective out there. You need to let them do their job, Thomas. You aren't a cop."

Tom squeezed the phone in anger.

"I'm well aware of that. Julie just got here. We are heading out to dinner. I need to go."

Tom picked up the toy resting at his feet and flung it down the hallway for Max to chase. Julie was nowhere around, but it was the only way he could think of to end the call.

"Are you driving? Don't drink and drive."

"Julie is driving."

"Well make sure she doesn't drink."

"Of course."

"Love you."

"Love you too."

Tom ended the call and looked for a possible missed notification from Julie. Still nothing. He flung the toy back down the hall. Max immediately raced for it.

Tom debated texting Julie to see where she was but decided to wait. His laptop was on the kitchen table. He flipped it open took a seat at the table. Tom opened his browser and searched for "Cape Cod candle stores."

Max tapped Tom on his knee and looked down at the toy sitting at his feet. Tom whipped it back down the hall.

The search online returned the same list it always did. He wasn't surprised, but part of him kept hoping that someday there would be a new entry. He modified his search to "Cape Cod FlickerWood candles." The results were also of no value.

Tom reached down to pick up Max's rope and ball. Max and the toy were not there. He looked down the hallway, and it was empty. Max began yelping from the living room. The deadbolt snapped open. Max ran to the front door just as Julie opened it.

"Max! Max! Max!" Julie yelled.

Max jumped up onto Julie, his front paws digging at her chest.

"Mind The Girls, buddy!" Julie said as she dropped to her knees and began to massage Max's ears. Max recoiled slightly and began to sniff her thighs. "You smell Mr. Fluffy, don't you? He was all over me tonight."

"Hey Jewels," Tom called out from the kitchen. "Umbrella?"

Julie waved her umbrella as she dropped it onto the floor.

She stood up and shook her hair out.

"It started raining like a bitch right after I left my apartment. I had to run back and grab an umbrella."

Julie took her jacket off and tossed it onto a chair in the living room. "What are you doing?" she asked as she entered the kitchen.

Tom spun his laptop so she could see the screen.

"Really, Tom?" Julie asked. "You are so obsessed with playing detective."

"You sound like my mom."

"How dare you! That's an insult. Is that wine open?"

Julie laughed as she walked past Tom and stopped at the island in the kitchen. Tom had a bottle of pinot noir sitting in the corner.

"Screw-top?" Julie asked in bemusement. "It must have been on sale."

"Buy one get one free."

Julie cracked the cap open and grabbed two glasses.

"Do you have any cheese?"

"No, sorry Jewels."

"You are wasting your time with those searches, Tom. You need to listen to me. Those candles are part of that urban legend. You won't find them in a store."

"There must be more of them out there, Jewels. Somewhere."

Julie finished filling the two glasses with wine and brought them over to the table. She sat down next to Tom.

"You used white wine glasses. You should have used the larger ones. They are off to the side in the cabinet."

"Seriously? It's going to be gone in less than five minutes. Just suck it down and don't be so anal about the glassware."

Julie held up her glass and nodded toward Tom. He nodded back. They clinked them together.

"My point about the candles, Tom, is that you should try and look elsewhere."

"Like where?"

"Those candles were taken from the store, right? Nobody has ever heard of them either. It was a one-time thing. What if they had set up shop elsewhere and sold some before?"

"They?"

"Mrs. Closed. And her mother. Remember she talked about her mother?"

"So, what are you suggesting?"

Julie drummed her fingers across the side of her glass and looked around Tom's kitchen. Everything was immaculate and perfectly placed. There was absolutely no clutter.

"Try searching for something like a yard sale," Julie replied. "Maybe a garage sale. Even an estate sale."

Tom entered a few different search parameters into his browser, trying to find Cape Cod sales that included candles. The results were inconsistent. He quickly grew frustrated.

"This might be something I need to do tomorrow," Tom said. "I can see this taking forever."

"Needle in a haystack, right?"

"Huge haystack."

Julie scanned down the list of links on the screen. She took a long sip of wine and gradually lowered her glass as one of the links caught her eye.

"Tom, try that one. Third up from the bottom."

Tom looked at the link. It was for an estate sale. The description included a list of different items including lamps, tables, candles, and artwork. He clicked the link. A new tab opened and the screen quickly filled with thumbnails of different images.

"Can you make the pictures full sized?" Julie asked.

Tom began to navigate through the rows of pictures. The image quality was poor, and the lighting was dull. Most of the images seemed to be paintings. Some were of individual lamps. One had a table with metal candle holders on it, but there were no actual candles. Tom began to click faster.

"Wait," Julie said. "Go back."

Tom clicked back. It was a picture of a table with a dark blue blanket over it. The table had two thin wrought-iron lamps and a small pewter candle.

"What am I looking at, Jewels?"

"Call me crazy, but look at the table leg sticking out from the blanket. Can you zoom in?"

With a couple of keystrokes, Tom was able to zoom into the

lower right corner of the picture. The image was blurry, but it was also quite clear in a different way.

"Holy shit ... Jewels isn't that ..."

"Oh my God!" Julie said, her voice dropping to a faint whisper. "It's the table from the store. Isn't it?"

"That pattern ... the metal and the blue inlay."

Tom and Julie sat in silence staring at the image. The dark blue blanket covered everything except the lower half of one leg of the table. The foot at the base of the leg had a few inches of inlay. It was the same unique pattern as the table they had come across in the store in Truro last December. The same table that had crashed to the ground, kicking off the nightmare that would soon follow them back to the townhomes of Seabreeze Village.

"I thought it would be hard to find those candles," Julie said. "I never thought we would find the table."

Tom clicked a few more times to zoom in closer. It only made the image more pixilated.

"That's it, Jewels. It has to be!"

"Are you positive."

"I ... I think so. I remember how unique that inlay was." Tom squinted at the picture again. "I don't know. I mean. This image is not that clear. There is definitely a metal and blue inlay going on."

Julie stared at the jagged pattern on the screen. The silver trim was slim on three sides and thicker on one end. In the middle was a bright blue filler. She closed her eyes and pictured the dagger from her nightmare.

"Maybe it's our imagination," Julie said. "We're seeing what we want to see. That image is really blurry."

"Well, there is only one way to find out. What if it's just a reflection or something stuck on it?"

Tom aimed his cursor at the address and phone number listed on the top of the screen. He picked up his phone and began to dial. Julie snatched the phone from his hand.

"Are you crazy?" Julie cried. "What if ... what if Mrs. Closed answers?"

"What if," Tom said with a smile. He grabbed the phone back from Julie. "Wow, your hands are soft."

"Cocoa butter. I'm addicted to it. I don't think you should call."

Tom ignored Julie and dialed the number listed on the screen. As it rang he put the phone on Speaker. He went back and looked at the location information on his screen. The property was in Eastham, Massachusetts.

Julie realized her wine was empty and poured herself another half glass. Suddenly the ringing of the call ended.

"Hello?" asked a woman's voice.

Tom and Julie stared at each other in silence.

"Hello?" asked the voice again.

"Hi," Tom finally said. "I'm calling about your ad for the estate sale. I see it's this weekend?"

"Yes, noon to five both days."

Julie hit the Mute button on the phone.

"It doesn't sound like Mrs. Closed, does it?" Julie asked. Tom nodded in agreement and then unmuted the phone.

"OK great," Tom said. "I was looking at the pictures online. You have a lot of great stuff."

"Thank you."

"I was curious about the table in one of the pictures."

"Table? Oh yes. I only have a couple for sale. They are a matching set. The metal and glass ones, right?"

"No, no. This was a different one. You have some metal lamps sitting on a blue blanket. There is a table under the blanket."

"A table under a blanket?"

"Yes. You can only see the bottom of it. The leg is rather interesting. It looks like metal and maybe turquoise."

Julie punched Tom in his shoulder.

"Oh, that table. Well yes, actually, it is nickel and turquoise. It was that obvious from the picture?"

"Just a guess," Tom replied. He looked over at Julie. She was shaking her head and mouthed the word "idiot" to him.

"It's not for sale. That's why I had the blanket on it. Would you be interested in the other tables? Or maybe the lamps?"

"Maybe. I will have to get back to you."

"Well if you have any questions feel free to call again."

"Sure thing. Thanks."

Tom ended the call.

"Oh my God!" Julie yelled. "Nickel and turquoise! That has to be it. It has to be!"

"Right?"

"Tom, why the hell were you so specific with the inlay?"

"Sorry Jewels, I wasn't thinking. I got caught up in the rush. That wasn't her, though, was it? That wasn't Mrs. Closed."

"You're right. Totally different voice."

"So, you know what happens now, don't you?"

"What?"

Tom pointed to the Eastham address on the top of the screen.

"Fuck me!" Julie said. "We are not going out to the Cape to that estate sale. Are you crazy?"

"Hear me out."

"No. Never! We need to be elsewhere. Both your mom and my ya-ya said the same thing. I talked with her this morning on a video chat. She wants us to come to Greece. I'm starting to think she was right. Anywhere but Cape Cod."

Tom held his phone up so Julie could see the image of the four of them holding their red plastic cups.

"Greece can wait, Jewels. This needs to be our focus. Finding that woman that attacked us and killed our friends."

Julie's cheeks were flush with blood as her heart pounded in her chest. The thought of going to Cape Cod terrified her. She shook her head as she stared at the picture on Tom's phone.

"I can't believe you still have that on your phone. How can you look at that every day? We have to move on. Put Max back on there as your image."

Max had been sprawled out in the hallway chewing on his toy. His ears shot up at the sound of his name. He jumped up and ran to Julie. She began to massage his ears.

"I can't even go through all of the pictures I have," Julie said. "There are too many. Too many memories. When I start to look at them I just ... I just can't relive it all."

"Too many? You sent them all to me after we got back. There were only a dozen or so."

"No, Tom. There are dozens. I only sent you a handful of

them."

"Why?"

"Why? Because I knew you would obsess like you are right now!"

"Show me."

Julie pulled her phone from her jeans and reluctantly scrolled through her photos. After a few seconds, she stopped and passed the phone to Tom.

"Here," she sighed.

Tom began to flip through the pictures. His emotions fluctuated as each image slid by. Many of the photos were of them unloading Marc's truck and setting all of the boxes into the condo. Suddenly an image appeared of Julie with a buff guy in a red thong and a Santa hat.

"The Jingle Bell Run!" Tom said with a laugh. "I totally forgot about that."

The photos were in chronological order, and Tom soon found himself looking at the images from the candle store. Julie had taken a great picture of him and Marc together at the back wall. She had sent him that one. The next few were ones of Julie and Chris in the store. Tom stopped at the last one of Chris and zoomed in.

"Jewels, look at this."

"Chris," Julie said with a heavy sigh. "That one was blurry. I know you two didn't get along, Tom, but we were having so much fun ..."

"No. Look behind her."

Tom zoomed deeper into the picture. Behind Chris was the table with the candles on it. Standing next to the table was Mrs. Closed.

"Oh my God," Julie said in astonishment. "It's her."

Tom zoomed in a bit more.

"It's a crappy picture. Worse than the one of the table we found online. You really can't make much out."

Julie took a long sip of wine. She closed her eyes and briefly remembered the woman standing over the toppled table and shattered candles, screaming at them.

Tom sent the picture to his cell phone. He then duplicated it and cropped it and did his best to clean up the image.

"What are you doing?" Julie asked.

"I'm sending it to Officer Stevens in Provincetown."

"Why?"

Tom fired off the email to the police officer that had helped them the night of the attack. He then dialed the cop's phone.

"Who are you calling?"

Tom put the phone on Speaker and placed it on the table.

"Hello Tom," Officer Stevens said. "What can I do for you this time?"

"It's more like what I can do for you," Tom replied. "Check your email."

"Hi Trevor," Julie said.

"Hello Julie, it's nice to hear your voice."

Julie hit the Mute button.

"He's so damn sexy," Julie cooed as she smiled at Tom. "Even his voice."

"Oh, I bet you would go to the Cape for *him*."

"Now you're talking," Julie said as she started to laugh.

"OK Tom, I've got your email. What am I looking at?"

Tom unmuted the phone.

"That's the killer," Tom said.

"The killer?" Officer Stevens replied. "This blurry picture?"

"We found it on my phone," Julie said. "That's the woman that attacked me at the Seabreeze Village condo. And most likely killed our friends."

"Tom this is very blurry. I don't know what good this will do."

"Well, I wanted to send it anyway. Every clue helps, right?"

"Of course."

"We found another one as well. We are going to check it out tomorrow."

Julie punched Tom in the shoulder again.

"What are you talking about?" Officer Stevens asked. His tone had turned from bemusement to concern.

"We came across a table at a yard sale. The table looks like the one that the candles were on. You can even see the table in that picture I sent you."

"Tom, all I see is a round wooden table. With candles."

"It's the legs. You can't see them in the picture. They have this unique nickel and turquoise inlay. This yard sale has a similar table. Well, we think it's the same. It's hard to tell from the blurry picture."

"Tom, I don't want you to go chasing some wild theory about a table, OK?"

"But ..."

"But nothing!" Officer Stevens voice went up in volume by several decibels. "It's been four months. There are multiple missing person investigations underway. You send me a blurry image of this woman that you want me to chase, while you chase a blurry image of a table. You need to stop. Let it go."

Officer Trevor Stevens paused and waited for a response. After several seconds he continued. "You are not to play detective and chase down clues. Remember, Tom, I have all of your contact information. Don't think I won't call your mother and tell her what you are planning."

Tom stared in shock at the phone. Julie started to laugh and had to walk away covering her mouth.

"Do we have an understanding, Tom?"

"Yes. Sorry, Officer. Goodbye."

Tom ended the call.

"Oh my God, even Trevor knows the power your mom has over you! That's priceless. Let me pee, and then we can get going."

Julie walked into the bathroom and closed the door.

Tom looked at the blurry image of Mrs. Closed and set it as the new image for his phone's lock screen. He then copied the address for the estate sale and saved it to his phone. He was determined to go to Eastham, with or without Julie.

FOUR

Dinner

Federal Hill, in Providence Rhode Island, was the city's very own "Little Italy." The area was spread across a section of Atwells Avenue and occupied a tiny part of the capital city. Atwells ran just west of Interstate 95. Some of the best restaurants and delis were scattered across roughly two dozen blocks. If you wanted the most exquisite Italian food in the state, chances are you would find it here.

Tom and Julie were seated at Primitivo. It was one of the newest restaurants in town. Johnson and Wales University – affectionately known as J&W – was located on the other side of the highway, not far from Federal Hill. The college regularly produced a stream of highly skilled chefs looking to make their mark on the city. Primitivo was the genius creation of Anthony Bonardi. Anthony already owned two other highly rated restaurants in town. However, this was his first to open in Federal Hill. He was proud of his staff, many fresh out of J&W. The menu was an innovative take on traditional Italian dishes, served up in a low-carb, low-sugar fare. He was primarily catering to the Paleo crowd. Traditional pasta dishes and loaves of bread were nowhere to be found.

Julie glanced through her menu, scanning for her favorites.

"Most of the pasta dishes are made with spiraled zucchini," Julie commented. "And where is the bread?"

"It's healthy style Italian, Jewels."

Julie took a sip of her pinot noir. They had ordered the wine as soon as they had sat down earlier.

"Call me old fashioned," Julie said, "but I would just love a slice of pizza."

"Pizza is on the third page."

"Really?" Julie flipped ahead in her menu, excited to see the options. "What the hell is a cauliflower crust?"

Julie frowned at her choices. She looked up as their waiter Angelo approached the table. He was in his early 20's and stood close to six feet tall. Broad shouldered with jet black hair and ice blue eyes, he smiled as came to a stop next to Julie.

"I hope you are enjoying the wine and the menu," Angelo said. His accent had a hint of Italian. "Can I answer any questions for you?"

"The wine is fantastic," Julie said with a flirtatious smile. "Do you have any bread?"

"Aren't you adorable," Angelo replied. "We don't do traditional here. However, we do have some great nut based crackers along with a selection of cheeses."

"Cheese!" Julie said with joy. "Yes, please! Wait, is it real cheese or some kind of soy thing?"

"It's real cheese," Angelo said with a grin. He turned to Tom. "Anything for you?"

"No, I'm fine," Tom said.

Angelo nodded before he turned and headed to check in on his next table.

"Wine and cheese," Julie said with relief. "I'm good."

Julie turned her head to watch Angelo interacting with the guests at the table next to them.

"Why are waiters always so sexy?" Julie asked.

"I think at a place like this one it's sort of a requirement."

"Speaking of which. Why did you pick this place? No pasta or bread. Seriously? Are you trying to tell me I need to diet?"

"No, Jewels. I picked it for Marc."

"Marc?"

"This menu was practically custom designed for him. He had been looking forward to coming here once they opened. I thought it would be good for us to check it out."

Julie flipped back through the menu scanning all of the different healthy takes on traditional Italian cuisine. Tom watched as Julie studied it. Her angst was woefully noticeable.

"What about the pepper and sausage dish?" Tom asked.

"As long as it's not from Truro."

"Truro?"

"Remember the other urban legend? The one about the sausage maker?"

"Jewels," Tom said with a sigh. "I think the sausage here is safe to eat."

Tom and Julie sat in silence and spent a couple of minutes reading through the detailed menu.

Angelo quietly returned with a basket of crackers and a small plate of various Italian cheeses including asiago, taleggio, fontina d'Aosta, and provolone. They were cut up into multiple cubes, slices, and wedges.

"Any questions?" Angelo asked. "Or are you ready to order?"

Julie looked over at Tom.

"I'm ready if you are, Jewels."

"I think I'm going to try the Chicken Marsala. I hope the nut flour is good. Sounds kind of weird."

"You won't notice the difference," Angelo interjected. "And for your side?"

"Can I get the mixed vegetables in a cheese sauce?"

"Of course," Angelo said. He turned toward Tom. "And for you?"

"I'll have the Spaghetti Squash Bolognese," Tom said as he closed his menu.

"Excellent choices," Angelo said with sincere approval. He collected their menus and excused himself from the table.

Julie watched their waiter maneuver his way through the chic restaurant on his way toward the kitchen. Tom grinned as he watched Julie study the waiter's every move.

"How's work, Jewels?" Tom asked.

"It's fine," Julie replied. She slowly turned her gaze back to her dinner companion. "I really can't complain. The life of a paralegal is never exciting."

"You really need to go back to school to finish your law

degree."

"It's on my list. How about you? Anything new?"

"Yes, actually. My company won a bid to do the marketing campaign work for this year's giant boat show. My boss asked me to lead the graphics design team."

"Wow! Tom, that's awesome."

"Thanks. I think my boss is prepping me for a promo. We are growing quickly, and the team may split in two, opening up another manager slot."

"So, do you think you will get discount passes or something VIP for the event?"

"I have no clue. If I do should I assume you would want to tag along as my plus one?"

"What do you think?" Julie replied with a hearty chuckle. "I love some free VIP treatment."

"I know Jewels, but you also hate boats."

"I don't hate boats, Tom. I hate falling off them and drowning in the ocean. I hate deep oceans, and you hate tall heights. It's always limited our adventure seeking activities."

"Which is probably why we stick to bars and booze."

Julie held up her glass of wine, nodded across the table, and took another long sip.

"Well, the job opportunity sounds promising, Tom. Are you excited?"

"To be honest, I'm just not that into it."

"Why not?"

"Why do you think?"

Tom held up his phone, so Julie could see his updated screen image of Mrs. Closed from the store in Truro.

"Oh my God! Tom! I can't believe you set that up. You really are getting too obsessed with this. You can't let this interfere with your job. Especially a possible promotion."

"I can't help it Jewels. I've been thinking. We have to go to that estate sale in Eastham tomorrow."

"No, Tom. We need to move forward. We need to ... we need to be elsewhere."

"Not me. I need closure, Jewels."

"I think we have all of the closure we can expect. Marc and Chris are gone. Mrs. Closed and her mother took them off to some barn and made them into candles. Mrs. Closed is probably walking around with a burned face from that candle you flung at her. Probably hundreds of miles away. The cops have found nothing. They have no leads. Marc's truck has vanished. Their bodies are yet to surface. It's been four months. You have to let this go!"

Julie grabbed a few pieces of cheese from her plate. She had yet to try any of the nut crackers. She pointed at her appetizer and nodded toward Tom. He took a few items and put them on his plate.

"So, let's walk through this scenario," Julie said through a mouth full of cheese. "What happens if we find Mrs. Closed? She's standing right in front of you. She just shows up at that estate sale to claim her table or whatever. What will you do?"

Tom lowered his head and stared into his glass of wine. He thought of Marc and Chris and whatever fate they may have suffered back at the barn. He remembered the woman attempting to kill Julie in the bed across from him. He remembered the night his father was murdered.

"Honestly, Jewels?" Tom said. He paused momentarily, concerned with how Julie would react. "If I came face to face with her again. If we were in that same situation again, and she was about to kill you. Or me. I'd ... I'd kill her."

Julie looked across the table at her best friend. Someone she had known since college. She set her glass of wine down. Tom and Julie kept their eyes locked on one another for several seconds, neither willing to blink. The drone of incoherent chatter throughout the restaurant faded away as they both studied one another.

"I can't believe you just said that. How could you ... Tom, you are...." Julie leaned forward and lowered her voice to a whisper. "You are *not* a killer."

Tom looked away, and let his eyes wander the restaurant studying the people at the different tables.

"I could never kill someone," Julie added. She was completely rattled by his confession. "Neither could you."

"Jewels, that woman tried to kill you." Tom turned his stare back to Julie. "She attacked you with that dagger. Or did you forget? If anyone should want revenge, it should be you!"

28

"I can't believe we are even having this conversation."

"Sorry Jewels, I just ... I can't let this go. She got away. We can't let her get away. I ... I can't."

"Tom I'm worried your anger is fueling this hate inside you. I've never seen this part of you before."

"Well, I guess I'm not as strong as you. You seem to have accepted things. No repercussions. You've healed much more quickly than I have these past few months."

Julie decided to try one of the nut crackers. She smeared some taleggio on it and popped it into her mouth.

"I haven't, Tom. My nightmares. They ... they still haunt me."

"I thought they ended weeks ago."

"They did. Until last night."

Tom reached across the table and opened his palm. Julie immediately clasped it and squeezed tightly.

"I'm so sorry, Jewels. Why didn't you tell me?"

"I figured the less I talked about it, then the less I would think about it, and then it will just go away. What's that saying about time healing all wounds? I just need time. That's what I kept telling myself. Hopefully, this was the last nightmare."

"Jewels, you say that every time you have that nightmare. Can't you see that we both need closure? We need to go to that estate sale. Face our fears. We need to at least take a chance. See what we can find out."

Tom ran his thumb across the back of Julie's hand and into her palm. He watched her eyes for any sign of agreement. He truly believed Julie needed to face her demons to move forward.

"What are you thinking, Jewels?"

Julie reached out with her other hand and cupped Tom's hand with both of hers.

"I'm thinking two things," Julie said. "First of all, I'm in. You're right. It might help with closure. My ya-ya told me I needed closure as well. Maybe even just by going to the Cape, it will help. But we are not going past Eastham. I don't want to be anywhere near Truro or Provincetown."

"Agreed," Tom said. He was both relieved and thrilled he had convinced her to make the trip. "What's the other thing?"

"Your hands are dry."

Tom yanked his arm back across the table.

"Seriously Tom. You need cocoa butter. It's the best."

"OK, so we each have our own obsessions. Yours is cocoa butter. Mine is Mrs. Closed."

Julie managed a smile and a quiet laugh.

"Tom, I remembered something else in my nightmare this time. Something I hadn't noticed in the prior dreams."

"Did it have to do with her melting face? Because that part of your nightmare really freaks me out."

"Her face always melts in the dream. No, this was something new. It had to do with the dagger."

"What about it?"

"The wooden handle on it. It had the same design as the leg of the table."

"The metal and turquoise inlay? Nickel, right? That's what she said on the phone. It was the same?"

"Yes."

Tom took a long sip of his wine. Julie sat across from him staring down into her glass.

"Then it's settled. We're going back to the Cape tomorrow."

"But not to Truro or Provincetown."

"Agreed. We stop at Eastham."

Julie let out a long nervous exhale as she scooped up the last bite of cheese.

"I've never been to Eastham. How far is it from P-Town?"

"Far away, Jewels. I think there are at least two or three towns separating them. Probably a good thirty or so miles. The National Seashore in that area is pretty amazing."

"Really?"

Tom nodded as he grabbed a nut cracker and popped it into his mouth.

Julie took a moment to glance around the restaurant. Angelo was standing at a table several feet away. He had just presented a slice of cake to a young woman. A small flickering candle pierced the frosted top. The man seated with the woman passed her an elegantly wrapped gift.

"Tom, I have an idea."

"What are you thinking?"

"Let's stay overnight."

"Overnight? In Eastham? Why?"

"Well ... a few reasons. Mainly, I feel like we need a break. We need some fun. A getaway."

"Kind of short notice, isn't it? I mean, I would have to find a place. I think my mom can take Max. But I would have to ..."

"You don't have to do anything. Leave it all to me."

"You?" Tom began to laugh. "We both know that I'm the planner in this duo."

"Exactly! Let me do this."

"Why?"

Julie looked back at the woman that had just gotten the slice of cake. She was opening the present the man had given her.

"Like you said, you plan everything."

"OK, but I need to call my mom to see if she can take Max."

"Leave that to me."

"Wow. Can I listen in on *that* call?"

Julie burst out laughing and let out a small snort.

"Right? What have I committed myself to?"

Tom paused for a moment and took a sip of wine.

"OK, Jewels, plan away. I'm glad you want to hit the estate sale. If we have a place to stay, we won't be rushed. Have fun explaining this trip to my mom."

Julie smiled and took another long sip of wine.

"What time should we leave?" Tom asked. "Can we do our usual physical therapy in the morning?"

"Totally. I don't want to miss it. I'm scheduled for ten tomorrow morning. You?"

"I was going to do the same."

"Perfect!"

"Meet me at my place at noon, Jewels. We can take Ruby."

FIVE

Family

Sara Johnson lowered the hood that was covering her face. She instinctively used her fingers to brush her long blond hair forward across her right cheek. The burn mark was not severe, but she had become very self-conscious of it ever since Tom Leblanc had scarred her face four months ago.

Her family barn was aglow with a warm yellow light, cast from four overhead propane-powered lanterns. They were almost as old as the barn itself and did not work very well. The barn also had three large electrical lights suspended from the ceiling, but they had shorted out over a year ago. Like many things in this old home, they were past due for some desperately needed maintenance.

It was Friday evening, a few hours after sunset. A chilly windy April night blanketed the town of Wellfleet. Sara was restless and needed to calm her mind. She looked over at the workbench near the stalls at the end of the barn. She had two portable battery powered lanterns set on the end. Next to them were a tattered, stained hand towel, a whetstone set, and a six-inch long knife.

There were over a dozen knives of various shapes and sizes spread out across the table. Sara had sharpened half of them earlier in the day. They all shared one thing in common – a wooden handle inlaid with nickel and turquoise. She had yet to master the art of crafting such an exquisitely detailed handle. *Someday,* Sara thought to herself as she admired her father's handiwork.

Sara picked up the knife and began to run the blade back and forth across the whetstone. The key was the angle. Choose the wrong angle, and you would end up with a dull blade. She may not have mastered making the handle of a family knife, but she had become quite adept at working the edges.

After every few sweeps Sara tested the blade's sharpness. Eventually, she felt it easily slice into the tip of her thumb. She stopped short of drawing blood and set the knife down next to a row of five others that were already completed.

Dad would be proud.

The creak of the front door of the barn broke the silence of the chilly breezy night. Sara looked up to see if it was just the wind. Instead, she noticed her mother looking around the edge of the doorway.

"I finally got the oven working, Sara," Laura said. "I know it's late, but you must be hungry. It's so cold out here. Winter simply refuses to leave. Come inside. You can pick this up tomorrow when the sun is up."

"I'll be right in, Mother."

Laura watched as her daughter walked to the back corner of the barn and turned a valve connected to a 120-gallon propane tank. One by one the lanterns along the back beam flickered off. The barn got progressively darker until all that was left was the cold white light cast by the two battery-powered lanterns sitting on the bench.

"Are you going to turn the valves off on the lanterns up top?" Laura asked.

"Not tonight," Sara replied as she approached the work table. "I'll get them tomorrow."

Laura frowned as she looked up at the four old rusted lamps. Sara grabbed the two small lanterns from the table and met her mother in the doorway.

***

The kitchen was filled with the smell of garlic and oregano.

Sara was sitting at the kitchen table, watching her mother tend to the food cooking away on the stove.

"Smells great," Sara said. "Pasta tonight?"

"No, this is for tomorrow night," Laura replied. "This sauce isn't finished. I have leftovers in the oven."

"Leftovers again?"

"Money is tight. You know that."

Sara frowned at the judgmental tone of her mother's voice.

"With that face of yours you can't just get any public job," Laura continued. "We are going to have to live off your father's pension checks until it's safe for you to find permanent work."

Sara stroked her fingers through her long blond hair until the entire right side of her face was covered. She had not bothered to cut her hair since the incident four months ago. Her mother had suggested she dye it. They had used a store-bought kit and turned her from brunette to blond. Sara liked the change but had become a bit of a recluse, afraid to go out in public unless it was an emergency.

Laura watched as her daughter nervously combed her fingers through her hair.

"Things will settle down eventually, Sara. You just need to be patient. We were both too bold and risky when we sold those Seabreeze candles last Christmas. I don't know how I let you talk me into that. We were lucky you weren't spotted. Remember, discretion is the name of the game."

"Discretion," Sara sighed. "I know. I'm just going stir crazy stuck here all the time."

"Your face is healing nicely. That limp is gone. Another month or so and I'm sure you will be good as new. They still have the police sketches up. I see them when I go into town. It really doesn't look anything like you."

"I miss my life. I miss my Jeep."

"What's done is done. You have to let it go. Be a dear and go clean up for dinner, OK?"

Sara left the kitchen and went to a small bathroom off the main hallway. The light switch was an old metal one that made a loud audible snap when you flicked it. Only one of the two bulbs came to life. The light fixture that was secured to the right side of the mirror was dead.

Sara turned the hot water faucet and waited for the water to warm. She stared into the sink, not wanting to look in the mirror. These days she hated her reflection. It reminded her too much of the night that Tom had flung the candle at her, and how she had failed to kill her prey.

The water coming from the tap was still cool to the touch. Sara grabbed a bar of soap and began to wash her hands anyway. She reluctantly looked up into the mirror. With only the left light working, the right side of her face remained in the shadows. The burn mark was no longer visible. Sara managed a brief smile at seeing her reflection looking somewhat normal.

Seeing her mirror image with only half of her face illuminated suddenly reminded Sara of a poem. It was a simple limerick from her childhood. She began to recite it to herself. As she did, she ran her index finger against the mirror, circling her face.

> If I'm unsure and feeling blue,
> It only takes a look from you.
> Do I see me?
> No ...

Before she could finish the rhyme, there was a loud knock at the kitchen door. Sara heard her mother yell out in shock. She turned off the water and ran back toward the kitchen.

"Bobby!" Laura said with surprise.

Sara stopped in the hallway entrance to the kitchen to see Bobby Mason standing outside the porch door, staring in through the glass. Laura rushed over and opened it.

"Hi Laura," Bobby said. "I brought you more sausage. As requested. It's still frozen. Feel free to keep it on ice or thaw it."

"Come in, come in," Laura said as she took a small brown bag from Bobby. She leaned forward and gave Bobby a hug.

Bobby Mason was five foot ten and towered over the diminutive woman. They had known one another for over forty years. Despite being seventy-one years old, he was still a broad-shouldered and rugged man. He had a full thick crop of hair on his head, although it had faded from brown to white well over a decade ago. His tanned skin, once smooth, had weathered over the years.

He kissed the top of Laura's head and held her close to his chest. Bobby looked up to see Sara standing in the doorway.

"How are you doing, Sara?" Bobby asked. He kept Laura in his embrace. "How's the face?"

Sara pulled her blond hair forward as she walked over to the kitchen table. She pulled one of the old metal and turquoise vinyl chairs toward her and sat down.

"It's fine as long as I don't look in the mirror," Sara replied.

"It's really not that bad," Bobby said. "You look good as a blond."

"Bobby," Laura said as she pulled herself away from his embrace, "I've got chicken and vegetables in the oven. It's just leftovers. Would you like to stay for a bite?"

"I can't tonight, Angel."

"But you've been so kind and helpful to Sara and I these past few months. Ever since last December. Please. I insist."

"I can't. Besides, I've told you many times there is no need to thank me. You know I'd do anything for you two. In fact, I wish you would let me do more. You've got no power in the barn. Your stove is always breaking. That front porch is a safety hazard. The roof is a mess. This place is falling apart. Truro is only one town away. I can be here as often as you need me to be."

"You are simply too kind," Laura said.

Sara watched as her mother held onto Bobby. He had been a godsend these past few months. She knew she was right – they would not have evaded the police without his help.

Bobby leaned down and gave Laura a kiss on the cheek. He glanced up at Sara and winked. She smiled back.

"I'll talk with you this weekend," Bobby said. He nodded, turned, and stepped outside, slamming the door behind him.

Laura placed the bag of sausage on the counter next to the stove and opened the oven door. She was glad to see the old appliance was still cranking out heat. She turned it off and grabbed an oven mitt and removed the pan.

Sara brought two plates over to the counter next to the stove and quickly filled them with the chicken and vegetables. Laura and her daughter returned to the table to enjoy a much-needed meal.

"Bobby really has been incredibly kind to us," Sara said.

"He's always taken care of this family. In ways you are not even aware of. He's just been an angel always watching over us and protecting us."

"He seems very … affectionate with you."

"He's always cared for me."

Laura looked out the window at the old barn and let her mind drift off to memories long ago. She smiled, as she recalled all of the family cookouts they'd had over the years. All of the delights and surprises.

"Mother, can I ask you something?"

"Always, dear."

"Are you still mad at me for killing that couple that owned the store? I mean, that's why you had to teach me how to make the candles in the first place."

The question startled Laura and quickly erased the nostalgic memories she had been enjoying.

"I told you, Sara, what's done is done. There's no going back now."

"I know that. But sometimes I feel … I feel like I've disappointed you in some way."

Laura took a bite of her chicken and slowly chewed her food. She frowned as she felt her dentures shift a bit.

"You have never been a disappointment to me. None of my children have. It's just your temper, Sara. You've always been the hothead in this family. You take after your father. You and your sister are so identical, and yet so opposite."

"Can we not talk about her? Don't change the subject."

Sara felt her anger rising. She did not like her mother telling her she had anger issues. She was also well aware of how ironic her reaction was.

"You murdered two innocent people, Sara."

"I told you it was self-defense! I didn't mean to!"

"So much like your father."

"But they were the ones that …"

"But nothing! Like I said, what's done is done. It was a moment of rage. Accidents happen. Trust me, they happen quite a bit in this family. We just have to move forward."

Laura paused to pull her lower teeth out and inspect them.

She picked out a small strand of chicken at the back corner and returned her dentures to her lower jaw.

"Well if the past is the past then why aren't you being more supportive of carrying on the family tradition? I'm trying to do everything the right way including how we make the candles."

"Because you got sloppy!" Laura said with frustration. She slammed her fists down onto the table, causing the utensils to rattle. "We've been doing this on and off for thirty years. Do you know why nobody in this family has been caught? Discretion. We always cover our tracks, Sara. Always."

"I did cover my tracks!" Sara suddenly found herself on the defensive. "There were no clues left behind. I took the book, the dagger, and even the candle."

"Nothing left behind? You left two eyewitnesses! Not to mention your burned face. You were sloppy."

"I did my best!" Sara cried. "I fell two stories, Mother! It could have been worse."

"You're right, it could have been much worse."

"All I'm trying to do is make you proud. To do these family candles again. Just like dad did with the first one."

Laura smiled and nodded. The truth was her husband did not create the first candle. That was a myth of its own. But she felt it was best for her daughter to believe that he did. Sara worshiped her father. Laura was not about to tarnish that image.

"I'm sure he would be proud of you, Sara. I'm proud of you too. I am. Together we made the Ginger, Sesame, and Seabreeze candles. And we have not been caught. Yet. That's why we need to lay low."

"I understand."

"You really did a wonderful job making all three scents. Even the texture of the wax was perfect."

"Thanks," Sara said with a smile.

"But ... But I do have one criticism."

"What?"

"You shouldn't have made those damn labels. That was a mistake."

"What's wrong with labeling the scents?"

"Not the scent. The name you created."

"FlickerWood? I thought it was fun! Besides, it can't be traced back to us. Search the web, and you won't find us."

"But it's a calling card. A clue. Never leave any hint of evidence. Always clean up loose ends. Always."

"I'm sorry, Mother. FlickerWood does have meaning to me. It's personal."

Laura could see her daughter was genuinely disappointed. She knew that Sara meant well. Ever since the death of her father the girl had always strived to do her family proud.

"Remember dear, another reason we've lasted this long is we would let years go by before we make another batch of candles," Laura continued. "This was your first experience making them. We don't make the candles for fun. We don't seek out people to melt down into candles. They come to us. They disrespect us. They pay the price. The candles are simply part of how we dispose of them."

Sara stared into her mother's icy blue eyes. No matter how much prodding and pleading Sara tried, her mother had kept the family candle making a bit of a mystery. Years ago, Sara had discovered many different candles hidden beneath the property. Her mother had glossed over them as if they were not important. Then the incident happened with the store owners, and Sara learned about the family recipe that her father had started. Beyond that, she knew very little.

"I just feel so trapped here, Mother. Everything feels … unresolved."

"This is just as frustrating for me as it is for you. You had to quit your job to go into hiding. Money is tight. Your father's pension has not been the windfall I'd hoped for. We need to proceed with caution. The shop owners have been taken care of. So, have the other two we made into the Seabreeze candles. But the two that escaped. What were their names?"

"Tom and Julie," Sara said. Her anger had finally subsided. "Tom is the one that burned my face."

"Those two are still out there."

"Are you saying we should go after them where they live?"

"No!" Laura was disappointed with her daughter's cavalier attitude. "What part of *discretion* do you not understand?"

Sara shoved her plate away toward the middle of the table. Despite only eating half of her dinner, she was no longer hungry. Laura stared at her daughter, saddened with the confusion and anger spread across her face. She got up and walked around to the empty chair next to Sara and sat down next to her.

"Listen, child, I know this is all so confusing and frustrating for you." Laura tucked Sara's blond hair behind her ear, exposing her burn mark. "You never intended to kill that Asian couple. It was a confrontation that escalated out of control. Murder is nothing to be taken lightly. Accidents happen. Death happens. We cover it up. We always have. I will do whatever it takes to protect you. The day will come when Tom and Julie will pay the price. The choices I am making today are all to protect you. We are family. Blood runs warm through the bonds of love and family. We stick together and take care of one another. At all costs."

Laura kissed her daughter on her burned cheek and gently squeezed her hands. Sara slowly turned her gaze toward her mother.

"Mother, if family is so important then how come you and Aunty Jen no longer talk?"

Laura was surprised that her daughter decided to bring her estranged sister into the conversation.

"Don't speak about a family history you don't fully understand," Laura said sternly as she sat upright in her chair.

"But you and Aunty Jen were so close when we were kids. I know there are many secrets you are afraid to tell me. I have so many memories ..."

"I've reached out many times to make amends with my sister. Do you really want to talk about the bonds of siblings? We can talk about you and your sister Emma if you would like."

Sara frowned. She was disappointed she had set herself up and let her mother turn the tables on her.

"Emma is no longer family to me. You know why. That drifter dad brought home. Everything changed after that."

Laura ran her worn fingers across her daughter's damaged face.

40

"Sara, we both know that Emma spent years trying to patch things over with you. If you were still close, she could have helped you with this injury. She could have helped us the way Bobby has been helping."

Sara whipped her hand against her mother's, pushing it away from her face.

"You couldn't make amends with Aunty Jen way back when she wanted to. I wouldn't with Emma. I guess I have dad's temper and your stubbornness."

Laura sighed. The discussion was going nowhere. She stood up and began to collect the plates from the table. The food had grown cold, along with the conversation. Sara was indeed a combination of her parents' worst traits. She knew her daughter well, and all would be fine after they both got a good night's rest.

"This family has never been the same since dad died," Sara said. She was still sitting at the table. "You speak of bonds. I feel like his death was the beginning of the end of our family bonds. It's like once his love for you was gone the family started to fall apart. I know you both loved each other so much. He was your world. He was mine, too."

Laura walked over to her daughter and kissed her gently on the top of her head.

"You head up to bed, Sara. It's been a long day. I need to finish making the pasta sauce. I'll clean everything up when done."

Sara stood up and kissed her mother on the cheek before leaving the kitchen. Laura turned and looked out at the barn. The hulking building sat in peace, quiet, and darkness.

So many, many secrets, Laura thought to herself.

SIX

Passion

1979 Saturday 16-Jun 4:00 p.m.

It was a beautiful, cool, crisp afternoon in Wellfleet, Massachusetts. The air was dry and breezy. Clear skies and a temperature of 70 degrees blanketed the outer Cape. Days like this were idyllic and cherished this time of year – the last week before summer officially started.

The front corner inside the Johnson family barn was still set up for tutoring. Two rows of four small school chairs were lined up facing a blackboard that hung on the wall next to the front entrance. Laura Johnson taught weekend lessons for local students in grades three through four that were struggling in math. In the colder months, she held class in her living room. When the weather allowed for it, she preferred to run classes in the barn. Tutoring was done for the school year, and Laura finally had some time to herself. She was putting that free time to good use.

In the large loft across the back of the barn, above the cow stalls, Laura was in ecstasy. Her naked body was covered in a thin film of sweat. She pulled herself higher as she wrapped her legs tighter around her partner's waist. He was deep inside her, filling her with a level of sensuality she used to think was impossible to achieve. Making love in a pile of hay in the

42

family barn had always been her favorite sexual escape. Making love with this man took her joy to another level.

"Deeper," Laura moaned.

Bobby Mason was more than happy to oblige. He smiled as he felt Laura lean back. That was his signal to take on a more dominant role. He pulled himself forward until he was fully upright on his knees. He groaned as he looked into Laura's ice blue eyes. She nodded in approval. Bobby fell forward, pushing her against a mound of straw. He began to thrust deeper and deeper into her. Laura pushed her hands against Bobby's muscular hairy chest. His dark Portuguese skin was drenched in sweat. Sex with her husband was mechanical and awkward. She cherished every moment she could steal to be with Bobby. He gave her everything her husband Fred could not.

"I love being inside you," Bobby said before nibbling on Laura's lower lip.

Laura and Bobby were in a rhythm now. It had become a dance of passion. The intensity increased with each thrust. Laura knew he was close.

"Bobby, you have to pull out. Please."

Bobby grabbed Laura's wrists and flattened her arms against the buttery gold strands of hay above her head. He pushed harder and deeper.

"Not so rough," Laura moaned.

Bobby eased his aggression but continued to push as deep and hard as he knew Laura could handle.

"Bobby! Bobby!"

"I love you so much Laura," Bobby cried as he exploded inside of her. Bobby flung his arms around his lover and continued to thrust, moaning with each lunge.

Laura clutched Bobby's broad shoulders. She knew this was a dangerous game she was playing. They had stopped using condoms weeks ago, but Bobby would always pull out. Almost always. Her mind was awash with a mix of confusion, fear, desire, and pleasure.

As always, Bobby continued to pleasure Laura even after he had climaxed. He was never a selfish lover. Not with her.

"Your turn," Bobby cooed into Laura's ear.

Bobby and Laura locked eyes longingly. They were four months into a torrid affair, with no end in sight. Laura smiled as she looked at his ruggedly handsome face. She wrapped her legs up and around the small of his back, grinding hard until she couldn't take it anymore. Laura screamed out in short rapid bursts as she finally climaxed.

Bobby smiled as he felt Laura's tense body slowly uncoil and relax. Her legs slid down past his waist. Laura let her hands run across his shoulders and down his muscular arms as she melted into the moist, golden hay. Bobby rolled over and put his arm around her, pulling her against his chest.

"You were supposed to pull out," Laura muttered.

"I'm sorry, Angel. I couldn't help myself." Bobby kissed her on the top of her head. He chuckled as he felt a piece of hay stick to his lips. "You drive me crazy."

"I love you dearly," Laura said. She pulled herself closer to Bobby's warm body. "But I can't get pregnant. The last time I got knocked up I ended up marrying the fool."

"Are you calling me a fool?" Bobby asked sarcastically.

Laura plucked at several of the hairs scattered across Bobby's flat, taut stomach. She knew this was his sensitive area. He playfully smacked her hand away and then quickly grabbed it and began to massage her fingers.

"Fred knocked me up at eighteen years old. Then we got married, and I had the twins. They are enough of a handful. That Sara is a hothead like her father. Fred and I rarely have sex anymore. If I got pregnant by you ..."

"Relax my love."

Laura propped herself up on her elbow and pulled back slightly so she could look Bobby directly in his warm chestnut colored eyes.

"I'm serious, Bobby. You know what a temper he has. If he found out about this affair, one or both of us would be dead. You know about his past."

"So, fuck him."

"What?" Laura was genuinely confused.

"Be a good wife and have sex with your husband."

"Are you serious?"

"Completely. When he comes home tonight, fix him a nice

meal. Pour him a few chilled beers. Tell him you are horny and it's been awhile. Men are pigs. We never say no to sex. Trust me. He will welcome the attention."

Laura shook her head in disappointment.

"So right after you finish fucking me and telling me you love me you tell me to go have sex with my husband. That makes no sense."

"Angel, if you are worried about getting pregnant at least he will think the kid is his. Better to be safe than sorry, right?"

"The safe thing to do is for you to pull that big Portuguese meat stick out *before* it erupts!" Laura laughed as she grabbed Bobby's still erect cock.

Bobby glanced at his watch. It was 4 p.m.

"I have to get going," Bobby said. He kissed Laura before he stood up. The backside of his body was covered in hay.

Laura smiled as she watched Bobby wipe himself down. She was so in love with him. He had a beautiful body. He was kind and caring. He made her feel desired, loved, and safe. She hated to see him leave.

"What do you have planned tonight?" Laura asked.

"I have several orders to fill this weekend. Mostly just going through paperwork to make sure I have everything ready. You?"

"Did you forget already? I'm going to be riding my husband's little dick. Per your request to fuck him."

Bobby laughed. Laura stood up and began to brush the dampened yellow straw off of her thighs. Without Bobby to keep her warm, she realized how chilly the late afternoon air truly was. She quickly began to put her clothes on.

"Like I said, Angel, better to be safe than sorry. And don't you worry about Fred's temper. I will always protect you. The girls too. Someday we will all be together as a family."

"When? How? I'm so unhappy with him. I'm twenty-five years old and miserable. This marriage was such a mistake."

Bobby walked over and pulled Laura close to him. He buried his face into the top of her head. Even smelling of hay, he found her scent intoxicating.

"I just want to be happy," Laura continued. "Look at my sister Jennifer. Her husband Carl worships her. He has her on a pedestal. I tell her that all of the time. She needs to appreciate what she has. She knows I am not happy with Fred."

"You didn't tell her about us, did you?"

"Of course not. Nobody knows."

"Good. And I wouldn't worship your sister's relationship with her husband. Carl is one of the most socially awkward people I have ever met."

"True, but he's her husband. And he loves her. He treats her like gold. That's how it's supposed to be."

Bobby and Laura slowly descended the ladder back down to the ground level of the barn. Bobby grabbed Laura by the waist while she was still two rungs from the bottom. He pulled her into his arms and swung her around twice before lowering her to the floor.

Laura glanced out the partially open front door of the barn to make sure Fred had not come home early. He and the twins were not due back for another hour. The driveway was empty. She turned around toward Bobby and tilted her head back and stood on her toes. They kissed.

"Are we still on for Sunday?" Laura asked.

"Of course we are. I'll see you then."

***

Bobby glanced at his watch. It was 10 a.m. Sunday. He rolled out of his bed and walked over to the window above the old radiator. He cranked the twist rod on the blinds to let a bit of light into his bedroom. His cock, still hard and dripping, banged against the dusty slats of the window covering. He bent down and pulled on a pair of boxer shorts and glanced over at the young naked woman panting in satisfaction in his bed.

"You should have pulled out," Jennifer Campbell said with disappointment.

"We both know you love it," Bobby said in a reassuring tone.

Jennifer grinned, knowing he was right.

"Be that as it may, we really can't take the chance."

"You and Carl have sex all the time. What's the worry?"

"The worry is I get pregnant by you."

"Relax, Angel," Bobby said. He walked over and sat down on the edge of the bed. Jennifer slid over and rested her head on his thigh, letting her long brown hair cascaded over his leg and dangled off the side of the bed. "You need to get dressed and get home. Carl is going to wonder why it took you so long to come get your sausage order."

Jennifer rolled her head over and brushed her lips against Bobby's crotch. She could feel his cock bulging through his white cotton boxers.

"And get your sausage I did," Jennifer said with the glee of a young school girl.

Bobby laughed as he pushed her head away.

"Speaking of which, don't go home without it. I have it wrapped up for you. It's on the top shelf of the fridge."

Jennifer smiled as she rolled out of bed and started looking for her clothes.

"I won't forget it. But I'm serious, Hon. I'm tired of pretending to enjoy sex with Carl. Pretending to love him. This affair of ours needs to move to the next level."

Bobby paused as he pulled a light blue T-shirt over his head.

"Next level?" Bobby asked. He was genuinely confused.

Jennifer, still naked, came around to his side of the bed. She slid her hands around Bobby's trim waist and locked her hands behind his back. At five foot five, she was five inches shorter than him. Bobby draped his arms over her shoulders and pulled her close. She pressed her lips against his chest and closed her eyes.

Jennifer had spent all week fretting over their affair and her mix of emotions. What started as a drunken night of passion five months ago had turned into a recurring weekly liaison. With each passing week, her love for Bobby had grown, and her affection for her husband Carl had faded.

"I want to get a divorce."

Bobby let his arms fall away. This was something he never saw coming. He looked down at Jennifer. Her face was still buried in his chest. He took a small step back and slid a finger under her chin, tilting her head up.

"A divorce?"

"I want it to be just the three of us. You, me, and Susan."

Bobby was rather stunned. He had only started having sex with Jennifer a month before he began his affair with Laura. He cared for them both, but he knew in his heart that Laura was the one he ultimately wanted to be with. Jennifer let him be much more aggressive with her. Their sex was primal. It was pure animalistic lust. He could not get enough of it. But it was just sex, not love. Although he could not be as rough with Laura as he wanted to be, he cherished her deeply. He knew Jennifer was becoming more and more attached but had chosen to ignore it, hoping it would not become an issue.

"Jennie, how can you even be thinking that?" Bobby's tone was calm. He knew Jennifer could be emotional and he wanted to keep that in check. "Carl is going through a rough time right now. Are you ready to destroy him? To destroy your family?"

Jennifer was disappointed and confused over Bobby's reaction to her news. She had spent all week role-playing this very moment in her mind. She always assumed Bobby would welcome her suggestion to move forward. Jennifer yanked her chin away from his hand and walked back over to her belongings that were scattered across the floor.

"Why are you concerned about my husband?"

"Think of your daughter. What would this do to Susan? She'll be eight years old this month. What would she think of her mother leaving the family? Carl also needs you. If you really want us to be happy, this isn't the time to end your marriage."

Jennifer paused to consider his words. In all of her inner rehearsals of this moment with Bobby, she never did give much thought to the aftermath. She always assumed he would just say yes and they would run off and live happily ever after.

"I guess, but ..."

"But you know I'm right," Bobby said as he fastened the button on his denim jeans. He walked over to Jennifer and took her by her hands.

"Our time will come, Angel," Bobby whispered calmly into

her ear. "Let's not rush this. We have a good thing going here. Day by day, OK?"

"I just love you so much," Jennifer sighed as she threw her arms around Bobby.

"I love you too," Bobby said flatly.

SEVEN

Physical Therapy

Elite Fitness in Providence was quickly filling up as the clock showed 10:50 a.m. The early morning crowd had finished their weekend workouts and long departed. The current members were younger. Most were pushing through a recovery workout, with some of them sweating it out on the cardio equipment.

Julie was propped up on her left knee and drenched in perspiration. The white hand towel she had brought here an hour ago sat in a damp lump by her right foot. The sweat coming down her brow filled her eyes, blurring her vision. Her hands, enclosed in boxing gloves, struggled to pick up the towel.

"Do you need a hand?" Julio Castano asked with a smirk. The kickboxing trainer was patiently waiting for his student to complete her mini break. "I don't want you to get those pretty little gloves dirty."

Julie maneuvered her forearms like salad tongs, eventually snatching the towel up off the floor. She exhaled deeply as she cleared the sweat from her face. Next up was the water bottle. She dropped the towel and repeated her clamping move to take a long, much-needed drink of water.

When done she stood up and turned to face the mirror. Julie took her gym clothing just as seriously as she did her training. She thought she looked stunning. Everything was pink and black – sneakers, gloves, shorts, and her T-shirt. Her hair was pulled back in a bun, and she had a pink scrunchie to secure it in place.

"Oh, these pretty little gloves are going to get dirty," Julie said through heavy breathing. The sweat had already started to run down her face again. It had been a very full hour in the ring. "Dirty all over you, trainer boy!"

Julio laughed as he motioned Julie back to the center of the ring. He was a few years younger than Julie, as well as a few inches taller than her. The two had immediately bonded when she had first approached him about learning to kick-box. Of all of his students, Julie had not only been the most dedicated, but also the most impressive. Her confidence had grown exponentially with each passing week.

"OK Julie, I'm going to mix the combo up this time. We are going to do one-two, one-two, one-two, and then three and end with a four. I want your one-twos to be fast and accurate. All about speed. When you drop to three use a bit more power. But four is where I want you to fully unload. Make that your power shot. Don't rush it."

Julie knew the drill. She had been working with Julio for the past three months, once a week. Julio would hold his boxing mitts at different positions. Each location had a number assigned. That number correlated to a swing. One and two were left and right hooks, up high and out at head level. Three and four were jabs to the chest. Five and six were hooks down low to the abdomen. These covered three basic swings. Julio would continuously mix them up, holding his mitts in the proper spot and letting Julie figure out the right punch to use.

"Ready," Julie said as she positioned her feet and hands.

Julio held his left mitt up and out away from his head. Julie rotated her body and swung her arm in a wide arc. She quickly fired off three sets of alternating left and right upper hooks. Julio quickly dropped his mitts down toward his chest. Julie thrust forward with her left hand, hitting his mitt dead center. He lowered his hands a few inches more.

"Nice, Julie! OK give me all your power now."

Julie plunged her right hand toward Julio's mitt with all her might, rotating at her hips. Her glove, wet with sweat, missed the center and slid off the edge of his mitt, hitting Julio right in the stomach.

"Oh my God!" Julie yelled as her trainer leaned forward and stumbled a few steps away from her. Julio took a couple of gasps and then coughed. His cough quickly turned into a laugh.

"Kick his ass!" yelled someone from the cardio deck next to the boxing ring. Several people started to clap and laugh. Julie waved at the group of observers and took a slight bow.

"You've got some serious power," Julio said as he regained his composure.

"I'm so sorry!"

"It's OK. Honestly. It happens more than I would like to admit. Last week some guy completely missed the mitt and clocked me right in the jaw. I'm used to it. Occupational hazard."

Julio looked over at the huge digital clock hanging on the wall across from the cardio deck. It was 10:55 a.m. Standing several feet from the ring stood his next client, Brad. Brad was young, tall and muscular but had absolutely no coordination. Julio was dreading their training session.

"We're almost out of time," Julio said. "Why don't we switch things up a bit. I think you are ready for something new. A little preview for next time."

Julio walked over to the corner of the ring and tossed his mitts to the ground. He picked up a large vinyl-covered full body pad. He quickly strapped it on, securing it with several oversized Velcro fasteners.

"We're moving onto legs. There are three different moves I want to teach you, OK? I'm going to show them to you quickly. We will focus on these over the next few sessions."

Julie nodded in approval. Her breathing had finally returned to normal. Julio moved within a foot of Julie and placed his hands around her neck, grasping it from behind.

"This first one is for when you are in close contact with someone. Pay attention."

Julio pulled Julie's head down into his chest and at the

same time thrust his right knee up toward her stomach. The body pad prevented him from making any sort of impact.

"Notice there are two moves happening here," Julio explained. "I pull you down at the same time I knee you in your gut. My hands are locked on you. I can hold you here clamped against my chest and repeatedly knee you in your stomach. Give it a try. With our difference in height just lock my head down onto your shoulder. I've got the body pad on so don't hold back."

"I'll try not to hit your nuts," Julie said with a grin. Julio laughed as she wrapped her arms around his neck. She quickly yanked his head down against her shoulder and flicked her right leg up, kneeing him dead center in the pad.

"Excellent, Julie! Give me a few more, alternating legs."

Julie complied and rapidly did six more, three on each side. Julio pulled back, signaling her to stop.

"You're my star pupil, Julie. You keep impressing me."

Julie smiled as she gasped for breath. For what looked like such a simple move it took a lot out of her.

"You just want to keep me as a client," Julie said.

"Well that too," Julio said as he winked at her. "OK we are out of time, so we can pick this up next week."

"You said you were going to show me three new ones. What about the other two?"

Julio looked at the clock and then over at Brad. Brad was leaning against a treadmill texting on his phone.

"OK," Julio said. "Very quickly."

Julio removed his body pad and stepped out of the ring. Julie followed him. Off to the side of the ring were two boxing stations with long bags hanging from the ceiling. Neither of them was in use.

"Watch," Julio said. He then quickly did six roundhouse kicks – three with the left leg, and then three with his right. He stepped away from the bag and waved his arm, motioning Julie to get into position. She was amazed that he was barely breathing heavy. "Just like I showed you. It's all in the rotation. In your hips. Pivot on your lead foot. Take it slow to start."

Julie stepped up to the bag and positioned her legs the

same way Julio had them. She then stepped in, spun, and completely missed the bag. She continued to rotate until she crashed to the floor.

"Fuck!" Julie yelled in disgust.

Julio chuckled as he helped Julie get back on her feet. He glanced over at Brad to see if he was upset that Julio was late starting their session. The guy still had his face buried in his phone. Julio wished he could just do another hour with Julie.

"You aren't trying to kick a ball, OK?" Julio explained. "You want a straight line from your shoulder down to your toe. Observe."

Julio stepped forward and quickly nailed the center of the bag with his right foot. Julie shook her head.

"You make it look so easy. Try doing it with these tits."

"C'mon now, they should help with your rotation."

The two of them laughed. Julie often used The Girls as an excuse anytime she had trouble with her form.

"Just show me the other one," Julie said. "I know we are way past time."

Julio stepped a few feet from the bag and took a long deep breath.

"Front kick. Super easy, OK? Two variations on this depending on the leg you use. Either defense or offense. I'll show you the defense one first."

Julio leaned back slightly and struck the bag hard with his forward left leg, knocking it away. Julie watched intently. She was always amazed at the power he could generate.

Julio caught the bag and steadied it before he got back into position.

"Offensive," Julio said as he focused on the bag. "Watch for the difference."

Julio took a small step forward with his lead left leg, leaned back, and thrust his right leg ahead, extremely hard. The bag flew back, almost hitting the wall behind it. He turned to see Julie's reaction. She watched the bag swing back toward Julio. He stepped aside to let it sway back and forth.

"You are stepping in," Julie said. "You are sort of attacking when you use your back leg. Like you are going after the bag. That first one was almost a blocking kind of move."

"Exactly," Julio said. "You have much more power with the offensive move. Give it a try. Defense first."

Julie got into position and did a few with her lead leg. It felt awkward to her. She was surprised by how difficult it was to keep herself steady and upright throughout the move.

"Not bad," Julio noted. "Watch your hand position, though. We'll work on that next time. Try your offensive strike. Think of yourself like a pendulum as you lean back and thrust that rear leg forward."

Julie took a moment to compose herself and did a few offensive kicks. She still felt off balance, but definitely noticed the difference in power.

"Nicely done, Julie."

"Thanks. It helps to have a great teacher."

Julio glanced over at Brad, still buried in his phone. He reluctantly secured his mitts, in preparation for his next training session.

"Trust me. It helps having a great pupil as well."

Julie smiled and headed back over to the ring. Her towel was still sitting in a lump, and she desperately needed to clear her brow.

"Hey, Julie?" Julio asked from behind.

Julie turned back and was about to ask what he wanted when Julio lunged forward and swiped his left mitt sideways toward her head. She immediately bobbed below his reach.

"Four!" Julio yelled as he dropped his glove down. Julie instinctively did a hard jab into his mitt.

Julio clapped his mitts together in approval.

"You really have the fastest reflexes, Julie. That's something that can't be taught. It's instinctive."

Julie gave him a nervous smile. She thought back to her recurring nightmares and to the attack that happened at the Seabreeze complex a few months ago. She thought of how she blocked the woman's assault with the book. At the time it didn't feel instinctive at all. All she could recall was being filled with terror.

Julio could see Julie getting lost in her thoughts. He knew of her past and why she had signed up for lessons with him. During their first lesson, Julie had actually freaked out a bit when he began to swing at her to teach her how to avoid taking a blow. They had to take a ten-minute break so she could tell him what happened in the condo and her desire to never feel that helpless again.

"I know that look, Julie. Are those nightmares back?"

"I'm fine."

"Julie, there is only so much I can teach you. If you are still haunted by what happened, it may do you some good to talk to someone. A professional."

Julie used her teeth to tear into the Velcro strap holding her left glove on.

"I told you I don't do talk therapy. I just need to learn how to defend myself."

"You can, Julie. You can. I believe in you."

"Thanks."

Julio did not like her less than enthusiastic tone.

"What separates us?" Julio asked with a grin.

Julie immediately smiled back. The day she signed up with him they both joked that they had almost identical first names. There was just a single vowel separating them. Once Julio understood her goals and drivers he had given her a mantra, based on that letter.

"I" Julie replied.

"I what?" Julio asked.

"I am strong. I am confident. I believe."

Julio stepped closer and gave her a big hug.

"I believe in you. You just need to believe in yourself."

***

Ocean State Archery in Lincoln, Rhode Island was the largest archery club in the state. They had a mix of indoor and outdoor fields for members to use, including an advanced field course with a variety of 3D foam animal targets.

It was a damp morning. The temperature was a cool 50 degrees. Tom had decided to take advantage of the weather and use the outdoor practice range. The club was quiet today, and the few patrons that were there were all using the indoor field. He had the outdoor range all to himself.

Tom looked down the field trying to decide how he wanted to end his session. He wasn't sure if he should try something different or continue doing what had become a seemingly impossible task. It was almost 11 a.m., and he had to be home and ready to leave at noon for the Cape. Time was running out.

The left side of the course had a series of targets spaced in 5-yard increments, starting from 5 and stopping at 30. After that, they went up in 10-yard increments until reaching 70 yards. The right side had another series of targets. These had similar spacing; however, they were done in meters, resulting in a staggered distance from what was on the left side of the field. At the very far end of the right side of the range was a small single target at 90 meters.

All of the target mats on the left side were round and used a white covering with a standard set of concentric rings that went from black to blue to red and finally to yellow. This was your classic bullseye target.

The mats on the right side took a different approach. These were all rectangular, and stood either upright or sideways depending on the paper image wrapped around it. The images covered a wide variety of items, including different animals as well as a mix of zombies, replete with dangling limbs and torn clothing.

Tom studied the last arrow resting by his side. He had done plenty of research before buying his first archery set. His arrows had alternating red and white fletchings. The shafts were blue. He thought back to December when he and Marc were in the candle store in Truro. Marc had marveled at the lightweight arrows with the yellow vanes.

I wonder if he would like the set that I bought? Tom pondered.

Tom looked down the range and set his sights on the target set at the 60-meter mark. The mat was a hooded zombie. The image was a female with long brown hair jutting out from the edges of her hood. She had white eyes, and an exposed jaw with the flesh rotted off. Tom had been trying to hit this one for the past half hour, but he kept striking the corners of the mat or missing it altogether.

Tom placed his arrow onto the nock on his string. He

wrapped his fingers around the string, placing one above the shaft and two below. He made sure to keep his hand flat and not let his fingers touch the arrow or the nock.

He closed his eyes and took a long deep breath. In his mind, he imagined himself in the upstairs guest bedroom in Marc's townhome. The room was dimly lit, and the bed close to the large arched window was empty. When Tom finally opened his eyes, he looked at the target at 60 meters and pictured the killer standing over Julie's bed. He could see her bed sitting on the practice field.

He extended his arm and rotated his elbow out. Slowly he raised his bow. Once in position he used his back muscles to pull the bow back toward his face, being sure to keep his drawing elbow up at ear level, forming a complete T shape with his body. He then anchored his hand against his jaw.

Tom continued to stare at his target. It was no longer a mat covered with a zombie. It was Mrs. Closed. She paused as she held her dagger up over Julie. She looked up at Tom and said "Mother is waiting. There are candles to be made. Time to pay."

Tom exhaled as he gently released his fingers from the string. The red, white, and blue projectile flew across the field. It felt like an eternity, but in reality, it took but an instant. The blunt tip of the arrow struck the target dead center. From Tom's point of view, the arrow hit Mrs. Closed directly in the heart. The image suddenly shattered into glass fragments. In an instant he saw himself back at Seabreeze Village, standing in the guest bedroom, watching her fall through the jagged arched window.

"Bullseye," Tom whispered.

"Nicely done," Rick Peterson said. He had been standing several feet behind Tom, quietly observing his technique.

Tom blinked several times and shook his head to try to get the image of Mrs. Closed out of his mind. He lowered his bow and turned to face his instructor.

"Sorry, Rick, I didn't even know you were standing there. I sort of got lost in my thoughts. I thought I was alone."

Rick had been with the club since it first opened five years ago. At 52 years old he was the oldest and most experienced instructor on staff. He zipped up his blue canvas coat, disappointed that it was a struggle to get it over his ever-expanding stomach.

"I just finished with some kids inside, and I looked out the window and wondered who the hell would be out here alone in this chilly weather. Of course, it ended up being you. I can count on you to be here every Saturday. It's like clockwork with you."

"Yeah, well I still need the practice. But I can't really focus today."

"What are you talking about? You hit her dead center."

Tom glanced at the zombie target. His final arrow was resting in the center red spot. He frowned.

"Well, it took me all day."

"Is that really what matters? 60 meters is a new record for you, right Tom?"

"It is," Tom said with a slight grin. "Good point, Rick."

Tom looked around to make sure it was safe to walk down the field. He was still the only one using the outdoor range. He turned and began to walk toward the 60-meter target. Rick joined him by his side.

"You've really improved a great deal since you started three months ago," Rick said. "I like that you set these goals and stick to them. Meter by meter, target by target, week by week. You just keep improving. Your dedication is really impressive. I mean look at this shitty day. That breeze certainly isn't making things easy for you. But you nailed it."

"Well, it took me over two weeks to go from 50 to 60 meters. And I had to use every arrow. Repeatedly for the past hour. So, I'm not that happy."

"You should be proud. 10 meters is a big jump. What you need to do now is stick with the 60-meter target until you are consistently striking it. Don't be in a big rush to get to the next one."

"That makes sense, Rick. This last one may have just been a lucky shot."

"Don't sell yourself short, kid."

They arrived at the 60-meter target. Tom had four arrows that had hit the target, including the one in the bullseye. The other eight were spread out across the grass behind the target. Rick began to remove the arrows from the mat, taking care not to tear the zombie image that covered it. Tom began to search for the ones that had missed.

"You've got skills, Tom." Rick continued. "You are going to be a real killer once hunting season gets here later this year. Have you bought the right tips? These bullet tips you are using are only good for targets. You need some nice broadheads."

"Hunting?" Tom asked somewhat surprised.

"Isn't that what all of this is for? When you signed up, I thought you said it was for hunting. Are you a hunter?"

"Oh ... well, yes. Eventually. To be honest, right now my focus is just confidence building. A friend told me archery would be good for me. This was the place he told me to go ..."

Tom stopped, not wanting to complete the sentence.

"Who's your friend?" Rick asked. "Is he a member?"

Tom glanced around the empty field. There were two arrows still unaccounted for.

"He was," Tom replied. He took a moment to collect his thoughts. "Not anymore."

"Damn," Rick sighed with disappointment. "Did he switch clubs? I can tell you this is the best one in the state. And not just because of the size. I've tried them all. Where is he now?"

Tom noticed the last two arrows sitting just past the 70-meter target. He walked over and grabbed them. Rick waited patiently for him to return. Tom turned and slowly walked over to his instructor.

"He died. A few months ago."

"Holy shit. I am so sorry, Tom. Honestly, if I had known ..."

"It's OK, Rick. I purposely didn't bring it up when I signed up because I really didn't know who might know him. I honestly was not ready to discuss it."

"I understand."

Tom took the four arrows Rick was holding and began the long walk back toward the main building. Rick waited a few seconds before following him.

"Tom, is it something you can talk about now?"

Tom did not reply. The wind was beginning to pick up. The air felt damp and cold as it blew across his face. Tom took a deep breath, trying to take solace in the scent of the freshly cut grass. The silence of the morning wrapped itself around him. Even the birds were not singing. He suddenly felt very empty and alone.

"Can you at least tell me his name?" Rick asked.

Tom stopped but did not turn around to face Rick.

"Marc. Marc Sirola."

Rick was stunned. He quickly walked up to Tom and rested his hand on his shoulder, pulling him back to turn him around. Tom could not look Rick in the eyes. Instead, he looked past him, at the various targets spread out across the field.

"Marc's dead?" Rick asked as he shook his head in disbelief. "I was wondering what the hell happened to him. He hasn't been here in months. I tried calling him the other week, but the call would not go through. What the hell happened?"

"It's a long story, Rick. I really don't know that I can ..."

"Hey, hey, it's OK, Tom. I didn't mean to press you. Marc was a fantastic archer. Not to mention a total beast! I used to tell him he was wasting his time with a bow and arrow since he was big enough to wrestle any animal to the ground."

Tom finally managed a broad smile at the thought of Marc taking down a huge deer with his bare hands. He looked up at Rick and nodded in approval.

"I could see Marc doing that too."

The two men turned and walked in silence until they reached the equipment area. Tom dropped his arrows next to his case and began to load them in, one by one, taking the time to wipe them clean of any debris they had collected. Rick smiled at how methodical Tom was with the care he took with his equipment.

"Was he a good friend?" Rick asked, unsure if he was pressing too hard.

"He was the best," Tom responded. He felt his eyes begin to well up.

"So sorry for your loss, Tom."

"Thanks, Rick. Truth be told, I had promised Marc I would take up archery. It was a promise I made before he died."

"Well, I can tell you he would be proud of you. You're really quite good."

Tom finished loading his case. He looked around one more time to make sure he had not left anything behind. He noticed his cell phone sitting on the edge of the table.

"You really need to think about taking up hunting," Rick said. "Hunting season begins late September. I can just imagine how good you will be five months from now. Have you thought about what you want to hunt?"

Tom grabbed his phone and looked at the screen with the blurry image of Mrs. Closed on it.

"I have," Tom said with decisiveness. "Take care, Rick."

EIGHT

Departure

Julie rummaged through her duffle bag one last time. She wanted to make sure she had everything she would need for the weekend ahead. Mr. Fluffy was hiding under the couch, watching her every move. Julie walked over to the couch and got down on all fours.

"I won't be gone long," Julie said.

Mr. Fluffy purred quietly but kept his distance. Julie stood up and wiped the dust from her pants. A faint knocking came from her front door, startling her. She walked over to the door and looked through the peephole.

"For fuck's sake."

Julie debated opening the door or waiting to see if she would leave. Another series of knocks came. These were even louder. Julie sighed as she flicked the deadbolt sideways and opened her door.

"Mrs. Leblanc," Julie said with a half-smile. "What a surprise."

Tom's mother stood patiently on Julie's porch. Her flowered scarf was knotted tightly beneath her pouting chin.

"Did you want to come in?" Julie asked.

"Thank you," Mrs. Leblanc replied.

Julie took a few steps back and allowed her to enter the apartment. Mrs. Leblanc looked around the small one-bedroom unit, taking time to quietly inspect everything. She frowned as she noticed the dust covering the table next to the front door.

"I'm sorry to show up unannounced," Mrs. Leblanc said. "I didn't want to do this on the phone. Can we sit?"

"Sure."

Julie closed her front door and escorted Tom's mother over to the couch in the living room. Mr. Fluffy stayed hidden below as the two women sat down. Mrs. Leblanc untied her scarf and folded it neatly before resting it on her lap.

"Are you not able to take Max?" Julie asked. "When I called you last night you said you were more than happy to take him."

"This isn't about Max," Mrs. Leblanc said. "I'll swing by and get him after you leave today. It's this trip you are doing to the Cape. I'm worried. I'm worried about Tom. He's become too obsessed with what happened last December."

"Well, he's kind of an obsessive guy. In case you haven't noticed."

Julie flashed Mrs. Leblanc a grin, hoping to lighten the old woman's dour mood. The blank stare told Julie her smile was not effective.

"Julie, what do you know about the death of Tom's father?"

Julie folded her feet beneath her thighs and leaned back against the backside of the couch. She clasped her hands and began to pick at her cuticles.

"His dad? Well, I know … I mean … What … what does his dad have to do with what happened in P-Town?"

Mrs. Leblanc looked Julie up and down, taking in her tone and apparent discomfort.

"You do know that he was murdered, don't you? You and Tom are very close. I assume you know what happened."

"To be honest, Mrs. Leblanc, Tom doesn't like talking about his dad's death. I know he was killed when Tom was only twelve years old. I know Tom saw it happen. But that's about it."

Mrs. Leblanc's raised her eyebrows. She turned her attention to the dusty coffee table next to her knees.

"Really? He never told you the details?"

"No. He can be a bit of a clam."

Mrs. Leblanc managed a slight chuckle.

"He can indeed, Julie. My husband ... my husband was murdered. I was out of town when it happened. A horrible snowstorm delayed my return. I often wonder if things would have turned out differently had I been home. It was his birthday, and ..."

"Tom's birthday?"

"Yes. My, he really has kept the story from you. There was a break-in at the house. My husband struggled with the intruder. Tom ... Tom walked into the kitchen just as his father was killed. He was stabbed. It ... it was a fatal blow."

"Oh my God. Stabbed?" Julie closed her eyes as the image of a knife-wielding Mrs. Closed materialized in her mind.

Julie opened her eyes and looked at Tom's mother. She didn't know how much Tom had told her about the events that had happened last December.

"Stabbed," Julie said. "I ... I had no idea. Tom never told me how he died. Only that he saw it happen."

"Then I'm guessing he never told you what happened later."

"Later?"

Mrs. Leblanc sighed as she closed her eyes. Recounting the death of her husband was something she hated to do. She opened her eyes and looked at Julie.

"They never caught who did it. The bastard ran out the back door, leaving Tom alone with his dying father. The police searched for months. To this day it remains an unsolved murder."

"That's horrible."

"Thomas went into therapy. I ... I couldn't help him deal with it. I thought I could. I tried. I tried everything. But it was beyond me. The trauma of seeing his father killed was bad enough. But then he just became obsessed with finding out who did it. He would ride his bike to the police station and ask for updates. The detective was so kind and supportive. But this went on for years, Julie. He would read about a local break-in or assault or murder. Then he would run to the police to see if there was a possible connection. It was a long time before he finally let it go, and stopped bothering the police.

But I know that deep down he never really has. You know?"

Julie reached over and took Mrs. Leblanc by the hand.

"Thank you for sharing this with me."

Mrs. Leblanc squeezed Julie's hands and pulled her closer.

"When you called me, you told me you were taking him to the Cape this weekend. I need you to promise me this is not about what happened last December. That's why I came here. To make sure you knew about Tom. I know the woman that escaped has not been caught. I don't want him going off on some wild chase trying to play detective."

Julie looked into the old woman's pale blue eyes. She could see the worry and concern that she was carrying.

"Like I told you last night, I'm just taking Tom away for a belated birthday escape."

"Hyannis, right? That's what you told me on the phone."

Julie smiled nervously.

"Yes."

"Good. Hyannis is almost an hour from Provincetown."

"Trust me, we won't go anywhere near Provincetown. Or Truro. That's the truth."

Mrs. Leblanc studied Julie's smiling face as she squeezed her hands. She let out a sigh of relief and smiled back.

"You're a good friend, Julie. Thank you."

***

Max was curled up, fast asleep in his woven brown canvas dog bed. Max often liked to fluff his dog bed to try and get it into the perfect shape. This daily habit would end up shredding holes in the outer material. Max destroyed several during his first year of adoption. Tom finally settled on an oversized, heavy-duty bed. It had proven quite durable since being put into service a year ago. Max's left front paw dangled from the edge of the cushion, quivering ever so slightly, along with his upper lip. The dog was in the middle of a very happy dream. Several small yelps managed to escape from his deep slumber.

The creak of the front stairs was subtle but enough to get Max's attention. First, his left eye slowly opened. Another creak followed. Max's right eye popped opened as he lifted his head and turned toward the front of the house. Another creak. Both of Max's ears shot upright as a low rumbling grow began to churn in his throat. Max jumped up and ran to the window, ready to bark if he did not like what he saw outside.

"Is that Aunty Jewels?" Tom called out from the kitchen.

Max pressed his nose against the window and began to whimper. His tail whipped in a circular clockwise motion. The bolt to the front door snapped open with a loud thump. Max ran to the hallway just as the door flew open.

"Max! Max! Max!" Julie yelled. "Aunty Jewels is here!"

Max jumped up onto Julie, planting both paws right under her chest. Julie dropped the duffle bag she was carrying and slid it off to the side. She then kicked the front door shut with a slam.

"Watch The Girls!" Julie said with a laugh. She dropped to her knees and began massaging Max's ears as he nibbled on her nose.

Tom walked down the hall from the kitchen, carrying a mug of Earl Gray tea. He was wearing slippers that Julie had bought him for Christmas. They were brown bear faces that Julie had pre-mangled a bit to wear them out. One had a missing eye. The other had an ear that had slice marks through it. She had even taken the time to run them through some mud and snow. She told him they were Zombears, to match her own set of worn out Zombunnies.

"You're late," Tom said.

"Are you moving?" Julie asked as she continued to massage Max. He had dropped and rolled onto his back and was enjoying a vigorous belly rub.

"What?" Tom replied somewhat confused.

"There is a 'For Sale' sign at your curb."

Tom glanced out the front window.

"Wow, they are finally selling the unit upstairs," Tom said with a smile of approval. "They must have put that up after I got back from walking Max. It wasn't there earlier."

Tom's condo made up the first floor of a three-story home. Years ago, it used to be three separate apartments. Then someone bought it and converted it to condos. The first floor, purchased by Tom at a foreclosure, was a small two-bedroom one and a half bath unit. The two upper levels had been converted to a large three-bedroom two-bath townhouse style home. The current owner bought it as an investment and rented it out.

"I hope you get some better neighbors," Julie said.

"Me too. Ideally, someone nice and quiet that lives there. The current renters have lead feet."

"Right? I have the same issue at my apartment."

"So, when are you going to tell me the name of the place you got for us in Eastham?" Tom asked. "Why all the secrecy?"

"You plan everything. Besides, it will add to the birthday fun."

"Birthday? Jewels, my birthday was in January. That was three months ago."

"I know. We never did any sort of celebration. I never got you a gift. Just a lame card. It was too soon after ... after everything that happened out on the Cape. I owe you something. This weekend is on me. I got us a fab place. It looked so adorable online!"

"That's too sweet. It's really not necessary."

"It is. You're twenty-nine now. End of an era. You hit thirty next year. I hit thirty in November. We need to enjoy our twenties before we become old."

Tom looked down at his Travel Checklist that was resting on the kitchen table. He had packed everything late last night. All that was left to do was to lock down the condo. He began going window to window to close the blinds.

"My mom is coming by to get Max, right?" Tom asked. "What time?"

"Actually, she ..."

"She what?"

Julie briefly considered telling Tom about her surprise visit, but quickly determined it was best not to discuss it with him.

"She told me she had some errands to do here in Providence and would swing by shortly after we leave."

"What kind of errands does she have here in Providence?"

"I have no idea. Can you finish your anal little list so we can get going? Or do you want to still be here when she shows up?"

"God, no."

Tom laughed as he closed the last of the window blinds. He returned from the living room and went into his bedroom to get his backpack.

"Any new toys for this trip?" Julie asked as she nodded towards his bag.

Tom reached into his pack and retrieved a pair of binoculars. His mother had given him a gift card for Christmas, and he used it to buy them. They had a 10x-30x adjustable zoom range.

"What are those for?" Julie asked.

"Surveillance!" Tom said with a grin.

"Such the detective."

Tom brought his bag to the front door and sat it down next to the rest of the bags. Max walked into the hallway and laid down in front of the door, blocking the exit.

"Someone knows what's going on," Julie said.

"Hey, Max," Tom said as he knelt down next to his dog. "Mémé is coming to get you. You're going to spend the weekend with her."

Max did not budge.

"I'm not seeing much excitement from him," Julie laughed. "Are you sure he loves staying with your mom?"

"Max loves her. She spoils him rotten. He just lays the guilt trip on me anytime I leave."

"See, Mr. Fluffy could give a shit. I walk out the door and say goodbye he doesn't even look over. Cats are easy."

"Dogs are a lot more work, but you get so much love back. We both know our pet choices reflect ..."

"Don't even, Tom," Julie said with frustration.

"You aren't big on commitments, Jewels. Admit it. Mr. Fluffy is easy to care for. Max is a lot more work. Commitment."

"Or maybe I am just a low maintenance type of gal?"

"Are you implying I am not?"

Julie burst out laughing as she reached for her duffle bag.

"No comment. Let's get this weekend escape started."

***

Traffic heading to Cape Cod had been free of congestion. Tom and Julie were making great time. It was 1:15 p.m. as they approached the Bourne Bridge. The bridge was a sister bridge to the Sagamore Bridge that sat to the north. Construction was completed in 1935. The large steel arched bridge glistened in the afternoon sun. Tom accelerated as they began to cross the Cape Cod Canal.

"What's our ETA?" Tom asked as they traversed the middle of the bridge.

"I think we have another hour," Julie replied. She pulled out her phone and opened up her map. She had plugged in the route to the B&B before they left. "Looks like 50 minutes."

At the bottom of the bridge, they entered a huge roundabout. Tom followed it until he could jump onto Route 6A running parallel to the canal.

"I have a good feeling about this, Jewels. That table in the photo is the key. I think the woman that is selling it will lead us to the killers."

Julie put her phone away and nervously clasped her hands together.

"I think it's a long shot, Tom. Don't get your hopes up."

"But she said the table had been in her family. The table looked to be the same as the one Mrs. Closed had at the store. That means the seller must know Mrs. Closed!"

"I get that your logical little brain has this all figured out. I just think it's a stretch. You are assuming that Mrs. Closed didn't buy that table someplace. You are assuming it is *her* family table as well."

Tom paused to consider what she had said.

"Good point, Jewels. I didn't think of that. But if this woman is clinging to the family relevance of the table, then one would assume the table that Mrs. Closed had at the store is just as relevant to someone else. We should at least be able to track down some history on the family that made the table."

"Touché, Tom."

Tom smiled at his deductive reasoning and logic. He knew there had to be a connection.

"We would make a great pair of detectives, Jewels.

Seriously. We could give your sexy cop in Provincetown a run for his money. Show him a thing or two."

"Oh, trust me, I have several things I'd like to show Trevor."

Tom slowed as the traffic began to pile up. They were nearing the on-ramp to Route 6 just below the Sagamore Bridge.

"You and me as detectives," Julie said with a chuckle. "We would be such a mismatched pair. We would be clashing all of the time!"

"No way, Jewels. We'd be great! We just need cool detective names."

"I can only imagine!" Julie laughed.

Tom hauled Ruby to a stop, as traffic on Route 6A came to a standstill.

"I was hoping it would have been lighter today," Tom said with a frown. "Maybe there's an accident. Check the map."

Julie lowered her window and jammed her head outside to try and see how far the traffic went. The wind was crisp and blustery coming off the canal.

"It's not that bad," Julie concluded. "I can see where it clears."

"That air smells great," Tom said. He lowered his window a few inches and let the cross breeze fill the Jeep.

"Do you have anything to drink?"

"There's a bag in the back. Not one of the ones that we packed. It's one of the other ones."

Julie turned around and looked at all of the bags behind them. There were so many for such a quick escape. She pulled a large canvas case forward and unzipped it. Tom's archery equipment was inside.

"Why did you bring your bow and arrow?"

"Not that one. The smaller one next to it. With the red piping."

Julie pulled a small gym bag onto her lap. It was heavy. Inside she found several road trip items. She smiled, impressed at all of the different articles that were in the bag. She pulled out a stainless-steel mug with a power cord connected to it.

"Is this to boil water?" Julie asked with a bit of amazement.

"Yup. There are bottles of water back there too. We can plug it in and make tea, cocoa, whatever. There should be a couple of insulated mugs in that bag with the heater. Red for me, pink for you."

Julie rummaged through the bag and smiled.

"You amaze me, Tom. Seriously. It's like I can wish for anything and like magic you just automatically make it appear. It's ... it's ... Automagical!"

Tom laughed.

"You're welcome."

Julie plugged in the 12v electric heater and filled it with water. She pulled out Tom's knapsack and quickly found tea and cocoa mix.

"So, Tom, what do you think we will find once we get to the estate sale? For real."

"Honestly, Jewels? I'm not too sure."

NINE

Twilight

The Johnson family Victorian house in Wellfleet, Massachusetts was in spectacular condition. Fred Johnson had recently completed giving it a new coat of paint, as well as replacing all of the floorboards that wrapped around the deep outdoor porch and stairs. He opted to keep the original colors. Fred liked tradition.

The posts supporting the porch roof, as well as the window trim, were all done in pristine soft white. The shingles covering the sides of the house were a pale blue-gray called "Morning Sky." The color reminded Fred of the horizon before the morning sun rose up over the Atlantic. It worked perfectly with the brown and gray stacked stones that made up the foundation of the house. This same stonework continued up across the front of the main entrance. Fred had even spent some time sanding the front doorway to give it a new coat of stain and gloss. The refurbished woodwork really made the stained glass stand out. The five-bedroom home had never looked better.

Set far back from the house, shrouded beneath several towering pine trees, sat the family barn. The barn, unlike the house, had never been painted. It was a sturdy wooden structure. Fred's family had made sure to overbuild it to withstand the occasional extreme weather that would come in off the coast. The plank siding had weathered to a grayish brown over the years. Several planks and shingles had been replaced recently and stood out from the rest of the older materials.

Sunset was less than an hour away. The light inside the barn was beginning to fade. Fred was busy trying to get things cleaned up before tomorrow's big cookout. He took a moment to turn on the large overhead electrical lights. Apollo, a six-year-old Doberman, was sprawled out against a wall. The hum from the lights woke him from his slumber. He raised his head to see what his master was doing.

Fred used a pitchfork to push fresh hay back into the stall behind the ladder that led up to the loft. After clearing up as much as he could, he slid the pitchfork – handle side down – between two of the rungs of the ladder. Fred let the tool slide through his hands until it caught a notch in the floor of the barn. After making sure it was secure he went over to the large workbench several feet away.

A handful of small daggers were spread across the top of the table. Next to them was a whetstone. Fred spent a few moments admiring the collection of knives he had made. He was particularly proud of the inlaid nickel and turquoise detail he had crafted into the handles. Fred picked up the dagger closest to him to inspect the handle. He nodded in approval.

"Someday I'm going to try to sell these, Apollo. They will make for a nice income and hobby when I'm retired."

Apollo yawned in response, rolled over onto his back and closed his eyes.

Fred made his way around to the backside of the workbench to check the status of his latest creation. Sitting on a stained tarp was a small, glossy, dark wooden table. The top was circular and exactly three feet across. Fred had used two different types of woods to inlay into the top. The inlays were completely flush, and the difference in grain made for a lovely pattern. Fred was most proud of the rosewood legs. He was able to mimic the nickel and turquoise inlay pattern used on the daggers into the last few inches near the feet.

Fred gently pressed two fingers under the lip of the table. He'd spent the day doing multiple coats to seal the wood and wasn't sure if it had dried yet. It was still a bit gummy to the touch. He would have to let it sit for the night.

"Now they each have one," Fred said with pride.

Fred had made a similar table for his wife last summer. His sister-in-law, Jennifer, had praised Fred for his skills at creating such "works of art" as she had called them. He wanted to surprise her with a table for her to have as her own. Fred intended to present it to her at tomorrow's cookout as an early birthday gift.

Fred looked around to make sure he had finished his chores. He glanced over at Apollo. The dog was fast asleep. Fred turned off the lights, exited the barn and left the front door ajar for Apollo. As he approached the steps on the side of the porch, he detected a very unpleasant odor. With a heavy sigh, Fred glanced down and bent his right foot up at an angle so he could see the sole of his work boot.

"Shit," Fred said. His boot was caked in what appeared to be cow manure. Fred pushed the ball of his foot deep into a mound of grass to try and dislodge it. The deep pattern of his soles held tightly to the excrement. "I can't track this inside. I'll never hear the end of it."

Fred walked up the porch and tip-toed up the stairs, being careful not to get feces everywhere. There was a small bench between the kitchen door and window. He dropped himself onto the bench and began to unlace his boots. He could smell the scent of a freshly baked apple pie wafting out through the window.

Laura was seated at a large metal kitchen table. The shiny turquoise vinyl and chrome chairs were only a few months old and in excellent shape. She nervously drummed her fingers across the top of the chair that was beside her. Laura was shaking her head in frustration at the conversation she and Bobby Mason were having on the telephone.

"I'm sorry, but I just don't have time for this," Laura said. She paused and got out of her chair and walked over to the window to look at the barn. She was talking on an old corded phone, and the line barely reached to that side of the room.

Laura was relieved to see the door was still open. Believing she was alone, she continued her conversation.

"Because I'm too stressed planning the cookout. The girls are driving me crazy. I mean ... What?" Laura paused briefly, before letting out a slight chuckle. "Yes, including *our* daughter. That precious little flower! There are days she is worse than the twins. Thankfully her cousin Marilyn will be here tomorrow. Those two are ... Yes, yes, they are two peas in a pod."

Fred paused as he began to remove his right boot. *Did she say "our" daughter?" What did she mean by that?* Fred wondered.

"Before you hang up can I ask you something?" Laura said cautiously. "Things have seemed off with you and Jennie lately. There is this tension. Or is it my imagination? I'm just starting to wonder if ... if ... well, does she know about ... does she know about us?"

Fred's breathing became heavy and forced as the words he just heard began to sink in. He replayed Laura's last few words in his mind.

"Are you sure?" Laura said with concern. "Because we can't let her find out. Could you imagine? When I think about ... What? Fred? No, of course not. He's clueless."

Laura turned and walked back to the wall on the opposite side of the room. The strained telephone cord slowly drooped back toward the floor. Laura peered out the window again. It was quiet. Too quiet, in her opinion.

Fred sat outside, enraged. His temples throbbed from the beat of his racing heart. He slowly sat up. Fred took a few deep breaths and tried to collect his thoughts. *Did I just hear what I thought I did?* Fred said to himself. *Is my wife having an affair with Carl? Is my baby girl ... his?*

"I need to go," Laura said. "Fred is going to be here any minute. I will see you tomorrow, OK?"

Laura paused and smiled.

"I love you too," Laura replied. She hung up the phone and walked over to the refrigerator.

Fred finished removing his boots but decided to wait before going inside. It felt like an eternity. He listened to the clank of silverware and glasses as his wife went back to her work in the kitchen. Fred took multiple deep breaths to try and calm his escalating temper.

Fred walked over to the edge of the stairs and clapped his boots loudly, sending chunks of cow shit everywhere. Part of him wanted to barge in there and start a huge fight. His blood pressure was through the roof. He decided it was best to play it calmly and see what he could find out. Fred made a few loud thuds against the steps and then opened the side door.

Laura was standing at the counter enjoying a glass of white wine when he entered.

"What was all of that banging?" Laura asked.

Fred stood in the doorway glaring at his wife. He could not believe she was acting so casual given the conversation she had just had on the phone. He stared at her and did not respond.

"Are you OK?" Laura asked with concern. "You look ... red."

"To be honest, I don't feel so good right now."

"It's that sealant you were using on the table, wasn't it? I told you to keep all of the barn doors wide open for a cross breeze. Did you keep the side door open too?"

"The sealant?" Fred asked. His tone was dazed. He quickly realized he could use this excuse to his advantage. "I'm definitely feeling light headed. To make matters worse, my boots were caked in cow shit. I had to bend over out in the yard to try to clean them and I sort of lost my balance."

"Well come sit down. Relax."

Laura walked over and put her arm around her husband and guided him to one of the kitchen chairs. She held him by his elbow to help lower him to the seat. Fred played along and leaned on his wife for support.

"Who were you talking to?" Fred asked. He stared long and hard into Laura's eyes, looking for any hint of honesty ... or betrayal. "I thought I heard voices."

Laura clasped her hands and smiled. She then put one hand on Fred's forehead. He was red hot.

"I was on the phone," Laura said with trepidation. "Nothing important. You feel overheated. Let me get you a beer."

Laura turned and strolled over to the fridge. She was a bit

nervous that Fred may have overheard something. She retrieved a beer and brought it to her husband. Fred popped the can open as Laura took the seat across from him.

"So, who was it?" Fred asked.

Laura was starting to feel trapped. She needed an out.

"Carl called," Laura said casually.

Fred took a long sip of his beer. *I was right! Carl!* Fred wanted to explode. *She's fucking my brother-in-law? And she said "our" child!*

Fred took several long gulps from the can. The ice-cold alcohol felt good as it rushed down his throat. He took a deep breath and locked eyes with Laura.

"Carl?" Fred asked with an inquisitive tone. "What did he want?"

"It was nothing, dear. Just making some final plans for the cookout tomorrow. It should be a wonderful birthday party, don't you think?"

Fred stared at his wife in disbelief. He then turned his attention to his beer, taking another long chug from the can. His cheeks were still flush. His heart pounded rapidly in his chest.

Laura was concerned with how flushed he still looked. She walked over to the fridge and pulled out a second beer and left it on the table for him.

"I'm going upstairs to check on the twins," Laura said. "Oh, did you finish the table for my sister?"

"I did," Fred said. He forced a smile to appear.

"You are such a good husband," Laura said. She walked over and kissed Fred on his forehead. "My sister is going to love you to pieces."

Fred smiled as he looked into his wife's eyes. He was at a loss for words.

"She is going to be so surprised tomorrow!" Laura said as she turned and left the kitchen.

Fred sat alone at the chrome and turquoise table. He crushed the empty beer can in his hand and tossed it into the sink across the room.

"Tomorrow is going to be full of surprises," Fred said.

TEN

Eastham

Marsh Mellow Inn was situated at the end of a winding road in Eastham, Massachusetts. The small complex was made up of a large colonial home with two small cottages. The main house had thirteen rooms, several with a private bath. All three buildings had white trim and naturally weathered dark gray shingles. The complex spanned over twenty acres of open land bordering a vast salt marsh. The marsh was part of the Cape Cod National Seashore, which in and of itself covered over 43,000 acres along the Cape.

The state park was home to an abundance of wildlife, including dozens of protected species. Some were year-round inhabitants, while others would nest seasonally or use the space for migration. The park's ecosystem was heavily researched and monitored. In addition to the hundreds of animals that made the area home, the park was used to study coastal erosion, sea level rise, and other geological events.

Guests of the Marsh Mellow Inn had one of the most breathtaking unobstructed views of this ever-changing biome. It was a truly unique property on the outer Cape.

Tom and Julie were staying in one of the two stand-alone cottages. Their cottage was named "Red Cedar," as indicated by a small hand-painted sign affixed above the front entrance. The unit was named after the Eastern Red Cedar – one of many trees that thrived in the Cape's climate.

The small 800 square foot building had two floors and had recently been renovated. The original wide-plank pine flooring had been restored to a deep maple color. There was a small kitchenette area with a tiny fridge, sink, and microwave. Alongside the kitchen was a small pine wooden table with two chairs. A pale green cotton sleep sofa and an oversized white linen reclining chair made up the bulk of the rest of the space, along with a tight bathroom with a stand-up shower. The wall that ran along the east side faced out toward the marsh. Oversized windows sat on either side of a pair of French doors, that opened to a covered back porch. A narrow staircase ran along the north side of the cottage, leading to an open loft bedroom.

"This is adorable," Tom said as he placed his bags on the floor next to the sofa. "Well done, Jewels."

"It was pure luck I got this cottage. They just had a cancelation. The loft is all yours, Tom. I've got the sleep sofa."

Julie dropped her bags in the kitchen and slammed the front door closed.

"Are you sure?"

"Totally. Happy birthday."

Julie walked into the bathroom with her toiletry bag. She unpacked a pile of items including her cocoa butter. She poured some out to moisturize her hands. Tom stepped in and looked around.

"Cozy," Tom said with a smile.

"I think it's the honeymoon suite," Julie said with a laugh. "Cocoa butter, husband?"

"No thank you, wifey-poo."

"You have very dry skin. If you don't start moisturizing now, you are going to look like shit by the time you hit forty. I have a great face cream, too."

"I'm fine, Jewels."

Tom grabbed his carry-on and backpack and headed up to the loft. A white wood railing cut across an opening that looked down into the main room below. The bedroom had a white linen queen-sized bed decorated with green and yellow cotton pillows. The pale green walls had a variety of local artwork reflecting the thriving life and images of the marsh. A small door led outside to a second porch.

Tom walked outside for a quick look around. The porch was above the one down below, but had no roof, resulting in complete unobstructed views of the wetlands. Clouds hung off the coast, painting the sky a mix of pale blue with streaks of white and steel gray. Below was the lush marsh, dotted with rocks, sand, and trees. It was an endless tapestry of auburn and olive fabrics that wove their way from the cottage to the shoreline. Patches of purple flowers peppered the terrain that extended out to the Atlantic half a mile away. *I'm glad I brought my binoculars*, Tom said to himself.

Once back inside Tom walked over to the railing that overlooked the downstairs. Julie was still in the bathroom.

"Are you sure you don't want the loft?" Tom called out. "You paid for all of this. The porch has amazing views up here. It would get me closer to the bathroom, too."

Julie stepped out of the bathroom and looked up at Tom and smiled.

"I'm good! Remember, this is all part of your birthday present. Take the comfy bed. It's just the one night."

Tom spent a few minutes unpacking his clothes and putting them into a small white wooden dresser. He then rummaged through his backpack and grabbed his binoculars before heading downstairs.

"Did you check out the views yet, Jewels?"

Tom pressed his face up against one of the back windows and looked out toward the ocean. There were several small clusters of trees scattered along the property. They thinned out the closer they got to the salt marsh. Tom immediately started to do the math in his head to figure out how many yards or meters they might be, mentally aligning the trees to the targets on his archery range back home.

"It's stunning, isn't it?" Julie asked as she walked over to be by Tom's side. She opened the back door, startling a pair of deer that had been quietly strolling by. The animals bolted off into the nearby forest. The intense scent of the salt marsh wrapped itself around them as they stepped out onto the porch.

"I sometimes forget how tranquil parts of the Cape can be," Tom said quietly. "It's so easy to get wrapped up in the tourist stuff. All of the shops and restaurants. But this. This here is what it's really all about."

The air was cool, and the wind blowing in off the Atlantic Ocean was crisp. The two stood there in silence for a minute, enjoying the peace and quiet. Tom used his binoculars to study a deer at the edge of the forest.

"Sunrise tomorrow should be spectacular. This was a good idea, Jewels."

"I think this escape is just what we needed."

"So, what's this place again? Marshmallow Inn? Did you pick that because they make awesome hot cocoa?"

"No. It's two words. Marsh and mellow. Like relaxing in a mellow marsh."

"They definitely got the name right. But it's getting a bit too cold for me. It must be low 40's. We may want to come back here another time. Imagine sitting out here with this view when it is more like 70 degrees?"

"It would be heaven," Julie said as she nodded in agreement. "Add wine and cheese, and I would never leave."

Tom opened the door so he and Julie could return to the warmth of the cottage. Once inside they both turned to enjoy the view once more. A pair of egrets descended from the tree closest to their cabin and headed off toward the ocean.

"I read up on this place before I booked it. To answer your original question, yes, they do make hot cocoa. With milk! Oh, and they do a huge Sunday brunch, too. We will have to check it out tomorrow before we leave. It looks amazing."

Tom chuckled. Julie always had food on her mind. He glanced around the cottage looking for a clock. The one on the microwave showed it was 2:30 p.m.

"We should probably head over to that estate sale," Tom said.

"I wish you hadn't brought up marshmallows. Now I'm craving s'mores."

"Sorry, Jewels, I didn't pack any in my knapsack."

"I bet we can find a small market in town," Julie said.

Tom ran up the narrow staircase to get his backpack. He

spent a bit of time rummaging through it to make sure he had everything they might need for the rest of the afternoon.

"Bomb's away!" Tom cried as he dropped the backpack onto the couch down below.

"Watch it, Leblanc. The security deposit's in my name."

Tom laughed as he bounded down the staircase.

"It's a really great birthday present!"

Julie smiled as she slid her coat on. Tom joined her at the back door and snatched his keys and coat. They took a moment and stared at each other.

"Are you ready for this, Jewels?"

"I'm kind of starting to dread it."

"I know you think I'm crazy for thinking that woman is somehow related to Mrs. Closed because of the table," Tom said. He was starting to worry Julie was going to back out. "But I can't ignore my gut on this one."

"I don't think you are crazy. I just think it's a stretch. Do you want to hear my crazy theory?"

"I can't wait."

Tom opened the front door, and he and Julie stepped out into the chilly damp air. The western side of the cottage was protected from the winds coming off the ocean. It felt much warmer than it did just a few minutes ago on the back porch.

"Keys?" Tom asked before closing the door. Julie held up the key to the cottage and waved it across his face.

"Remember how Trevor told us there were other missing person cases?" Julie asked. "The one from the store. That Truro cop told us the store owners were Asian."

Tom's Jeep was parked several feet from the entrance to the cottage. Julie closed and locked the door before following Tom over to Ruby. The two jumped inside.

"I remember," Tom said as he closed his door.

"What scent were the candles at the store? The ones Mrs. Closed had."

"Sesame. I bought a sesame-scented one. I don't remember the other one. Wait, it was ..."

"Ginger. It was ginger. Do you see the connection?"

Tom fired up the engine and adjusted the heater to maximum.

"Connection to what?"

"The legend. From the book. Waxed in Wellfleet."

Tom glanced over at Julie and rolled his eyes. He decided a response wasn't even warranted. Julie frowned at his obvious disappointment.

"Hear me out," Julie continued. "The legend said the victims were made into candles. The couple that owned the store, and went missing, is Asian. The candles were Asian scented."

Tom shifted Ruby into reverse and began to roll back out to the driveway.

"I know that face," Julie said. "Look, I'm willing to buy your family table connection. Besides, I have more to support my theory. What did she say when she was trying to kill us in the condo?"

Tom finished backing out, turned, and shifted to drive.

"She said there were candles to be made," Tom said. "In the barn."

"Exactly! Those Asians were in the ginger and sesame candles, Tom. As morbid as this sounds, with Marc and Chris also taken by her, I guarantee you there is a set of candles ... with them inside."

Tom looked at all of the cars parked at the main house. It seemed to be about half full. He kept his pace slow as they made their way down the long driveway toward the exit.

"That makes no sense. The wicks were wooden. The legend said the wicks were bones."

"Mrs. Closed said something about that as well. About the book not being completely accurate."

"OK Jewels, so if that's true, then I have to ask you the most obvious question. If Marc and Chris were made into candles, what scent would they be? I mean, put aside that your Asian scented theory is sort of racist. How do Marc and Chris play into this? What would they have in common to be made into some sort of scent?"

Julie folded her arms across her chest in disgust. She turned and looked out her window toward the salt marsh and watched as it faded into the distance.

"I'm not being racist, Tom. I'm just connecting the dots.

Look, I have no idea what sort of candle they would end up in. You're connecting the family members and tables. I'm connecting the candles to the legend and the missing people. It's just something for us to keep an eye out for."

Tom's Jeep came to a halt at the stop sign at the end of the driveway. He turned and looked at Julie. He could tell that his reaction had upset his friend. He knew he needed to be more supportive.

"OK Jewels," Tom replied. "I didn't mean to rattle you. We're in this together, after all. We'll definitely keep an eye out for other scented candles."

Julie turned to face Tom.

"That candle jar was unique, Tom. That flip top lid. You don't see that every day. That's something else we need to look for. Don't you think?"

"Ditto on that, Jewels."

Julie held her hands out in front of the vent to warm them.

"Did you ever tell Officer Stevens about your theory?" Tom asked. "About the missing couple being in the candles?"

"No. I know it sounds crazy. I mean look at how you reacted. I can imagine what the cops would think."

Julie opened her handbag and pulled out a small bottle of cocoa butter and rubbed some on her hands. She offered it to Tom, but he shook his head no. Julie frowned.

"Tom, I just had an even more morbid thought."

"What's that, Jewels?"

"She said she was going to take us back to the barn. To make us into candles. Make *us* into candles. So, it begs the question. What scent would we have become?"

Tom and Julie stared at one another in silence for a few moments. He had no response. Tom turned his attention back to the intersection and empty road in front of them. A chill ran down the hairs on the back of his neck as he pulled out onto the main road, taking them away from the inn.

***

"I think that's the house," Julie said. "On the corner."

Tom drove past a large bungalow and took a right turn

around the corner. He slowed until he was a few houses past their destination, and parked his Jeep.

"Why are you parking way down here?" Julie asked.

"I'm being discreet," Tom replied. "What if I'm right about the family table connection? Or you are with the scented candles? What if Mrs. Closed is in there? I want to keep Ruby at a safe enough distance so that we can make a run for it if we have to."

"It's a good thing I didn't wear heels."

"Ditto on that, Jewels."

Tom and Julie both burst out laughing. It brought a much-needed release of built-up tension. The two had barely spoken during the ten-minute car ride through town.

"So, this will be our getaway vehicle," Julie said with bemusement. "You really do want to be a detective, don't you?"

Tom grinned as he turned off his Jeep.

"I do! We would totally kick ass!"

"OK, Detective Leblanc. If you say so." Julie tucked her handbag under the front seat, opened her door and started to exit the vehicle.

"Wait!" Tom said. He grabbed Julie's arm and yanked her back down onto the seat.

"What?"

"You just made me realize something. We shouldn't use our real names."

Julie frowned. She was anxious to get this over with.

"What the fuck are you talking about?" Julie asked.

"What if there really is some kind of connection? Let's play this out. We go in, and Mrs. Closed is not there. But we give the seller our real names. She turns around and tells Mrs. Closed and ..."

"Oh my God," Julie said. "I thought I was the one with wild connect the dot theories. You think this woman will know our names are related to what happened out in P-Town? I think you're being a bit too paranoid."

Tom shook his head in disagreement.

"Trust me on this one, Jewels. We need to protect ourselves."

Julie rolled her eyes and sighed.

"OK, Detective. What's your plan?"

Tom paused for a few seconds as he tried to figure out what to do. Then it dawned on him.

"I think we should use our porn names," Tom said with an evil grin.

Julie turned and stared at Tom in bewilderment.

"Absolutely not!" Julie cried.

"Why?

"Why? You know exactly why!"

"But Jewels, we have *great* porn names!" Tom was now giggling at the thought of them using these made up names as their alter ego detective names.

There were a variety of ways to create your porn name. Or your drag name. Or any other funny name. They always involved using some combination of pet and street name, such as first, last, or favorite. Last summer Tom and Julie found themselves at a party where this subject had come up. They went with the combination of using the name of your favorite pet as your first name, and the name of the street you grew up on as your last name.

"No, Tom, *you* have a great porn name."

"I do!" Tom said with pride. "Max Wood. It's like I was meant to be a porn star!"

"As I've told you before, I swear you named Max specifically knowing it would someday become your porn name."

"You know that's not true, Jewels. Max came from the shelter that way. I didn't pick his name. Besides, before I got him, the only pet I had was a dog back when I was five years old. I barely remember him. And his name was Black. So ..."

Julie folded her arms in protest and glared out the front window.

"Jewels, I think you have a fantastic porn name," Tom said with encouragement. "You grew up on Valley Drive. And you love your cat. You've told me many times he is your favorite."

"Tom, there is no way I am walking in there as Fluffy Valley!"

Tom started pounding on the steering wheel in laughter. Julie turned and glared at him.

"It's not funny!"

Tom could not stop laughing. Tears started to run down his cheeks. Julie finally cracked a smile and began to chuckle.

"Stop it!" Julie giggled.

"I'm sorry Jewels, but that really is a fantastic name!"

"Not for a Detective!" Julie said as she too began to laugh.

"Wait, what was the other one?" Tom asked as he began to regain his composure. "Was it a hamster? No, a guinea pig, right? When you were really young."

Julie began to laugh harder until she started to snort.

"Oh my God!" Julie cried. "Yes. His name was Baron."

"Baron Valley!" Tom howled. "You have so many great choices, Jewels. Will your valley be barren or fluffy?"

"Neither, asshole."

Tom burst out in laughter once more. Julie pulled a tissue from her handbag from under the seat and cleared her nose.

"That is too funny," Tom sighed.

"Well that certainly helped with my nerves," Julie said. She turned and looked at Tom.

"Fluffy," Tom chuckled.

Julie wiped her eyes and checked her face in the mirror to make sure she had not made a complete mess of herself.

"OK, let's get this over with," Julie said as she turned to face Tom. "But if you call me Fluffy Valley I will seriously knock you on your ass."

Julie opened her door and stepped outside. She was still giggling and shaking her head. Tom hopped out and joined her on the sidewalk.

"And who the fuck names a guinea pig Baron?" Julie said as she continued to chuckle.

"Right?"

Julie slid her arm around Tom's elbow and pulled him close. They began to walk toward the end of the block. The streets were empty. Clouds had rolled in, darkening the sky. The temperature had dropped a few degrees since they had first arrived on the Cape. The house on the corner grew closer with each step.

Neither one of them were laughing as they approached the old bungalow.

ELEVEN

The Table

Julie stood a few steps behind Tom at the base of the walkway that led up to the old bungalow. A small hand-written sign was scrawled out on a plain white matte poster board nailed to a wooden stake. The sign had an arrow on the bottom pointing toward the street corner. The words "Estate Sale" were scrawled across the top of the poster. Tom and Julie ignored the sign and kept their eyes fixated on the door at the end of the walkway.

The house was painted a butter-cream yellow, accented with dark forest green shutters and bright white trim. It was a traditional single-story bungalow with a deep front covered porch with four large white wooden support posts. The cloudy afternoon dampened the mood of the cheery, inviting color palate.

Tom turned and looked over his shoulder at Julie. He could see the concern in her eyes.

"We'll be fine," Tom said somewhat reassuringly. He wondered if he was saying that to comfort her or himself.

Tom's legs felt heavy as he made his way up the long flat cement walkway that led to the front steps. He stopped at the bottom and waited until he heard Julie by his side. He took her hand, and they walked up four brick steps. They paused briefly and then crossed the green wooden floor of the porch.

Julie looked down at her feet. A welcome mat with images of a cat and a dog greeted them. *Max and Fluffy*, Julie bemused.

Tom reached for the doorbell.

"Wait," Julie said anxiously. "Tom, if you're right and that really is the same table, what if Mrs. Closed actually lives here?"

"That wasn't her voice on the phone, Jewels. I'm positive." Tom reached for the doorbell again.

"OK, but what if Mrs. Closed is her sister, and it just so happens they live together?"

Tom lowered his hand and looked back at Julie.

"Fuck Jewels, it's a bit late to think of that now, isn't it?"

Julie walked back to the edge of the porch and looked around the intersection. The streets were empty.

"Maybe we should call Trevor?" Julie asked. She reached into her pocket to pull out her phone. The ring of the doorbell startled her. She spun around to see Tom pulling his hand away from the doorbell button.

"Tom!" Julie said as she ran back to his side.

Tom kept his focus on the front door. He felt his heart throbbing in his chest. The veins on the sides of his head began to pulsate. He took a couple of deep breaths to try and calm himself down. They waited for what felt like an eternity before the deadbolt snapped, and the door opened.

Tom and Julie breathed a sigh of relief as a woman appeared in the doorway. She looked nothing like Mrs. Closed.

"Hi," Tom said. His voice cracked as he spoke. He coughed to clear his throat.

"Can I help you?" asked the woman.

"We're here for the yard sale," Tom replied as his confidence returned. "I think we talked on the phone yesterday. I was asking about the table ... and the lamps."

"I'm so glad you saw my ad. I'm Susan. Please come in."

Susan stepped aside, and Tom and Julie walked into the house. They were in a large living room that was furnished in a mix of traditional and modern furniture.

"You startled me by ringing the front door," Susan said. "Everything is out back in the garage. That's why I had that sign at the walkway. I can't hear anything out back if I am in the garage. Lucky for you I was in the house checking on my mother."

Julie felt a weight sink deep in her stomach at hearing the word "mother." *Is it the mother from the barn?*

"Follow me," Susan said. She led them through the living room, past a dining room, and into a kitchen. As they walked through the house, both Tom and Julie looked around as much as possible, looking at the different tables and candles. Unfortunately, their pace was too fast for them to have any time to make a detailed assessment.

"You have a big house," Julie said as they entered the kitchen. "It's lovely."

"Oh, why thank you," Susan said with a smile. "It's my mother's house. I live here with her. To be honest, it is a lot of house for just the two of us. Especially the back yard."

Susan opened the back door of the kitchen. Behind the house was a large detached single car garage. The garage door was open. Susan led them across a small walkway that connected the house to the garage. There was a large yard out back. Tom thought it looked to be in disarray.

"Have a look around," Susan said as she motioned toward the inside of the garage.

"Thanks," Tom replied.

Susan remained outside as Tom and Julie stepped into the garage. It had been a slow afternoon at the estate sale, and Susan had only managed to sell two lamps and a few small pieces of art. She watched the pair, hopeful that they would buy something.

Tom and Julie stopped halfway into the garage to assess their options. It was a very odd mix of items, including an old rocking chair, various tables, boxes of dishes and towels, and a couple of racks filled with women's dresses, skirts, and blouses.

Julie noticed a small table off in the back corner. It had a few small lamps sitting on top of it. From a distance, the lamps looked like the ones from the online advertisement. The table was covered in a dark blue blanket, just like in the online ad. The blanket went all the way to the floor, concealing the legs.

Julie tapped Tom on the shoulder and pointed to the table. Tom nodded and together they made their way to the back of the garage. Julie felt her skin get flush with each step that led them deeper and deeper into the old building.

A quick scan of the table, however, revealed nothing resembling the FlickerWood candle they had bought last December. Julie grabbed one of the candles. It was a tall round glass cylinder. She inhaled it and was relieved to find it did not have a scent. She did not bother to check the twin that was sitting next to it.

"Is there something specific you are looking for?" Susan called out from the driveway. "Some of those boxes have a mix of different things in them. I apologize for not being better organized. I really didn't have the time to do this properly."

Tom ignored her and instead stared at the heavy blanket draped over the table in front of him. It looked like one of those packing blankets you would find in a moving van. He glanced at Julie. She nodded. Tom's hand trembled slightly as bent down and slowly lifted the blanket up. The coverlet rose like a curtain on a stage, exposing the star of the show – a single rosewood table leg with a nickel and turquoise inlay embedded near the foot.

"It's the same," Tom whispered.

A cool breeze shot through the garage, wrapping itself around Tom and Julie. Julie stood there frozen, her eyes fixated on the foot of the table. The nickel and turquoise seemed to sparkle in the damp darkness of the garage. She closed her eyes and recalled Chris back at the candle store crashing into the table, knocking the ginger and sesame-scented candles into the air. She remembered crawling around on the floor trying to collect the broken pieces, with the table laying on the floor next to her. Tom was right. That leg was an exact match to the one that was in the candle store in Truro.

"The same as what?" Susan asked. She was standing directly behind Julie. Julie jumped at the sound of her voice. She had no idea she had entered the garage.

"Are you OK?" Susan asked Julie. "I didn't mean to startle you."

Tom spun around. He too was caught off guard by Susan's stealthy approach. Tom could see the panic setting in on Julie's face.

"As the one in the picture," Tom said. "From your online ad. It's the same as that one."

"I remember your call now," Susan said with a frown. "You were more interested in the table, weren't you? Not the lamps that were on it."

"Well the design really interested me," Tom replied. He was doing his best to keep calm. "The detail work is impressive."

"You could see all of that detail from the online ad? I thought those pictures came out poorly."

"Well no. I mean yes. I mean ..."

Julie felt herself getting flush. Her heart was racing in her chest. She was getting nauseous. The walls of the oversized garage felt like they were beginning to close in on her.

"I'm sorry, I don't think I got your names," Susan said with confusion.

"I'm sorry," Tom replied. "I thought I did. When we first got here."

"No," Susan replied.

Julie's stomach began to churn and made an audible growl. Susan turned and looked at her with concern.

"I'm ... I'm Max," Tom sputtered. "Max Wood."

Susan turned back toward Tom and smiled. Julie broke from her panic-induced trance and glared at Tom. She couldn't believe he went with his porn name. Susan turned and looked at Julie and patiently waited to hear her name.

"This is Miss Val ..." Tom began to say.

"Valerie," Julie said, cutting him off. "I'm Valerie. Valerie Hope."

Julie smiled as she thrust her arm toward Susan to shake her hand. Susan obliged, somewhat startled at how vigorous and firm the young woman's grip was.

"It's nice to meet you both," Susan said. "Where are you from?"

Tom and Julie looked at each other. They had spent so much time debating their porn star detective names that they had not bothered to come up with any other details to their back story.

"Fall River," Julie blurted out.

Susan stepped past Tom and rolled the blanket completely up, resting it on the top edge of the table. The three-legged base was fully exposed now, along with part of the circular top.

"So, you like the detail?" Susan asked with a bit of pride. "It's impressive up close, isn't it? It's completely handmade."

Julie felt her chest tighten and her stomach churn. With all three legs exposed, there was no doubt in her mind that the table was completely identical to the one from the candle store in Truro.

"Handmade?" Tom asked. He was doing a much better job of masking his shock than Julie was.

"Yes. I'm pretty sure there are only two of these tables. Including this one."

"There's another?" Julie asked. The tone of shock in her voice was undeniable. Susan was a bit taken aback by her reaction.

"Yes. I think my cousin has it. Maybe my aunt. To be honest, I haven't seen it – or them – in ages." Susan sighed as she thought about her aunt and cousin. "There's some family drama there that I could bore you with for an hour."

Tom and Julie locked eyes. Julie turned and abruptly walked to the entrance to the garage. She bent over and took a long deep breath of the cold, damp April air.

"Are you OK, Valerie?" Susan asked.

Julie stared down the driveway and let herself enjoy the open space and breeze of the late afternoon.

"I just needed some fresh air," Julie said. She could not turn around to face Susan, the table, or any part of the garage.

"Wow, only two of these," Tom said. He dropped to his knees to inspect the leg up close. "And handmade? That's really impressive."

"I think my uncle made it," Susan replied. "I can't recall. The table is all rosewood. You should see the top. There's too much on it, but you can see a bit of the inlaid detailing." Susan pulled the top of the blanket back a bit. Tom couldn't remember what the top of the table from the store in Truro looked like, but he nodded in approval.

"It's really quite beautiful," Tom said.

Julie walked back into the garage but stopped halfway. Her queasiness had subsided, but she had no interest in getting any closer to the table.

"My mom really cherishes it," Susan said fondly. "She has some special keepsakes from the family that mean the world to her. This table is one of them."

"Your mother?" Julie asked. "You mentioned her before. Is … is that why you're having this estate sale?"

"Yes," Susan said. Her voice was a mix of sadness and relief. "My mother has been ill for quite some time. To be honest, she has not been herself for decades. But she has really spiraled out of control in the past few months. Dementia has set in. It's so sad to see her mind slipping away. Caring for her has become almost a full-time job for me."

"Sounds like a lot for one person to handle," Tom said.

"It is. My husband left me last year. He couldn't deal with it. He's got a business to run. PJW Auto Repair?" Susan paused, hoping they knew of her husband's shop. The blank expression indicated they did not. "Anyway, my son comes by when he can, but he works long hours. The same with my cousin. She's my mother, right? I need to care for her. It's all been too much. Too much. So, I finally made the decision to put her into assisted living."

"That might be best," Julie said, trying somewhat unsuccessfully to sound supportive.

"Now we fear she may not make it there. She has pneumonia. The doctor was just here this morning. I don't know how much longer my mom has."

"Sorry to hear," Tom said.

"I was selling all of this stuff to help with the anticipated cost of moving her out, but also just to clear things out. There is too much clutter. You should see her bedroom. It is still packed with stuff that I would love to get rid of. She would be so upset if she knew her favorite table was back here in the garage."

"It must be difficult for you," Julie added.

"My dad died a long time ago. My mom was never the same after that. Neither of us were. But my mom took his death quite hard. I was only thirteen and suddenly had to grow up overnight. I found myself doing things that my dad used to do and providing emotional support to my mom. I mean, can you imagine?"

Tom stared at the floor. He could easily imagine since he went through the same thing at almost the same age. Part of him wanted to tell her that he could completely sympathize with her. But Tom knew he needed to keep an emotional distance. This woman Susan was somehow tied to Mrs. Closed. He had to get more information from her.

"I'm sorry," Susan said. She turned and smiled at Julie. "I'm being quite a downer. Are you feeling better, Valerie? Did the fresh air help?"

"To be honest I am feeling a bit queasy," Julie replied nervously. "Must have been something I ate at the bed and breakfast earlier."

"You are staying in town?"

Julie felt her face get flush. She looked at Tom standing behind the woman. He mouthed the word "idiot" to her.

"I'm sorry but is there a bathroom that I could use?" Julie asked as she rubbed her hands across her stomach.

Susan paused as she looked the young woman up and down. Her color was going from pale to flush every few seconds.

"Of course," Susan said. "If you go back in through the way we came the bathroom is right off the living room."

"Thanks," Julie said. She spun around and headed toward the back door of the house.

"Can you tell me more about the table?" Tom asked. "You said it was rosewood, right?"

Julie listened to the voices of Tom and Susan fade away as she left them behind. She entered the house and closed the door. The warmth and lack of wind comforted her. Julie made her way back to the living room and easily found the bathroom.

As she was about to enter, she heard a voice call out from the partially open door to her right.

"Susan?" It was a faint whisper, wafting through the crack in the doorway.

Julie paused and took a step toward the door. She could hear labored breathing coming from inside. Julie rubbed her fingers together as she nervously reached toward the doorknob. Part of her wanted to look. Part of her wanted to run. Part of her wanted to be back in Providence snuggled up with her cat enjoying some hot cocoa.

Julie slowly pushed the door open. The old hinges released a long drawn out creak as Julie stepped into the room. The curtains were drawn closed, and a small dim Tiffany lamp next to a rocking chair illuminated the entire room. The multi-colored glass shade cast various warm colors across the walls and ceiling. Julie turned to see an old woman resting in a large four post bed.

Jennifer Campbell rolled her head toward the door. The lower half of her face was obscured by an oxygen mask. The sixty-six-year-old woman had recently entered Stage 6 of dementia. Jennifer constantly forgot where she was and who her doctor was. Sometimes she struggled to recognize her own daughter. Events from the past, however, were somehow still easy to recall.

Jennifer's breathing was shallow, as her lungs fought pneumonia that was slowly consuming her. She looked at the young woman that had just entered her room. She realized it wasn't her daughter. Jennifer turned her head back toward the ceiling and closed her eyes.

Julie watched as the old woman fell back to sleep. She looked around the bedroom. It was indeed a cluttered space. It also smelled like a hospital. There was a dank scent of sheets that had not been washed in weeks. The entire room smelled neglected and musty.

Julie walked over to a cherry wood dresser on the wall opposite the bed. It had a white marble top and was covered in a dozen picture frames, all in different shapes and sizes. In the center was an eight-by-ten rosewood wooden frame. The black and white photo was of two young girls. The younger one looked to be about four or five years old and had a short dress covered with flowers. The girl sitting next to her was several years older. She had on a flannel shirt tied at the waist, along with faded denim shorts.

What caught Julie's eye wasn't the picture but the frame itself. The corners had inlaid nickel and turquoise in them. Carved into the top of the handmade frame were the words "Sisters."

Which one is Susan? Julie wondered as she studied the picture.

Julie let her eyes wander across the other pictures. Next to the picture of the sisters was a smaller color photo of two young girls. One of them was obviously the younger one from the black and white image. The other had the exact same dress on, but different colored shoes. The two were sitting on a picnic table holding hands. They looked remarkably similar.

Julie glanced around the room. There was another eight-by-ten picture on the nightstand on the far side of the bed. It was a wedding picture. Julie assumed it had to be Susan's parents. She smiled at the thought of a grand wedding decades ago. Her smile faded as her eye caught the edge of a glass jar sitting behind the wedding picture. The top half of the jar disappeared behind the frame.

A sense of dread washed over Julie as she cautiously crossed the room and made her way around the bed. Jennifer remained in a deep sleep. Julie reached behind the frame, taking care not to knock it over. She pulled the glass jar out and stared at it in disbelief. It was a pale green candle, with a square base and rounded top. The lid was a flip-top design. Julie's heart raced in her chest. She immediately recognized it as the same design as the candles from the store in Truro.

Julie slowly turned the candle around in her hands. There were no stickers on it. In fact, it had no identifying marks whatsoever. The top was locked closed. She carefully opened the metal fastener and tilted the lid back. Two wicks protruded from the sage colored wax. They were barely exposed. The candle had never been lit, and the wicks were covered in a thin coat of wax. Julie realized they were not flat wood wicks like the ones from the store. These looked normal.

Julie placed the candle on the edge of the table and took her phone out. She quickly took a couple of pictures of it. The imitation camera shutter sound rang out loudly in the room. She looked down to make sure the old woman had not been disturbed. Julie put her phone away and went to put the candle back behind the picture frame where she had found it. She stopped as she was about to snap the lid closed.

But is it scented? Julie wondered.

She raised the glass candle jar to her nose and inhaled.

"Rosemary," Jennifer whispered as she grabbed Julie's arm.

"Oh my God!" Julie yelled in shock. She quickly yanked her arm away from the old woman's grasp.

Jennifer stared longingly at the candle. With all of her strength, she reached out to try and hold it. Julie's shock and sense of terror quickly subsided as she looked into the old woman's pale blue-gray eyes. Julie could see the yearning she felt as she reached for the candle.

Julie cautiously gave the woman the candle and rested it on her chest. She sat down on the edge of the bed, keeping one hand on the candle, so it would not tip over. Jennifer reached up with her other hand and slid the oxygen mask away from her mouth.

"Rosemary," Jennifer said, her voice filled with anguish. "It's rosemary."

"It smells lovely," Julie said with a smile. She was being honest, as the scent of rosemary was quite powerful.

"Susan," Jennifer said softly. Her voice struggled to get above a whisper. "You don't understand."

Julie suddenly realized the old woman had mistaken her for her daughter. Jennifer grabbed Julie's arm again. The candle rolled off her stomach toward the edge of the bed. Julie slowly unfurled the woman's hand from her arm and stood up. She closed the lid and placed the candle back behind the wedding photo.

"Susan, please," Jennifer whispered.

Julie pulled the oxygen mask back over the old woman's face and quickly left the room.

Once outside the mother's bedroom, Julie took a moment to collect her thoughts. The table and now the candle made it terrifyingly obvious that Susan was somehow connected to Mrs. Closed. Julie glanced at the door to the bathroom and realized she still had not used it. It didn't matter. All she could think about was getting Tom and leaving as soon as possible.

Julie made sure the bedroom door was slightly ajar just as she had found it. She then made her way back out to the entrance to the garage. Tom and Susan were still in the back next to the table draped under the blue packing blanket.

"I can see how gardening could be therapeutic," Tom said to Susan. "Does she still do it today?"

"No," Susan replied. "The entire herb garden is dead. It has been for quite some time. That whole backyard is such a mess right now."

Julie begrudgingly made her way toward the back of the garage, stopping halfway in.

"Feeling better?" Tom asked. Susan turned around to see Julie standing several feet away. She thought she still looked rather pale.

"Not really," Julie said earnestly. "I'd like to get going. I'm ready when you are, Tom."

"Tom?" Susan asked with confusion.

Tom's jaw fell open as Susan turned to face him.

"Nickname," Tom said nervously. "Long story. Thanks again for your time today."

"I'm sorry to see you go," Susan said. "I really can't sell the table that you like. Did you see anything else you might buy?"

"Maybe," Tom said as he maneuvered around Susan.

"I'm here tomorrow as well," Susan called out.

Julie shook her head as she realized she called Tom by his real name. Tom scowled at her as he got closer. She turned, and Tom pushed her from behind, eventually grabbing her arm to lead her down the driveway.

Susan watched with curiosity as they turned and disappeared around the corner of the house.

"What an odd pair," Susan said aloud.

TWELVE

Happy Birthday

1984 Saturday 25-Jun 12:00 p.m.

The 1980 Chevrolet Caprice sedan veered back and forth along the quiet two-lane road. The light camel metallic paint color glistened in the sun. Inside, Carl Campbell nervously adjusted his glance, alternating between the road ahead and the rear-view mirror. He was trying to keep an eye on his two daughters as they bickered in the back seat. At the same time, his wife Jennifer had spent the past several minutes lecturing him about his health. The distractions were becoming too much for him.

"Marilyn and Susan!" Carl called out in a calm but stern voice. "I need the two of you to stop fighting, OK?"

Carl watched the girls through the mirror. Neither of them looked up as they continued to tug on a plastic bag. Carl had no idea what was in it or why it was the source of such a disagreement between them.

"No fighting!" Jennifer yelled as she turned around to face the back seat. "Today is supposed to be a celebration. No fighting!"

The two girls stopped and looked at their mother. Susan yanked the plastic bag from Marilyn's hands and tossed it on the floor beside her feet.

"Mom, you've been yelling at dad since we got in the car!" Susan said defensively.

Jennifer unhooked her seatbelt and spun around onto one knee so she could lean further into the back of the car.

"Don't make this about me, young lady," Jennifer said. "I want this to be a fun day. We all do. It's your birthday, Susan. So, let's all stop yelling."

Carl smiled, hoping the commotion had finally ended. He pressed his foot deeper against the accelerator, and the Dualjet 3.8L V-6 growled as the huge sedan rushed ahead. Jennifer spun back and re-buckled her belt. She rested her left hand on her husband's leg.

"I'm sorry I have been yelling, Carl," Jennifer said. "I'm just worried about you. And when I worry, I get upset. And when I get upset, I yell. And then I realize it and calm down."

"I know," Carl replied. "You haven't changed a bit since high school."

Jennifer looked over at her husband and smiled. At five-foot-eight-inches tall, Carl's once lean frame had filled out with a bit of a pot belly. His red hair had started to recede. *How my fiery Irishman has changed,* Jennifer bemused to herself.

"Did you take your meds this morning?" Jennifer asked.

"Yes," Carl said with a long sigh. "You ask me every day, and every day the answer is the same."

"Well, you have to get out of this depression of yours, Carl. That doctor has to get the right combo figured out. You keep getting laid off, and you are starting to get a reputation around town as being unreliable. Pretty soon nobody is going to hire you! And then what?"

"No fighting!" Marilyn yelled from the back seat.

Carl slowed the big Chevy as he made a turn onto a dirt road. The car began to bounce as it traversed the various ruts that littered the roadway.

"I know this has been a long six years for you," Carl replied. "For us. I'm sorry, Jennie. Every time I think I'm getting better ..."

Jennifer took Carl's hand in hers and kissed his knuckles.

"I'm sorry, Carl. I didn't mean to yell. I just don't ... That boating accident. Being lost at sea the way you were. I'll never understand what you went through. But it's been six years. Six years of depression and anxiety and pills. At some point, it has to end. It has to."

Carl slowed to a halt before turning right into the narrow opening of the driveway. The car shimmied from side to side as they made their way down the narrow path.

"I'll try to do better, Jennie. It's these meds. Every time the doc changes them I go through an adjustment period. They all have different side effects. How do you think I feel? I know I'm no longer the man you married."

Carl looked into the rearview mirror. His daughter Susan was staring directly at him. He could see the disappointment in her eyes.

"Thirteen today, Suzie!" Carl said in an upbeat tone. "Are you excited?"

"I guess," Susan said solemnly.

"Well, you better be, because we are here!"

The narrow driveway expanded. Carl pulled his big Chevy alongside the sprawling Victorian home and parked it next to Fred's Cherokee. Jennifer smiled at the sight of Bobby Mason's Ford F-150 parked closer to the barn. Susan and Marilyn quickly unbuckled their seatbelts and began to gather the small bags they had spread across the floor. Apollo came running up to the car and barked loudly.

"I'm sure the girls are out back behind the barn," Jennifer said as she turned to face her children. "Marilyn, remember to play nice. No fighting. You have your dolls?"

"No fighting," Marilyn said with joy. The young child smiled as she waved a small canvas bag back and forth. The plastic dolls inside rattled as they banged together. Her almond eyes sparkled with anticipation of a fun day with her cousins.

"Susan, I need you to do me a favor," Jennifer said. "I want to get pictures of everyone before you all run off and get dirty. Get your cousins over to the picnic table for me, OK? We'll take pictures, and then everyone can go explore and have fun. Oh, and take those bags back there with you."

"Sure thing," Susan said as she popped open the car door.

It was an oddly cool day for mid-June. The temperature was 70 degrees and not expected to get much warmer. Susan didn't care. Spring, school, and that long bickering car ride with her parents were in the past. Summer was finally here, as was her birthday.

Susan stepped out of the car and dusted off her faded denim shorts. The sun felt great. She undid the lower buttons of her flannel shirt and tied the ends across her waist. She had a feeling it was going to be a spectacular day. Susan walked around to the other side of the car and helped her sister Marilyn out. Apollo immediately began to lick the young girl's face. Marilyn giggled as she pushed the slobbering dog away.

Susan had a few small bags in her right hand. She grabbed Marilyn with the other, and the two ran off toward the barn. Apollo pursued with excitement.

Carl walked around to the back of the big sedan and opened the trunk. Jennifer exited the car and met him back there.

"I'm sorry, Jennie," Carl said. His tone was calm and sincere. He took his wife's hand. "These new meds may be the solution. I know my mood swings are bad, but my depression is just about gone. I've really been feeling great. Positive. Maybe this is the magic dose, and we just need a few more days for my system to sort it all out. I promise to do better. I will make it all up to you. You ... you deserve better."

"Let's try to focus on the girls for today. On Susan. This is supposed to be a party."

Jennifer squeezed her husband's hand and kissed him on the cheek. She smiled as she turned to inspect the items packed into the trunk.

"Can you take the cooler?" Jennifer asked. "I can get these bags."

"Of course," Carl said. He quickly retrieved the cooler and dropped it onto the ground.

The side door of the kitchen opened, and Laura Johnson and Bobby Mason stepped out onto the porch. Laura was wearing a pink blouse with white cotton cropped pants, covered by a long white apron. The apron was smeared in barbeque sauce.

"I hope that cooler has your world famous rosemary

chicken," Laura called out from the porch railing.

"That and more," Jennifer yelled back.

Carl grabbed the cooler and made his way toward the porch. Laura ran down to the trunk of the car to help her sister. The two embraced. Laura took the last few remaining bags from the trunk and closed it.

"What have you done this time?" Laura asked excitedly. "I told you all we needed was your rosemary chicken. It's not a cookout without it! One of these days I'm going to make you give me that recipe. I've figured out most of your ingredients. But there is something else in there, Jennie. Something I can't quite place."

"We all have our family secrets," Jennifer responded. "I love you dearly, but I'm taking this one to my grave."

Bobby held the kitchen door open so Carl could bring the cooler inside. Fred was seated at the far end of the kitchen table having a beer. Once inside, Carl dropped the cooler onto the floor near the table.

"Hey Fred," Carl said as he tried to catch his breath

Fred nodded lightly and took a sip from his beer can. He had been dreading this moment since he overheard Laura on the phone with Carl yesterday. Fred could not bring himself to speak to Carl. It was hard enough to even look at him. Fred felt his blood pressure begin to rise.

"What do you have in there, Carl?" Bobby asked.

"Jennie's chicken," Carl responded. He was a bit winded from carrying the heavy cooler. "And beer. Lots and lots of beer."

Bobby laughed as he popped the cooler open to look inside. Fred watched silently from the other end of the table as Bobby and Carl laughed and joked. He felt like a stranger in his own home. Fred stood up, walked over to the cooler and grabbed a fresh beer.

"Excuse me," Fred said to Bobby as he headed to the porch door.

Bobby frowned as Fred abruptly pushed his way past him. He watched as Fred crossed the yard, entered the barn and slammed the door shut.

Jennifer and Laura arrived at the side door. Bobby held it

open for them.

"Hi Bobby," Jennifer said somewhat awkwardly.

"Hi," Bobby replied.

Jennifer placed the bags she was carrying onto the kitchen table. She glanced over at the barn. She had observed Fred march over there before she could even say hello to him.

"What's up with Fred?" Jennifer asked her sister.

"He's being an ass," Laura said. "You know him and his temper. He's been a pain in my side all morning. Completely useless. Best to leave him be until he finally comes around. He always does. Bobby came over early to help me out."

Jennifer looked around the large open kitchen.

"I love this kitchen," Jennifer said with envy. "You need to send Fred over to update ours."

Fred had remodeled the kitchen a few years ago and installed new custom-made pine cabinets. He had designed and built them himself. He also replaced the old countertops with butcher block. Laura had complained that it was too much wood, so Fred had agreed to paint the cabinet doors white. It made for a bright and airy kitchen.

"So, what's on the menu for today, Laura?" Jennifer asked.

"In addition to your spectacular rosemary chicken, I've got the usual suspects. Burgers, dogs, a big green salad, and a potato salad that I made earlier this morning."

"Just hot dogs?" Jennifer asked. She turned to Bobby. "Didn't you bring your juicy sausage? It's been a long time since I've had it."

"Of course, Bobby brought his sausage," Laura chuckled. She was busy rummaging through the various bags they had just brought in. Carl was helping her to empty them. Neither one caught the glare that Bobby gave toward Jennifer. She smiled and winked back at him.

Laura reached into the cooler and pulled out two huge plastic tubs. She popped one open. It was packed with boneless chicken breasts that had been marinating in butter, garlic, rosemary, and several other seasonings for the past twelve hours.

"That scent gets me every time," Laura sighed as she held her nose a few inches above the chicken. The aroma of garlic and rosemary immediately filled the kitchen.

"Oh, I've got something else for you, Laura," Jennifer said. She grabbed a large brown bag, reached in and searched for her surprise for her sister.

"Here you go," Jennifer said with a smile. She handed two gallon-sized plastic bags to Laura. "Dried herbs from the garden. Sage in one, parsley in the other."

"You are the best!" Laura said as she kissed her sister on the cheek. "I keep telling myself I should do my own herb garden, but I could never compete with the one you have in your backyard. So why even try?"

"Well, I can't take all of the credit. Carl has the fertilizer schedule down to a science. I swear, without his help, it would just end up being a garden of weeds."

Carl walked over to his wife and gave her a kiss on the cheek.

"But you give them the water and care they need," Carl said.

"It's a team effort," Jennifer added.

"Agreed," Carl continued. "I find it all very therapeutic. It's quite relaxing. We make a great pair in the garden, don't we?"

Jennifer looked into Carl's blue eyes and smiled. She put her arm around Carl and let her head fall onto his shoulder.

"We are pretty great in the garden," Jennifer concluded.

Laura smiled, feeling a bit envious at the level of affection her sister still shared with her husband.

"Oh, and one more surprise for today," Jennifer said. She reached into the cooler and retrieved a brown paper bag. She opened it up and dumped a small plastic bag onto the table. The bag was filled with green leaves. "I brought fresh mint."

"What's that for?" Bobby asked.

"Mojitos, of course," Jennifer said with a grin.

"I can tell this is going to be a fun day," Laura said as she clasped her hands together in joy.

Jennifer opened up another large brown paper bag. It had the rest of what she would need to make mojitos, including a jug of white rum. Laura ran over to grab a glass pitcher and the two of them quickly set about making up a batch of mojitos.

"It's not every day your baby girl becomes a teenager," Carl said. "They really do grow up fast. Your twins are next, right Laura?"

"Next year," Laura said. "October. Luckily we have a bit of a break before the little ones get that old."

"They were only born a few weeks apart," Jennifer said. "When they finally do hit their teens, we will have to throw them a double party."

"I can't think that far ahead," Laura said with a chuckle. "Those two munchkins. The twins that aren't twins."

"They sure act like it," Jennifer said. She poured some of the mojito mixture into a small glass and gave it a try. She looked at Laura and nodded in approval.

"Speaking of which," Laura said. "I noticed you put Marilyn in the white and yellow flowered dress."

"You told me to!"

"I know. Thank you for that. You know they love to dress the same. White shoes too?"

"No. Her buckle broke this morning. She has her new yellow shoes on."

"Oh well, they won't be perfectly identical today. You know one of them will complain. It doesn't matter, however. I'm sure both will be covered in mud before we serve lunch."

"Oh shit, that reminds me," Jennifer said in a panic. "Carl, can you take the camera and get pictures of the girls before they get dirty? You know how they love to go explore. I've got a few other bags to sort through."

"Sure thing, Jennie," Carl said. He grabbed the camera from the table along with a beer. "Laura, you want to give me a hand?"

"What, you can't manage to get five girls to sit still by yourself?" Laura said with a laugh. She grabbed her mojito and followed Carl out the side door.

Bobby and Jennifer were alone in the kitchen.

"Mojito?" Jennifer asked.

"No, I'm good," Bobby replied. "How's Carl these days? He seems better."

"He seems that way right now, Bobby. You should have seen him in the car just before we got here. His mood swings are so unpredictable. I feel like I can never say the right thing.

It's becoming an issue with the girls too. I can see it on Susan's face. Marilyn not so much. She's too young and doesn't really understand."

"I'm sorry. Truly I am."

Jennifer took two big gulps of her mojito and immediately topped the drink off. She stared out the kitchen window toward the barn. There was nobody around. Not even the dog.

"I'm thinking of leaving Carl," Jennifer said cautiously. She turned to look at Bobby. His jaw was agape. She waited several seconds to see if he would say anything, but he remained silent.

"I just can't deal with it anymore, Bobby. He is never going to change. Ever. I'm trapped in this endless cycle. Every time it seems like his meds are finally working something happens. His depression returns. He becomes unstable. He got fired again. The only way it will end is for me to make it end."

"Jennifer I ... I don't know what to say."

Jennifer placed her drink on the table and took a couple of steps over to Bobby. She quickly threw her arms around his waist and buried her head into his chest.

"I've made up my mind, so don't try to talk me out of it. Not this time."

Bobby kept his eyes focused on the door that led to the porch. The last thing he needed was to be caught holding Jennifer in his arms. However, he could not ignore her current emotional state. Bobby slid his arms around her back and squeezed her tight. Jennifer exhaled a sigh of relief. She forgot how amazing it felt to be in his arms. He ran his strong hands up and down her back to try and comfort her.

"Bobby, I was thinking that once the dust settles from the divorce, that maybe ... well ... maybe we can try again."

Bobby let his hands slide down her waist and then fall by his side. Jennifer loosened her grip and took a step back. She looked up into his eyes hoping to see a hint of joy. Instead, she saw nothing but hesitation.

"Jennifer ..." Bobby said with caution. "You need to stop. This is why I ended our affair years ago. You need to focus on your family."

"I know what you are thinking, Bobby, but hear me out. In

the past, I wanted to run right into your arms. To go right from Carl to you. All I'm asking is for you to think about it. Let me get my divorce and get set up someplace with the girls. Make sure Carl is OK on his own. And then, well, maybe we can ... we can, I don't know, go on a proper date."

Bobby walked over to the kitchen door and looked outside at the barn. Apollo came running around the corner. He could hear the laughter of the children off in the distance.

"Jennifer, this really isn't the time or place to have this discussion." Bobby opened the side door and stepped out onto the porch. He turned to look at Jennifer. Her face was pale. He could tell he had upset her. "Today is about Susan. Focus on your daughter. Focus on your family."

Jennifer walked across the kitchen and stood in the doorway facing Bobby. Her mind fluctuated between resentment, regret, and sadness.

"I'm very much thinking about my family, Bobby. Shouldn't you? Do I have to remind you that Marilyn is *our* daughter?"

THIRTEEN

Scent of a Theory

Julie's eyes sparkled as she admired her master creation. She was hunched over the counter in the tiny kitchen staring at a small plate. The plate had what Julie considered to be a work of art. The bottom had a three-inch square graham cracker to serve as the base for her tower. Next was a layer of thick dark chocolate squares, topped by four marshmallows. She had sprinkled them with cinnamon before capping it all off with another giant graham cracker.

"I still can't believe you talked me into stopping at the market to get stuff to make s'mores," Tom said. He was sitting at the kitchen table watching Julie construct her snack.

"You will thank me once you have one in your mouth. Microwave baked s'mores are the best. Especially the baking part. It's better than watching a popcorn bag expand!"

Julie could not contain her excitement as she placed the dish into the microwave and flipped it on. Tom joined her near the microwave. They watched in amazement as the marshmallows slowly grew in size. Julie stood close to the microwave, with her finger resting lightly on the Stop button.

"It's all in the timing," Julie said.

She kept her focus on the ever-rising tower of decadence inside the oven. Once she felt the marshmallows were at critical mass, she turned it off. The gooey white gelatinous blob began to deflate, smothering the melted chocolate beneath it.

"Are the drinks ready?" Julie asked.

"Yes, master baker," Tom said. Julie had put him in charge of the drinks as soon as they had returned to the Marsh Mellow Inn. He had cocoa and tea set simmering at the kitchen table.

Julie opened the microwave and placed another plate with a pre-made s'more inside. She turned it on and brought the dish with the hot dessert over to the table.

"Try this," Julie said with pride.

Tom picked up the warm cracker sandwich and cautiously took a bite. The chocolate and marshmallow oozed out the opposite side and down onto the plate. Julie spun back to the microwave to monitor the progress.

"Holy shit! That is really good, Jewels."

"Right?"

Tom went to grab some napkins. It was a messy concoction to consume. Julie removed her s'more from the microwave and met him back at the table.

"We used to make these in college all of the time," Julie said.

"You do realize we are having dessert before dinner. It's only 4 p.m."

"Isn't it the best?" Julie asked with a grin. She took a huge bite of her s'more and exhaled in elation.

"Jewels, I still can't believe you picked 'Hope' as your last name back there at the estate sale," Tom said as he licked melted chocolate off the tips of his fingers.

"We went through this at the store," Julie said. "I told you I panicked."

"That's the street I live on. What if she makes the connection?"

"How could she know you live on Hope Street? She has no clue who we are."

"You called me by my real name."

"I'm sorry. You rattled me when you started to call me 'Miss Valley.' There was no way I was going with that dumb porn name idea. Besides, it could have been worse. We really didn't think that whole thing through. At least I didn't tell her we lived in Providence."

"True. Maybe telling her we were from Fall River will throw her off."

"See, I didn't screw *everything* up."

"I forgive you ... Fluffy."

Julie flicked a piece of graham cracker at Tom. They both let out a much-needed laugh.

"I'll tell you one thing, though," Julie said through a mouth full of sugar. "Seeing that candle in the old woman's room was a complete mind fuck. The table in the garage freaked me out enough. But then the candle, too! It was the same design as the ones Mrs. Closed was selling. The FlickerWood one that you bought."

"But no sticker, right?"

"No."

"Are you sure? Because that would be critical."

"I'm positive. But it was scented. Rosemary. And it had two wicks."

"You said they weren't wood wicks. So really the only link that candle has to Mrs. Closed is the jar."

Julie pulled her phone from her pocket and quickly retrieved the image of the rosemary candle she had taken earlier. She slid the phone over to Tom and pointed at the picture.

"I just wonder what's inside."

A blank stare covered Tom's face as he studied the image of the candle.

"Wax, Jewels. It's just rosemary-scented wax."

Julie frowned as she wiped smudges of chocolate from the corners of her lips. She took a loud sip of hot cocoa. Julie snatched her phone back and looked at the picture one last time.

"I just can't help but wonder ..."

"Does every scented candle now have to be filled with dead people?"

"You don't buy my theory, do you?"

"Jewels, we burned that sesame-scented candle I bought for hours. There were no bones in it, were there?"

"No, but ..."

"Maybe her mom has a rosemary-scented candle because she used to love to tend to her herb garden and the scent helps remind her of the past. You have a chocolate scented candle in your living room because you love chocolate."

"True, but ..."

"And I'm pretty sure if they made cheese scented candles you would have those all over your apartment. That's all this is, Jewels. She was an herb gardener!"

Julie stopped to consider the concept of a cheese-scented candle. *That would be a bit much,* she concluded.

"I get the connection with her garden," Julie said. "It's just with that jar being the same as the sesame and ginger ones, and everything that happened back in December ..."

"Let's not overthink this," Tom said. "The only real link we have with the candle is the glass. That mason jar design is a match. That's really all we know for sure. Put your detective hat on. What would your cop boyfriend think of our evidence so far?"

Tom licked his fingers and ran his damp fingertips over the crumbs and drops of chocolate and marshmallow scattered across his plate. He nibbled on as much as he could before grabbing his mug and heading over to the couch. He enjoyed a long sip of tea as he stared out at the spectacular panoramic view of the salt marsh.

Julie was almost done with her s'more. She took her plate, napkin, and mug, and joined Tom on the couch.

"OK, so we know the candle jar and the table are a match," Julie said. "Did you learn anything else about the table while I was snooping around in the house?"

"Not really. We only talked about her mom's illness and love of gardening."

"Didn't she say that an aunt or cousin had the other table?"

"Yes. But she wouldn't give me any real details."

"And didn't she say something about being estranged from them?"

"She did."

"But she wouldn't give up any other info on her?"

"No, Jewels. I could tell I was upsetting her with all of my questions. I had to keep pivoting to other stuff so that she wouldn't get too suspicious."

"So, explain this to me, Tom. She also said that her cousin was helping her take care of her mom. Which is it? Estranged or helpful? I think she's hiding something."

"Or you are being paranoid, and she simply has more than one cousin."

Julie took a sip of cocoa and stared out at the marsh.

"Shit. I didn't think of that."

"I agree that something seems off with her and her family. And the candle jar could very well be a key link. We have the table, the jar, and know that she has family tied to the table. See, Jewels, you are really getting into this whole detective thing. I told you we would make a great team."

"Well thank you, Max."

"No, thank *you*, Miss Valley."

Julie popped the last of her s'more into her mouth and washed it down with a few gulps of hot chocolate.

"Should I make more s'mores?"

"No. I don't want to fill up before dinner."

Julie frowned and began to pick at the last remnants of graham cracker on her plate.

"We need to figure out what we are going to do tomorrow," Tom added.

"Tomorrow?"

"With the information that we gathered today."

Julie wrapped her hands around her mug of cocoa and stared out the French doors. Several deer were roaming along the edge of a line of pine trees.

"I say we call this in," Julie said with conviction. "Let's call Trevor."

"Are you crazy? We aren't calling the cops. He will go ballistic if he knows we are here snooping around."

"Maybe. But we aren't in Provincetown. We aren't even in Truro. I can calm him down if he freaks out."

"It's too soon, Jewels. We don't have proof. Just a table."

"A table that ties to the one back in the store in Truro, Tom! And the candle jar! It's enough to get the ball rolling with Trevor. We phone this in and let him run with it."

"And then?"

"Then go have a nice dinner in town. Cocktails. Tomorrow we enjoy a big breakfast and then head home by noon."

"What's the rush? This is supposed to be our weekend escape. We haven't really explored Eastham at all. We can do some sightseeing and shopping and stuff. This is my birthday getaway, isn't it?"

Julie frowned at Tom pulling out the guilt card.

"OK, but we are not going back to that estate sale. Or any further out onto the Cape. Like your mom said, we need to be elsewhere."

"Elsewhere? When?"

"I don't mean now. Or tomorrow. I mean our next adventure. Anywhere but the Cape."

"Such as?"

Julie and Tom stared at one another for several seconds.

"How about upstate New York to see my family?" Julie suggested. "We do those huge annual family reunions. You could be my plus one."

"Right. Because you love them so much and always have a great time when you go back there."

"Point taken," Julie said with a long sigh. "It would probably be torture for you. They do drive me crazy."

"How do those reunions work anyway, Jewels? I always wondered how you blend Latin and Greek. What's the menu? Gyro tacos?"

"That's both inaccurate and offensive. I'm not Mexican. However, my mom does make a mean pile of gyro stuffed empanadas. God, now I'm hungry for dinner."

Tom let out a hearty laugh. Before he could make another wiseass remark his phone rang. He ran over to the kitchen table to answer it.

"Shit, Jewels. It's your boyfriend from Provincetown."

"Trevor!" Julie said with joy. "Put him on speaker. I love that deep sexy voice of his. And he's *not* my boyfriend!"

Tom sat down on one of the kitchen chairs and accepted the call and put it on speakerphone. Julie tiptoed over to the table and sat across from him.

"Hello Officer," Tom said in a formal tone of voice.

"Good afternoon Tom, how are you?" Officer Trevor Stevens asked.

"I'm doing well, and you?"

"I'm doing OK. It's been quite the day here."

"Hi Trevor," Julie said.

"Julie!" Trevor said with pleasure. "I figured you would be with Tom. I'm so glad I caught you both. I ... I have some news to share with you. Are you sitting down? Are you in a private space?"

"Yes," Tom replied.

Tom and Julie quickly locked eyes. Julie's giant grin at hearing Trevor's voice slowly faded. Tom exhaled a long nervous sigh. Trevor rarely called them with news and when he did it was never the good kind.

"We've made a lot of progress on the case this week," Trevor said. He spoke with caution. "A public statement about it has already gone out, but I wanted to call you two directly given your involvement in all of this. The families of the victims have been fully briefed as well. I thought you should hear this from me."

Tom picked up his phone and walked back over to the couch. Julie followed him. He placed the phone on the coffee table, and the two best friends sat down side by side. Tom put his arm around Julie, and she clasped his other free hand with hers.

"OK," Tom said softly. "Go ahead."

"We found four bodies in a very remote stretch of the National Seashore. All four have been identified. Two were Mr. and Mrs. Hamasaki. They were the couple that owned the candle store in Truro. The other two, I'm sorry to tell you, were your missing friends – Marcus Sirola and Christine Becker."

Julie let out an audible gasp and quickly began to sob. Tom pulled her close and kissed the top of her head. He could feel the tears start to well up in his eyes.

"I know this is difficult to hear," Trevor continued. "Part of you accepted their deaths a long time ago, but in a missing person's case it's always different when you get that final confirmation."

Trevor waited patiently and respectfully, not saying

anything. He could hear Julie crying and wanted to give both of them time to gather their thoughts. Tom finally allowed a few small tears to run down his face. He quickly brushed them away.

"Can I ask where the bodies were found?" Tom asked.

"Little Pleasant Bay," Trevor replied.

"Is that near the store in Truro?" Julie asked. Her voice was shaky as she struggled to regain her composure.

"No, not at all," Trevor said. "That's what made this so difficult. The bodies were outside of Orleans, almost twenty-five miles from Truro."

Julie hit the mute button on the phone.

"Tom, this doesn't make sense. The legend said the bodies were meant to be discovered. Why so far? It sounds like they were trying to hide them."

Julie unmuted the call.

"Can I ask who found the bodies?" Tom said. "I mean, were they buried or something?"

"It was a young husband and wife," Trevor replied. "They were just out on a stroll with their dog. Like I said, this is a very remote part of the park. The bodies were buried fairly deep in a sand dune. The dog caught some scent and started digging. They weren't even supposed to have a dog out there. It was complete luck."

Julie grabbed a chocolate-stained napkin off the coffee table and wiped her eyes. She looked at Tom as tears continued to run down her face.

"I have a question," Julie said.

"Ask away," Officer Stevens replied.

"What ... what condition were the bodies in?"

Several seconds passed before Officer Stevens responded.

"I was hoping you wouldn't ask that," Trevor said. "I'm going to be direct. My apologies, but this will be a bit graphic. They were skeletons. No flesh on them at all."

Julie winced and squeezed Tom's hand tighter.

"Was that it?" Tom asked. "Anything else?"

"Yes," Trevor said. He paused before delivering the final piece of information. "The skeletons were also dismembered. The legs and arms had been cut off. But they buried all of the bones together."

"Cut off?" Julie asked with trepidation. "How ... how do you know they were cut off, and not simply broken?"

"It was obvious due to the shear marks through the bones."

Julie felt a chill run through her as if a door had suddenly blown open allowing ice cold air to permeate the room. She picked up her mug of cocoa and took a long sip. The cocoa had cooled, providing no warmth. Her mind was suddenly filled with images of Chris and Marc being carved up on an embalming table.

"I know this has to be very difficult for both of you," Trevor said solemnly. "You take some time to process all of this. It can't be easy. We have no way of knowing how or when they died. We just have the final condition of the remains. If you have any questions at all, please don't hesitate to call me."

"Thanks, Officer," Tom said. "Can I ask one more question?"

"Of course, Tom."

"Any new information on finding the woman that attacked Julie? She has to be your top suspect in those murders."

"That's still a work in progress. Unfortunately, I have nothing new to share with you."

Tom and Julie stared at each other in silence. Both were wondering if they should confess what they had found today.

"Anything else?" Trevor asked.

"I think we're OK for now," Julie said. "Thank you."

Tom ended the call and turned to check on Julie.

"Are you OK, Jewels?"

Julie stood up and walked over to the window to the right of the French doors. The sound of the wind coming off the ocean could be heard as it wafted past the panes of glass. Julie couldn't help but notice the egrets that had been circling and hunting were gone. The entire marsh appeared empty of life.

"We always knew this day would come," Julie said as she tried to keep from crying again.

"Deep down there was always a small part of me that held out hope. Hope that they would be found."

"Me too, Tom. Despite all my wild theories about the candles and the legend. Without the bodies ..."

Tom pulled himself off the couch and joined Julie by the window.

"At least now we know. No more questions. No more wondering. No more hoping. Maybe even no more sleepless nights."

"Maybe."

"Maybe your nightmares will finally be gone, Jewels."

"Maybe," Julie said. "But ..."

"But what?"

"She's still out there, Tom. The killer. Mrs. Closed is still out there. Somewhere."

FOURTEEN

Bonds

Sara paused at the entrance to the family kitchen. Her mother was seated at the large table near the window that overlooked the porch and barn. Laura was holding her cell phone in one hand and pensively twisting the silver chain around her neck with her other. Sara watched in silence as her mother stared out the window, seemingly lost in her thoughts. The sun had set long ago, and the old barn sat ominously in the darkness, enveloped in a cocoon of towering trees.

"What are you doing?" Sara asked as she stepped through the doorway. Her mother jumped slightly before she turned and smiled toward her daughter.

"I didn't hear you back there," Laura replied. "I'm getting ready to call your cousin. We haven't talked in several weeks. I need to find out how my sister is doing."

"I don't know why you keep trying to talk to Aunty Jen. She's ignored you for decades."

Laura slid the chair out next to her and motioned for her daughter to take a seat. Sara begrudgingly obliged.

"Whatever history we have, we are still family," Laura said. "She doesn't have much time left, Sara. Susan is going to ship her off to long term care. Her mind continues to slip away. Your aunt and I were very close at one time. My poor sister was never the same after her husband's death. She blamed herself for what happened to Carl. That guilt has truly taken its toll on her."

Sara studied her mother's face as she talked about the past. She could see she was quite distraught at recalling the death of her uncle.

"I don't remember Uncle Carl's death."

"How could you? You were ... how old? It's been so long."

"I remember the day, Mother. The details? Those were always kept secret."

"For a reason," Laura said with a sigh. "I'm thankful Susan takes my calls. The bonds of family should not be ignored. I regret not trying to make amends with my sister sooner. Waiting until she is on her death bed with her mind drifting away was ... it was a mistake. I can see that now. I wish you and Emma would reconcile."

Sara frowned at the mention of her estranged sister. Ever since the incident last December her mother had been trying to get her to talk to Emma.

Laura could tell by the expression on her daughter's face that she did not want to continue this discussion. She turned her attention to her phone and scrolled through her contacts. The font was small, and Laura squinted as she tried to read the names. Finally, she found it. She touched the screen and place the phone to her ear. After a few rings, the call connected.

"Susan?" Laura asked into the phone. "Susan, dear, is that you? It's your Aunt Laura."

Laura paused a few seconds waiting for a response.

"Hi," Susan managed to say. Her response and tone were curt and brief.

"I called to check on my sister. How's your mom doing? Are you still planning to move her into assisted living? Can I be of any help?"

Susan paced around her kitchen, gripping the cordless phone tightly.

"Mom's not doing well, Aunty."

"Is her mind getting worse?" Laura asked with genuine concern.

"Yes, but that's not the latest problem. She's got

pneumonia. Her breathing is getting more shallow each day. We've got her on an oxygen tank. I'm probably going to give the doctor a call tomorrow if she doesn't improve."

Laura glanced over at her daughter and shook her head in despair. She continued to twirl her silver chain around her fingers as she realized the severity of the situation. It suddenly dawned on Laura how many years she had lost with her sister. Years she could never get back.

"Susan, would it be alright if Sara and I came to visit?"

"Aunty, I don't think she has the strength. And if I am going to be honest, I don't think she wants to speak to you. Not after all of these years. She needs rest. I think your presence will only bring her stress."

"I know she hates me, but we are family. You are my niece. Our blood binds us. We have to let go of the past, dear. Your mother never could. I've been trying for years to reconcile with her. Especially these past several months. You know that, Susan."

Susan pulled the phone from her ear and let out a big sigh. She really did not want to put her mother through any kind of anxiety. Her aunt, however, was being truthful. She had been extending the olive branch often, only to have her mother reject it.

"I guess so," Susan said with apprehension. "Maybe ... maybe closure would be good for her. I ... I just don't know."

"You sound so stressed and tired, Susan. How are you holding up?"

"I'm ... I'm OK, Aunty. It's just a lot to handle. I've got this estate sale going on, and it has really drained me."

"Estate sale?" Laura was shocked to hear this. She looked over at Sara and frowned. "What are you selling?"

"Just a lot of her old stuff. Mostly junk."

"Now listen, Susan. What you call junk might be a family heirloom."

"Don't worry Aunty, I'm well aware of what my mom holds dear. Trust me. Remember, I've been taking care of her since I was a teenager."

"I would just hate for you to give away something special."

"I know all of her keepsakes," Susan said somewhat

defensively. She suddenly felt like she was a kid again and had to prove herself to her elders. "In fact, I had this young couple come in today looking at that old table. The one with the three legs with the inlaid nickel and turquoise."

Laura's mouth fell open. She turned to look at Sara. Sara just furrowed her brow. She found it difficult to follow the conversation when she could only hear half of it. Sara pulled the phone from her mother's hand, placed it on the kitchen table and turned the speaker on.

"What did they want with the table?" Laura asked.

"Why am I on speaker, Aunty?"

"I'm making some tea, dear. You can't sell that table, Susan. It can't leave the family. There are only two of those in existence. My husband made them."

"That's right," Susan said with relief. "Uncle Fred! I couldn't remember who made it. I knew it was important to my mom. I told them it wasn't for sale."

"Well, what did these two want? Were they married?"

"I don't think so. To be honest, they were very odd. The guy saw the table in my online ad. He was asking about the history of it."

Sara raised an eyebrow. Her mother held her finger up to her lips to make sure her daughter did not speak.

"That is a bit odd," Laura said. Her tone had become conversational and filled with curiosity. Inside, however, she was becoming very concerned. "Where were they from?"

"I think they said Fall River."

Laura shook her head signaling "no" toward Sara.

"Why were you advertising the table if it wasn't for sale?"

Laura got up and walked over to the kitchen pantry. She pulled out a small tin cookie jar hidden deep behind several cans of beans. The old maroon jar was scratched and dented. She placed it next to the phone.

"I wasn't Aunty. It was just displaying some old lamps. The weird thing is the table was covered for the most part. All you could see was the leg. That detail work Uncle Fred did with the nickel and turquoise is really beautiful. That seemed to catch his eye."

"Did they happen to mention their names?" Laura asked

nervously.

"That was the other weird thing, Aunty. First, the guy said his name was Max. Then when they were leaving, the girl, who seemed very flustered the entire time, called him Tom. At one point she ran out of the garage because she felt sick."

Laura and Sara locked eyes. Sara started to speak, but her mother held her hand up and pressed two fingers on Sara's lips. She slowly pointed to the cookie jar.

"What did this couple look like?" Laura asked. She did her best to hide the angst that was filling her chest.

"They were cute. Young. I would say mid or late 20's. He had pale skin, blond and blue-eyed. She was darker skinned. Killer rack."

Sara began to nod "yes" to her mother.

"Oh, and they were kind of short," Susan added.

"Well they sound adorable," Laura said in an upbeat tone. "I'm glad my husband's handiwork was so eye-catching. What was the girl's name?"

Susan paused before responding. It dawned on her that her aunt suddenly seemed more interested in the table and the buyers than in her dying sister.

"Why so many questions?" Susan asked.

Laura frowned.

"Well, I wonder if maybe they somehow knew your uncle. Fred made many things with nickel and turquoise inlay. Maybe this couple somehow knew that? Maybe they have some other pieces of his?"

"Uncle Fred passed away so long ago, Aunty. They were very young. I don't see how ..."

"What about the girl? Did you get her name?" Laura's tone was terse and to the point. She was growing tired of tiptoeing around with her niece.

"Valerie."

Sara frowned and shrugged.

"Valerie Hope," Susan continued. "Like I said, she seemed out of it. Ill. Nervous. It was odd."

"Well, it sounds like no harm was done," Laura said with relief. "You never know what kind of strangers will show up at these things."

"I can take care of myself."

"I'm sure you can, dear. I wish I'd known you were doing the estate sale. We could have helped you."

"No worries, Aunty."

"Did they say if they would come back?" Laura asked. Her tone was genuinely casual now. She had all she needed from her niece and no longer felt the need to pressure her. "Were they going to buy anything you had? *Did* they buy anything?"

"No. They sort of left in a hurry. The weather was so dreary today I really had very little business."

"Maybe you will have better luck tomorrow, dear."

"Maybe. They said they might come back tomorrow."

"Tomorrow? Are they here in town?"

"The girl said they were staying at some bed and breakfast in town."

Laura smiled, as she felt herself feeling renewed and optimistic.

"Well, I hope they come back and buy something. Listen, Susan, I really must see my sister. Please. Let us say our goodbyes. Would it be OK if Sara and I come by tonight?"

"Sure thing, Aunty. Just promise me you will not do anything to upset her, OK? I think it's best to leave the past buried."

"Of course," Laura said with affection. "Goodbye, dear."

Laura ended the call and looked over at her daughter. She could see that Sara was ready to explode with questions.

"That sounded like them, Mother," Sara said with excitement. "But what's with those names? Max? Tom? Valerie Hope? Maybe it was just a coincidence?"

Laura glanced down at the cookie jar and smiled. She popped the top open, reached inside, and withdrew the luggage tag she had kept from Tom's backpack. She handed it to her daughter.

"Tom Leblanc lives on Hope Street, Sara. I don't know who Max and Valerie are, but what are the chances that two twenty-somethings that fit their physical description show up here on the Cape because they saw a picture of a table – *our* family table – online? It's them. It has to be."

Sara took a quick look at the tattered luggage tag and

nodded in approval. Her mother snatched the tag from her hand and put it back into the small tin jar.

Laura pushed her chair away from the table and stood up. She ran her hand down along the back of her waist. She let out a groan as she walked over to the kitchen pantry and returned the cookie jar to its hiding place.

"So, do we still need to lay low?" Sara asked. Her tone had a hint of condescension in it. "They are staying somewhere in Eastham! Are we still going to be discreet?"

Laura walked back to the table and rested both palms on the table top. She leaned close to her daughter's face and took a few moments to inspect the burn mark that Tom and Julie had left on her.

"No," Laura said adamantly. "We can't have any loose ends."

"Good," Sara replied as she smiled with relief. "They need to pay. Both of them."

***

Sara lifted her foot off the gas pedal and slowed as she approached her aunt's yellow bungalow. Sara was driving a very old Jeep Wrangler that her dad once used for fun on the beach. The huge off-road tires hummed loudly as the vehicle slowed. She pulled to the curb, parked, and turned off the engine. The old motor hiccupped and sputtered as it shut down.

"I miss the Cherokee," Sara said with a sigh.

"I'm not having this conversation again," Laura said. "We had to dispose of it. Just like that couple's big pickup truck. No loose ends."

"No loose ends."

"You go first," Laura said as she squeezed her daughter's hand for comfort. "It might be a bit much for us to both be there at the same time. It's been too many years."

"Why me?"

"Family bonds, Sara. Reconcile with your cousin. Now. You need to do this without me."

Sara sighed as she pulled her hoodie up over her head. It

had become such an instinctive move every time she stepped out into public that she almost wasn't aware of her actions. She opened the door and walked around to the curb. The sight of her cousin's home gave her pause. She couldn't remember the last time she had stepped foot into the house. *Decades?* Sara wondered as she walked up to the front door. She was surprised to see her handle tremble as she rang the doorbell. After a few moments, the deadbolt unlocked.

Susan opened the door with trepidation. She couldn't remember the last time she saw her cousin. Her Aunt Laura had come by every few years in an attempt to make amends with her mother. But Sara had stayed very far away. The shadowy hooded figure stood motionless. Her face was hidden from the light of the front porch.

"Sara?" Susan asked cautiously.

"Hi, Susan. Can I come in?"

Susan took a few steps back and motioned to Sara to step into the living room. She closed the door and watched as her cousin stood awkwardly with her hands jammed tightly into her coat pockets. Sara turned her back toward her cousin.

"I thought your mom was coming," Susan said. "Did she change her mind?"

"No, she's out in the Jeep. She wanted me to come in first."

Susan felt a bit frustrated that her cousin had not turned to talk to her. She walked around to her side and put her hand on her shoulder.

"It's good to see you again," Susan said.

Sara sighed as she took a step back from Susan, forcing her to release her hand. Sara knew she couldn't leave her hoodie up all night. She slowly slid it off, and quickly adjusted her hair to cover the right side of her face.

Susan smiled at finally seeing her cousin's face, if only in profile.

"You look so much like your sister," Susan said with amazement. "Well, other than the hair color. My, my ... even after all of these years. So similar. You just missed her. Emma. She was here an hour ago."

Sara felt her entire body tense up at the mention of her twin sister's name. The last thing she wanted to do was run into her. Sara turned to directly face her cousin. Susan's smile at their reunion quickly faded as she noticed the marks across Sara's cheek. She slowly reached her hand up to brush her hair aside.

"What happened?" Susan asked with concern. Sara immediately pushed Susan's hand away and pulled her hair further forward.

"It's nothing. Just a minor accident at the barn. I don't want to talk about it."

Susan briefly considered pushing her cousin on the topic but decided it was best to try and keep the conversation positive.

"I'm glad you came by," Susan said. "It's been so long since I've seen you. Too long."

"It's not like I had a choice. Mom was pretty insistent. She said time was running out."

"It's unfortunate that it takes someone to be near death in order to pull a family together. I do give your mom credit, however. She really has been trying to make amends for quite some time."

"I know. She kept lecturing me about the bonds of family blood."

"Blood bonds," Susan muttered softly as she rubbed her fingers together.

Sara felt her body tense up. The two cousins, once the best of friends, stood motionless staring at one another.

"So, how is she?" Sara asked cautiously. "Your mom."

"She's not well," Susan replied. "I've spent the past couple of months planning to move her to long-term care. To be honest, I don't think she's going to live much longer, Sara. Her pneumonia keeps getting worse."

Sara studied her cousin's face. She looked tired and much older than a forty-six-year-old should. Sara knew her aunt had suffered from mental issues for many years. It was now very obvious to her that playing caretaker had taken quite a toll on her cousin.

"I'm sorry, Susan. I'm sure this hasn't been easy for you."

"You could say that," Susan said. She let out an audible chuckle at the understatement her cousin had made. Sara managed a smile at hearing her cousin's trademark cackle.

"I heard you were doing some kind of yard sale," Sara said.

"I am. Care to take a trip down memory lane?"

Sara nodded, and the two walked through the house and out to the garage. Susan unlocked the side door to the garage and turned the light on. The harsh white light from the overhead fluorescent bulbs cast a sterile glow across the interior of the garage.

Sara strolled past a few paintings that she vaguely remembered used to hang in the living and dining room. She ran her hands across a twin set of metal and glass end tables before making her way to the back of the garage. The rosewood table was there waiting for her. Even though it was partially covered, she immediately recognized the shape and size. Sara raised the blanket and smiled.

"Wow, this is in fantastic condition," Sara said with admiration. She knelt down on one knee and lovingly ran her fingers across the nickel and turquoise inlay. "The one we have has seen a lot more wear and tear."

"Mom always kept that table in her bedroom. It had a candle and some pictures on it. But I had to move it out for the medical equipment. I didn't want it to get damaged."

"Mom said you had a couple come by today that wanted to buy this."

"No, they never asked to buy it. The guy just had a lot of questions about it."

Sara stood up and let the blanket fall to the floor, covering the table completely.

"People like that bother me," Sara said. "Too many questions. I wonder if they will come back to try and steal it."

"I highly doubt that, Sara. They were just an odd pair."

"Did you catch what were they driving?"

"Why?" Susan thought it was a genuinely odd question to ask. She felt her cousin was acting as nosey as her aunt.

"Like I said, you can't trust people. You should keep an eye out for them. Make sure they aren't stalking your house."

"Stalking?" Susan asked with a dismissive chuckle. "You are being overly dramatic. They were just ... annoying. I watched them as they walked off down the street around the corner. I went to the end of the property and saw them leave. They got into a bright red Wrangler."

Sara smiled as she remembered talking to Tom in the store in Truro last December. He had told her all about the new Jeep he had recently bought. *It's definitely them*, Sara said to herself.

"I'm really not worried about them," Susan said as she made her way to the door.

Susan and her cousin stepped out into the cool evening air. Sara immediately pulled her hoodie up around her face while Susan secured the garage. Sara looked up into the night sky and took in a long deep breath of cold April air. They walked back over to the house. Susan opened the kitchen door and turned off the outside floodlight in the driveway. The two stepped into the kitchen.

"I should go see Aunty Jen," Sara said. "My mom must be wondering why it's taking so long."

"She may not be awake, Sara. Please don't wake her if she's not. She really needs her rest."

"I understand. I just want to say goodbye."

Sara made her way to her aunt's bedroom, pausing outside the entrance to collect her thoughts. It suddenly dawned on her that the aunt that she had adored as a child was going to be on the other side of the door. She wasn't quite sure what to expect.

As she stepped into the bedroom, the first thing Sara noticed was how little of it had changed. The bedroom set was the same old wooden and marble one that she remembered from her childhood. Sara was surprised by the dozens of picture frames, both small and large, that covered the furniture. She took a few moments to browse through them. Many were unfamiliar to her. So many events had happened in the past thirty years. *I missed a lot,* Sara realized.

Sara walked over to the bed and took some time to study her aunt's face. Her hair was the same wispy gray and silver color as her mother's. She was very frail, however. Sara barely recognized her face beneath the oxygen mask.

The wedding photo next to the bed caught Sara's eye. That was the image of her aunt that she remembered. Young, vibrant and full of joy. Something else caught Sara's attention. She walked to the side of the bed and reached around the wedding photo. The glass candle jar with the flip top lid was very familiar to her. Sara popped it open and was surprised to see the two wicks inside. She had never seen that design before. *I may have to consider doing a two-wick candle some time*, Sara thought to herself.

Before putting the candle back, she took a moment to take a whiff. She held it close to her nose and inhaled deeply. *Rosemary.* Her mother had never mentioned a rosemary-scented candle as being part of the family history. She placed the candle back on the table and turned to look at her aunt. Sara studied the old woman for several seconds before she bent over and kissed her on the forehead.

"Goodbye, Aunty Jen."

As Sara headed for the door, she passed another picture that got her attention. It was of her, Susan and Emma from a cookout in 1984. Sara immediately remembered the event. It was Susan's birthday party.

"Those were such different times," Susan said from the doorway. She had been silently watching her cousin the entire time.

"It was a lifetime ago," Sara said with sadness.

Sara maneuvered her way past Susan and made her way toward the front door. She stopped and pulled her hoodie up before opening it and stepping out onto the porch. Susan quickly followed her and grabbed her by the shoulder to turn her around.

"Sara, before you go. Your sister. Emma. I think ..."

"Don't, Susan. Just don't."

"You mentioned family bonds, Sara. Well, why don't you try and show them?"

"You know why, Susan!" Seeing her cousin and aunt had brought back memories and emotions she was not prepared to deal with. "You and your family took my sister from me!"

"We both know that's not true!" Susan was filled with disappointment. She thought they'd had such a nice visit and could not understand why her cousin had become so angry so quickly.

"We're not having this discussion, Susan. The past is the past."

"We were the best of friends, Sara. How can you just ..."

"We were, Susan. *Were.* Past tense. Not anymore. There are some things I just can't forgive. What happened with Emma is one of them. Goodbye cousin."

Sara turned and marched down the front stairs and across the long cement walkway. She could see her mother in the front seat watching. The passenger's window was ajar. She wondered how much of the discussion she had heard.

The driver's door to the old Jeep rattled as Sara got inside and slammed it shut. She glared ahead, waiting for her mother to say something. She could feel her staring at her. Judging her. Her mother remained silent.

"Susan keeps acting like we are still friends like when we were kids," Sara finally said. "We aren't."

"No, you aren't," Laura said with disappointment. She quickly changed her tone to that of a mother that knows what's best for her daughter. "But you kids were all so close once, Sara. Those were happier times back then. I know why you carry the anger that you do. Ask yourself. Do you want to end up like me?"

"What do you mean?" Sara asked as she turned to face her mother.

"Here I am at sixty-four years old about to say goodbye to my older sister that's about to die. We've barely spoken to each other since Emma went to live with them. You don't even know the entire story, Sara."

"And how would I? Secrets and accidents, Mother. That's what this family is all about."

Laura frowned. Her daughter was stubborn and thick headed and only heard what she wanted to hear. She looked out her window and could see her niece was patiently waiting in the front doorway. Laura opened her door and looked down at the sidewalk. Her husband's old Wrangler sat high off the road due to the oversized tires. She cautiously lowered herself to the ground.

"This family is about much more than that. I want you to take this time to seriously think about family. Our family.

Everyone. With all that we've been through lately, the blood bonds of our family should be something we look to renew. Keeping Susan, Emma, and even my sister away was poor judgment. I can see that now. We are stronger together than apart. We always were. We can be again."

FIFTEEN

Mirrors

1984 Saturday 25-Jun 12:15 p.m.

Susan quickened her pace as she rushed along the sandy path that led from the Johnson family barn out to the pond. Although she had never measured the distance, supposedly the winding trail was almost a mile long. She had taken this path endless times and was well aware of the spots that required caution. Poison ivy and other odd and potentially abrasive plants randomly appeared along the way. Huge pine trees shaded sections of the trail. Other areas were wide open, many with hills that let you catch a glimpse of the Atlantic Ocean not far to the east.

A smile spread across Susan's face as she heard laughter up ahead of her. She had been searching for her cousins since her dad had finished taking pictures earlier. She quickened her pace and ran to the end of the path.

"There you are!" Susan said with exhaustion.

Sara and Emma were sitting on the end of a short wooden dock, dangling their feet above the water. Their flipflops were piled together at the start of the pier, just off the sandy path. A small woven pink and blue beach bag was slumped against some seagrass. The dock jutted several feet over a dark murky pond. Its planks were warped and weathered from years of being exposed to sun and sand.

The pond was a small freshwater kettle pond. Kettle ponds were scattered throughout Wellfleet and Truro. They formed over 10,000 years ago after the last ice age. They varied in size, shape, and depth. The one on the Johnson family property was not very wide, but it was extremely deep.

"I thought we were meeting at the beach?" Susan asked.

"That was the plan," Emma said. "Then grumpy changed her mind."

"It's too windy today," Sara said sternly. "The waves are way too rough. We can't go swimming."

Emma turned and looked at her cousin Susan and rolled her eyes. Susan suppressed her laughter because she knew it would only upset Sara. She kicked her flipflops off and made her way to the end of the dock. Once there she squeezed herself in between her two cousins, taking a seat by the pond.

"I was worried you were avoiding me because I'm a teenager now," Susan said sarcastically. "I might be too grown up and sophisticated to be seen with."

Emma and Sara laughed in unison. Susan wrapped her arms around the necks of her younger cousins and pulled them backward. All three girls fell back until they were lying flat across the dark gray planks of the old dock. Their legs dangled off the edge, leaving their feet just inches above the water. They laid there in silence, listening to the rush of the wind blowing in from the ocean.

"Thirteen," Emma finally said. "Does it feel any different?"

"No," Susan replied. "Should it?"

"How would we know?" Sara asked. "We're only eleven."

"Maybe you will be more popular with the boys now," Emma pondered.

"That's me, Miss Popular!" Susan said with a chuckle. Her laugh quickly turned into a series of short giggles.

"That laugh of yours!" Sara said. "That's what keeps the boys away!"

Susan laughed harder as she pulled herself upright. The twins followed her lead. All three looked out across the pond to the northern shoreline. Old pine trees towered over patches of seagrasses. Several egrets monitored the area, searching for food.

"Did your family ever name this pond?" Susan asked.

"No, but Sara did," Emma replied. "Like a month ago."

"I got tired of saying I was going to 'the pond' all of the time," Sara said. "I call it Flicker Wood."

"Why?" Susan asked with confusion.

"Because when I come down here at sunset, there are usually fireflies dancing around those pine trees on the other side. They flicker on and off. You know, in the woods."

"I like it," Susan said. She nodded and smiled as she looked out across the pond.

"I think it's kind of dumb," Emma said.

"It's not dumb!" Sara yelled. "You are just jealous because I thought of a name first!"

"I bet I can come up with a better name," Emma said calmly. "We both know I'm the smarter one."

"You are not!"

Susan began to laugh again. This time louder than before.

"You two crack me up," Susan said through her cackling. "For twins, you sure do disagree a lot!"

"Sara has always been the hothead," Emma said with an air of superiority. "She's just like dad. It's easy to push her buttons. Mom taught me that."

Sara turned toward her twin sister and flipped her middle finger up at her.

"You've got the brains, but I've got the brawn," Sara said. After a brief pause, she began to laugh.

"Oh please," Susan said. "You two are more the same than different."

"You know we are mirror twins," Emma said. "We aren't completely identical."

"I know!" Susan said with joy. "I love that you two are mirror twins!"

Mirror twins were identical twins with features, either physical or otherwise, that were opposite one another. This type of twinning occurred in about a quarter of all identical twins. The creation of mirror twins all came down to timing. During the embryonic stage, identical twins were created when the egg split within the first week. If the split happened after twelve days, a conjoined twin would form. Mirror twins were created when the egg split within that short time frame of seven to twelve days.

These twins often had features that were reversed, including hair shape, birthmarks, or even dental structure. Their faces would have contrasting features. In some rare cases, even their internal organs sat on opposing sides.

With Emma and Sara, their faces were completely asymmetrical. To the casual observer, this would not be that obvious until you looked closely at the level of their eyes and the shape of their nostrils. Emma was also right-handed, and Sara left-handed.

Susan jumped up from the dock and clasped her hands together. Emma and Sara twisted around in surprise to see what she was doing.

"I have a birthday request!" Susan said. "Do the mirror rhyme for me. Please? I love that poem!"

Emma and Sara turned to look at each and smiled. They had done this many times for family and friends, and were more than happy to entertain their cousin on her special day.

One year the twins had come home from school with a new homework assignment. Their English teacher had asked everyone to write a poem. It could be in any style that they chose. The assignment would include them reciting the poem in front of their classmates. The girls decided to write a limerick, which they read together in class.

Emma and Sara stood up and faced each other. Susan smiled as she stared at them. Seeing them sideways with their hair parted made their mirrored features all the more obvious. Emma raised her right hand, and Sara her left. They gently rested their palms together. As they recited their poem, they moved their arms in a slow circular motion around their faces.

> If I'm unsure and feeling blue,
> It only takes a look from you.
> Do I see me?
> No, I see we!
> Your eyes will tell me what to do.

Susan always thought it was the most brilliant poem, and immediately began clapping loudly.

Despite their joking that Emma was the smarter one, the

twins had written it together. Sara had even picked the general theme they should do. Their teacher had given them an A+.

"I know you two aren't feeling blue," Susan said, quoting the poem. "So, what do you want to do now?"

Emma and Sara were still smiling from doing the rhyme. It always seemed to bring them closer. Emma squinted at Sara. Sara nodded in agreement.

"Birthday hugs?" Emma asked.

"Birthday hugs!" Sara said.

The two turned and quickly embraced their cousin. The three girls held each other tightly as they giggled and laughed. Susan could not suppress her cackle from escaping.

"You two should be movie stars!" Susan exclaimed. "You could take Hollywood by storm!"

"I know!" Sara said.

"Seriously!" Susan continued. "There are plenty of famous acting twins. You two could be the first mirror twins to win Oscars! Golden Globes! All of the awards!"

"They would have to make the statues mirrored," Sara said as she continued to laugh. "I would love to be a movie star. Fame and money are in my future for sure."

"We aren't going to Hollywood," Emma said.

"Here we go," Sara said as she rolled her eyes.

"I want to do something meaningful when I grow up," Emma said. "Maybe help people, you know? I could be a doctor. Like a brain surgeon."

"The only brain you need to work on is your own," Sara said as she walked back to the edge of the dock. "I'm going to Hollywood. Or maybe start in New York."

"We can live happily here on the Cape," Emma continued. "What's so great about living in a big city?"

"There's nothing wrong with dreaming," Susan added as she joined Sara at the edge of the dock. "There's no reason we have to stay here. There's a whole world out there waiting to be explored."

Emma joined her cousins on the end of the dock and looked down into the murky dark green pond below.

"Speaking of exploring, where's Marilyn?" Emma asked.

"She's off playing somewhere with your sister. Mom told

me to keep an eye on her, but it's impossible these days. Especially when she gets with her cousin."

"Those two are quite the pair, aren't they?" Emma asked.

"I think it's kind of annoying how our moms dress them the same," Sara said.

"I think it's kind of sweet," Susan said. "They are twins at heart. They insist on dressing and acting alike. I think they are jealous of the bond that you two have."

"You don't have to be twins to have a special bond," Emma said. She took her cousin's hand and squeezed it tightly. "We've always been close. And we always will be. Even if you are going to become a stuck-up teenager!"

"And you become a world-famous brain surgeon!" Susan replied.

Susan and Emma hugged and began to laugh. Sara kept her focus out across the family pond.

"Don't laugh," Sara said with a somber tone. "I don't want things to change. I don't want us to drift apart. Ever."

"I'm not going anywhere," Susan replied. "I'm only sixteen months older."

"Let's make a bond," Sara said. She walked over to the beach bag at the edge of the dock and pulled out a leather sheath. Sticking out of the end of it was the wooden handle of a dagger. The handle had a nickel and turquoise inlay.

"What did you do?" Emma asked incredulously. "You took one of dad's knives! He's going to be so pissed! Are you crazy?"

"He has a bunch of them," Sara said in a dismissive tone. "He won't miss it. Besides, I can return it later. He'll never know."

Susan reached toward Sara and cautiously unsheathed the dagger. All three looked at the weapon in silence. The newly made knife had never been used. The edge of the blade was razor sharp.

"There is no way I am doing one of those stupid blood bonds!" Susan cried as she passed the knife back to Sara.

"You have to!" Sara said sternly. "It's the only way we will stay family forever."

"Emma?" Susan asked as she looked at her cousin for support. "You don't want to do this crazy thing, do you?"

Emma spent a few moments looking at Sara, Susan, and the dagger. Her initial shock at seeing the stolen knife had subsided. Prior to Susan's arrival, Emma had confessed to Sara that she was worried that things would change in the next few years. Susan was always ahead of them in school. She felt they had been and always would be playing catch up – middle school, high school, college. She did not want them to drift apart.

"Why not?" Emma finally said. "You just said there was a whole world out there waiting to be explored. What if our lives lead down different paths? I agree with Sara. Let's do the blood bond. Family forever, right?"

"Family forever," Sara repeated.

Sara held her right hand out and pointed the tip of the dagger at the end of her thumb. Her confidence quickly faded, and her hands began to tremble. She took a deep breath to try and steady her nerves.

"Oh, let me," Emma said as she snatched the dagger from her sister. "You never did like blood."

Emma took Sara's right hand and held it out over the water. She pricked the end of her thumb with the blade. The blood began to drip down into the pond. Emma was surprised at how smoothly the tip went in. Sara did not wince from the cut. Emma quickly punctured the thumb on her own hand and watched the blood drop down into the murky water below.

Emma turned and looked at her cousin, who's face appeared slightly green.

"Susan?" Emma asked.

Susan swallowed the saliva that had been pooling in her mouth. She closed her eyes and held her right hand out. Emma quickly poked the tip of her cousin's thumb. Susan opened her eyes, shocked at how fast it had happened.

"Together," Emma said as she held her thumb upright. All three girls pressed their thumbs together.

"Blood runs warm through the bonds of love and family," Sara said.

"Family forever," Emma said.

"Always the best of friends," Susan said quietly.

After a few moments they each took a small step back. One

by one they inspected their thumbs. The cuts were minor and would heal quickly. Emma began to suck on her thumb. Susan did the same. Sara let hers continue to drip blood down into the pond. Susan watched the drops as they disappeared into the inky black water.

"How deep is it?" Susan asked. "The pond."

"Nobody really knows," Emma said as she sucked on her thumb. "My dad said there is an old family legend about it. Supposedly it's bottomless."

"I heard mom say it had family secrets buried in it," Sara said. The dripping from her thumb had slowed. She shook her hand a few times and began to lick her wound.

"Well now it has something else," Susan said. "Our blood."

"Our bond," Sara added.

The three girls stood in silence staring into the murky waters of Flicker Wood Pond. The wind coming in from the Atlantic Ocean was strong. It wrapped them in the scent of sand and salt. Susan checked her thumb. The bleeding had stopped.

"This is turning out to be a great birthday," Susan said.

SIXTEEN

Shop to Shop

Tom took one last sip of Earl Grey tea from his insulated mug before resting it on the railing along the back porch of their cottage. A fog bank had rolled in, obscuring his view of the ocean. He had spent the past hour walking the trails that snaked their way throughout the marsh. The cold morning air did not bother him. It invigorated him. He'd had a surprisingly deep and sound sleep last night.

A seagull flew by and began to circle the area directly in front of him. Tom watched as it methodically hunted for food. He took a seat in one of the oversized white rocking chairs and listened to the crashing of the waves far off in the distance. As he rocked back and forth, he thought about what he and Julie had discovered at the estate sale yesterday. Part of him wanted to go back to talk to Susan and ask more questions. Deep down he knew that Julie was right – they were out of their league and needed to call it quits. Still, though, he could not shake the feeling that they were very close to finding Mrs. Closed.

The handle on the French door snapped open, and Julie stuck her head outside.

"Oh my God!" Julie said. "It's fucking cold! How can you just sit there?"

"It's awesome, Jewels," Tom replied softly. "I can't get over this view. I could watch it for hours."

Julie disappeared back inside for a moment. She returned with a thick woven cotton blanket from the sofa. She stepped out onto the porch and sat down in the rocking chair next to Tom, wrapping herself deep within the warm blanket. Each rocking chair had a small matching footstool. Julie had her Zombunny slippers on and propped her feet up on the stool. She took a moment to scan the horizon. The fog was beginning to burn off, and the purple flowers that sat closer to the shoreline were becoming visible.

"This really is peaceful," Julie said. "Did you sleep OK?"

"I slept great. You?"

"Totally. Like you said last night, we had some closure with that news from Trevor. But I'm ready to get back home. I feel like ... like my life has sort of been on hold these past few months. And now I can go home renewed. Somewhat."

"I know what you mean, Jewels."

"I miss ... I miss having fun. We've been a couple of zombies these past few months."

"Like our slippers!" Tom said with a laugh as he wiggled his Zombear slipper covered feet back and forth.

"Exactly!" Julie replied with a chuckle.

"That feels good."

"What does?"

"Laughing."

"We need more fun when we get back home, Tom. We rarely go out anymore. I've been avoiding dating. Even sex. I need to get my mojo back. Maybe this closure will help."

"I'll notify the single men of Providence."

"Thank you. Although, now that I think about it, I may have burned through most of them. You might want to expand that radius."

"I'll notify all of Rhode Island."

"How about you? Are you ready to dive into the dating pool yet?"

"It's the last thing on my mind."

"How about sex? At least go and get laid. Have you done any of those apps? What am I saying? Of course not. You are too innocent and sweet."

"Fuck you," Tom said in jest. "For your information, I've

done the online thing."

"When?" Julie asked with surprise. "This is news to me. Another secret? We said no more."

"This was last summer. I did it for like a week."

"A week? What happened?"

"It was all a big game. Everyone just wants to get laid."

"I think it depends on what app you are using. There are legit ones."

Tom watched as two deer appeared from the forest. They began to roam through the grass together. One glanced up and briefly stared at the cottage.

"I want more. I want love. Romance. I'll never find that in an app. It's like shopping for milk at the hardware store."

"Oh my God, that's brilliant! But you have to know that going into it. Try a different app. Look, I have a dating app and profile, but also another one just for hookups. With my hookup one, I am online knowing I am in a hardware store. And looking for a good solid screw."

Tom laughed as he turned his gaze back out toward the marsh. He raised his binoculars to watch the deer that were beginning to move further away.

"Are you hungry yet?" Julie asked as she stood up. "It's after 11 a.m., and I'm starving. I want to hit that big Sunday brunch in the main house."

"Give me a second. I want to see where these deer go."

Julie opened the French door and went back inside the cottage. The cold air outside had dried her skin. She ran to the bathroom and began to moisturize with her cocoa butter.

Tom came in from the porch and secured the back door. He jiggled the handle to confirm it was locked. Tom had become extra cautious with home security, ever since the events in Provincetown. He pulled out his phone and opened an app he wanted to show Julie.

"I made a list last night," Tom said.

"Of course you did," Julie said as she emerged from the bathroom. She held out the bottle of cocoa butter to Tom. He declined the offer. Julie squinted at the phone but did not bother to read it. "Dare I ask?"

"It's a list of stores for us to check out. I looked up tourist shops and furniture stores."

"Furniture?"

"Remember the table? Maybe we can find other pieces with the nickel and turquoise inlay."

Julie frowned and walked back into the bathroom. She checked her hair and turned off the light.

"Last night at dinner we agreed that we were doing a lazy day and not playing detective."

"We also agreed we would check out the town a bit. Birthday weekend getaway, remember?"

Tom and Julie stared at each other in silence. Julie crossed her arms and furrowed her brow. Tom slid his hands in his pockets and kept a hopeful smile spread across his face. Each studied the other, looking to see if either seemed willing to budge. After several seconds Julie conceded.

"OK fine, Tom. But don't get all obsessive about it."

"Me?" Tom asked with feigned shock. "Now when have you known me to be obsessive, Jewels?"

Julie let out a smile and managed a small chuckle.

"I'm serious, Tom! If we see something we just sort of make a note and move on. Use one of your little apps to document it all."

"OK, Detective Valley."

Tom grabbed his windbreaker and made his way to the front door. Julie quickly followed.

"Do you remember what else we agreed on last night?"

"What?" Tom asked.

"We are calling Trevor. We can do it when we are back in Providence if you want. But we are telling him everything we found. Agreed?"

"Ditto on that, Jewels."

***

After a very hearty brunch, Tom and Julie had gone for a lazy one-hour trek through the trails along the National Seashore. Prior to the hike, Julie had made Tom go back to the cottage to get an insulated mug so that she could fill it with the homemade hot chocolate they had served at the brunch. They spent most of the walk reminiscing about Marc and Chris. Julie had slept just as deeply as Tom had. They both hoped that the news from Trevor had brought them some much-needed closure.

They had checked out of the Marsh Mellow Inn just after 2:00 p.m. It was too far to walk to town, so they ended up driving in and parking at various small retail shopping lots scattered along Route 6, as well as some of the side roads. The pair had spent the past two hours scouring the stores on Tom's list. They were currently parked at a small plaza on Brackett Road.

"Another dead end," Julie announced as they stepped out of a small T-shirt shop. "Where to next, Max?"

"To be honest, Fluffy, I just don't know. I think we are out of options." Tom glanced down at his phone, and double checked the list of shops he had made last night. "That was the last store on my list."

Julie breathed a sigh of relief. She was anxious to get back home. It was almost 4:30 p.m. and she missed her cat.

"Wait," Tom said. "Check out across the street. That wasn't on my list."

Tom pointed to the other side of the road. There was a small building with four stores in it. It was newly constructed and resembled a classic Cape style home with faux dormers across the front. The shingle siding was a soft pale blue. All of the trim was bright white. A covered porch spanned across the store entrances. The shops included a bakery, deli, liquor store, and gift shop. The bakery and gift shop were both open, but the other two had "Coming Soon" signs posted in their doorways. A flag in front of the "Eastham Eden" gift shop flapped in the afternoon breeze and proclaimed "Now Open."

"What do you think, Jewels?" Tom asked hopefully.

"I think we need to hit the road," Julie replied flatly. She could tell by Tom's frown he was not happy. "I'm wiped. Who knows if we will hit any traffic on the way home. Honestly, I'm tired of playing detective."

"OK, but let's take a look. I promise this is the last one. My last birthday weekend event. Please?"

"The birthday guilt card has now expired," Julie said. "Last one. We are done after this."

"Agreed! We can leave Ruby here and just walk over. It's not that far."

Tom headed toward the edge of the parking lot. Julie stayed in front of the shop they had just left and proceeded to dig out her phone. She wanted to send a text to her cat sitter to let her know they would be back after dinner. Julie used a woman that her boss had recommended. She would stop in twice a day to check on Mr. Fluffy and take care of any issues with food, water, or the litter box.

Traffic on Brackett Road was light this afternoon. Tom was about to cross when he looked back to make sure Julie was with him. He was disappointed to see her standing all the way back at the store with her face buried in her phone.

"Jewels!" Tom yelled out.

Julie kept her head down but managed a quick dismissal hand wave toward Tom. Tom shook his head and turned back to cross the road. Much to his surprise, an old Wrangler approached from the east. As a Jeep fanatic, Tom's reaction was one of excitement. He loved classic Jeeps almost as much as he did the newest models. This one appeared to him to be an old Wrangler that had been heavily modified. He could not quite place the age. Right away he noticed the winch kit attached to the front. *I'm going to have to get that for Ruby*, Tom thought.

The trees spread along the edge of Brackett Road scattered the sunlight. The paint color of the Jeep flickered as it passed in and out of the shadows. One moment it was a deep gray. The next it was a faded blue. Tom walked to the very edge of the road to get a closer look at the vehicle. The oversized tires intrigued him. He wondered what other customizations it might have.

The Jeep slowed as it approached Tom. Then, just as the vehicle was next to him, he looked through the passenger's window at the driver. All he could see was a figure wearing a hood. For a brief moment, the driver turned and glanced at Tom. They locked eyes. He felt his heart stop. *Mrs. Closed?*

The engine on the old Wrangler roared as the vehicle sped away. Tom watched the Jeep as it continued to accelerate down the road.

"What are you doing?" Julie asked.

Tom jumped and spun around to face Julie.

"Shit, Jewels!" Tom exclaimed. "You scared me! Did you see it? Did you see that Jeep?"

"No. What did I miss?"

Tom looked back down Brackett Road. It was empty. He closed his eyes and replayed the drive by in his mind.

"Nothing," Tom said. "It's just that I thought ... I thought I saw a Jeep. With Mrs. Closed inside."

Julie began looking around the parking lot, the main road, and to the lots across the street. She felt her heart begin to race.

"Are you kidding?" Julie asked in a panic. "The old Cherokee from the candle store?"

"It's gone. But it wasn't the Cherokee. It was a really old Wrangler."

"You said you saw her!"

"I thought I did. I'm ... I'm, not sure. It happened so fast."

"If it wasn't the Jeep from the store then why do you think it was her?"

"The driver was wearing a hoodie. I got a brief look at the driver's face. I swear the right side looked ... well, scarred. And her face seemed ... I don't know. It seemed ... familiar. Maybe it was the shadows."

"Did you get a license plate?"

"No, Jewels. I was so shocked that I froze. I didn't even think of taking a picture. There wasn't time. Maybe ... maybe I was wrong."

Julie frowned and punched Tom in the shoulder.

"Well then don't freak me out like that," Julie said with frustration. "Let's go check out that last store and then get the hell out of here."

Julie glanced up and down the street and then crossed over to the lot on the other side. Tom followed but stopped in the middle of the road to look westbound one last time. Julie did not wait for him. She was still trying to calm down from the false alarm he had set off. Julie walked up to the gift shop and stepped inside. Her goal was to get back on the road in ten minutes tops.

"Can I help you," asked the young male clerk behind the counter.

"Just browsing," Julie said with a strained smile. She had repeated that line way too many times this afternoon and had grown weary of playing the role of tourist.

A glance around the store revealed nothing new. Julie sighed as she noted the T-shirts, souvenirs, and knick-knacks scattered throughout the shop. There was a small display along the back wall that looked to have several different candles on it. She debated going to check it out. Tom walked in, and Julie pointed to the table at the back. He smiled and headed to inspect it.

Julie looked back at the clerk behind the counter. He was tall, with dark hair and broad shoulders. She pegged him for early twenties and thought he was kind of attractive. She unzipped her purple jacket and adjusted her chest. *Milk in a hardware store*, Julie wondered to herself as she strolled over to the counter and smiled at the young man.

"New store?" Julie asked. She leaned onto the counter and rested her chin on her right hand.

"Yes, we opened yesterday," the man replied. He blushed as he looked Julie up and down, trying not to stare at her chest.

"Busy?"

"Not really. But it's early in the season." After a brief pause, he cleared his throat. "My girlfriend works the morning shift, and she said it was slow then, too."

Julie stood up and zipped her jacket closed.

"Milk," she said softly.

"Oh, I'm sorry we don't have any of that here."

Julie chuckled at the misunderstanding and began to skim through the display of sunglasses. She already had too many pairs, but couldn't resist something unique. One pair immediately jumped out at her. They had a tortoise frame with red and blue stripes down the side. She quickly realized they were similar to the Gucci pair that Chris had.

"Is there a mirror?" Julie asked the young clerk. He pointed to a display up near the front window.

Julie walked up to the front counter and checked her hair in the large mirror. The wind had made quite a mess of it. She sighed and pulled her hair back before she slipped the glasses on. The fit was great. She briefly thought of Chris and the fun ride in Marc's truck when she asked to see her Gucci rims.

As Julie tried a few different poses in the mirror, she was suddenly startled at another image looking back at her. A figure, their face shrouded in a dark gray hoodie, was watching her through the front window. Julie still had the sunglasses on so her shock was somewhat hidden. She focused on the person watching her. The lighting was poor, especially with the hoodie, but she could easily see the long blond hair sticking out from the corners of the hood. As Julie was about to turn around the person hurriedly spun around. As they did Julie noticed the sun illuminate the person's face. It only lasted for an instant, but she thought the person's cheek looked scarred. Julie stared in the mirror in shock and watched as the figure disappeared from her view.

"Hey, those look like the frames that Chris had!" Tom said. He was standing at the end of the front counter, a few feet from Julie.

"Did you see her?" Julie asked in a panic. "Did you?"

"See who?" Tom asked. He began to look around the store.

"Her!" Julie hissed, as she spun around and ran out the front door. Tom followed her. Julie looked back and forth across the parking lot. Several people were strolling around, but nobody was wearing a dark gray hoodie. She turned and looked at Tom. "Mrs. Closed!"

"What?" Tom asked. His jaw fell open, and he began to look around in a panic. He took a few steps out into the parking lot trying to find the old Jeep he had seen earlier.

"Excuse me, are you going to buy those?" The young clerk was standing in the open doorway looking nervous and confused. Julie handed him the sunglasses and stepped out into the sunlight next to Tom. The clerk grimaced and went back inside.

Julie's heart pounded rapidly in her chest. Her throat began to close, and the air became harder to inhale. She took a few more steps out into the lot.

"What did you see, Jewels?" Tom asked. He tried to stay calm, but he too was suddenly filling with anxiety. He grabbed Julie by the shoulders and shook her to get her attention. The two friends locked eyes. He could see she was terrified. "Talk to me."

"I ... I was looking in the mirror. I noticed someone looking at me through the window. She had a hood covering her face, but when she turned away, I could see there were faint marks on her cheek. Sort of like scars."

"What side?" Tom asked, his voice elevated due to a mix of fear and urgency. He tightened his grip on his best friend's shoulders.

"Behind me," Julie replied somewhat confused. She stopped looking around the lot and looked back at Tom.

"No, I mean what side of her face was it."

"Oh ..." Julie paused and played the event back in her mind. "The left. No, wait. The right. She was in the mirror. It was the right side. That's the one, isn't it?"

Tom eased his grip on Julie and took a step back. The wind had picked up, sending brush and debris tumbling across the parking lot. They were now the only two people standing outside in the plaza. Tom noticed there were only a few other cars in the lot. None of them were an old blue Jeep Wrangler. He looked across the street at Ruby in the other lot. She looked like she was a mile away.

"Tom?" Julie asked. The shaking in her voice had subsided. "Do you really think it was her?"

"You tell me, Jewels."

"I ... I ... I don't know. Her face was covered. All I noticed was that mark on her face. Or was I just imagining it?"

"You mean like I was? So, we're both imagining we saw her? It has to be her. I told you that the driver of the old Wrangler that drove by me also had a hoodie on."

A car horn went off behind Julie, causing her to jump. She turned around, and a young girl in a jet-black Toyota Corolla was waving at her to move. Tom and Julie realized they were still standing in the middle of the parking lot. The two walked up to the edge of Brackett Road and took refuge under a large maple tree.

"One thing, Tom. The person watching me had blond hair. Mrs. Closed had brown hair. So maybe we are wrong?"

"It's too much of a coincidence. I bet that was her. She must have seen me on the edge of the road and then came back looking for us."

"What now? Call Trevor?"

Tom scanned the parking lot and main road. His nerves had finally calmed down, and he was thinking clearly again.

"Wait here," Tom said. He began to walk back to the building they had just left.

"No fucking way!" Julie cried. She jogged ahead and joined Tom. "Where are you going?"

"Follow me," Tom said.

Tom lead Julie around the side of the building. They stopped at the far corner of the back lot. From there they could see behind all of the plazas on that side of the road. Most of the lots were empty. There were several SUVs lined up in a row against a large white cement building. They sat beneath a sign that read "Parker, Jones, Walker Auto Repair." None of the vehicles were Jeeps.

"Let's get back to Ruby," Tom said.

Tom and Julie sprinted across Bracket Road. His Jeep was parked at the far end of the lot in front of a small T-shirt store. Julie slid her arm around Tom's and pulled him close for comfort as they approached Ruby.

Sara Johnson watched her prey run toward the bright red Wrangler parked off in the distance. She was standing next to a donut shop two blocks away. Her Wrangler was tucked deep around the corner in a different lot, far from prying eyes. She reached into her pocket and pulled out her phone and called her mother. Sara kept her eyes locked on Tom and Julie as she waited for the call to connect. Finally, her mother answered.

"I've got them," Sara said.

SEVENTEEN

Detour

The engine in Tom's Jeep burbled quietly. Warm air gently wafted from the dashboard vents throughout the SUV's cabin. Tom stared ahead through the windshield as he contemplated the different options he and Julie could pursue as next steps. He tried his best to ignore the glare from his best friend in the passenger's seat. Her icy cold look continued to break his concentration.

"Just do it already," Julie said impatiently.

"I'm thinking," Tom snapped back.

They were still parked in the lot across the street from where Julie had seen Mrs. Closed. Tom was desperately trying to think of their next course of action. He hoped that the old Jeep would miraculously appear and they could simply follow her.

"Thinking of what?" Julie asked with frustration. "We have to call Trevor! Enough of this detective bullshit!"

"Jewels, you know he is going to freak out when he finds out where we are. What if ... what if we go back to Susan's house and wait to see if Mrs. Closed arrives?"

"Are you fucking crazy?" Julie yelled. She reached into her pocket and pulled out her cell phone. "If you aren't going to call him then I will."

Tom reached over and yanked her phone away.

"Hey!" Julie said.

Tom cradled the phone against his chest and leaned back towards his door.

"Enough," Julie said. Her tone had calmed down. She opened the palm of her hand. "You know I'm right. Give it up, Max."

Tom took a deep breath and slowly handed the phone back to her.

"You win," Tom said. "But let me make the call."

Tom pulled up Officer Trevor Stevens' number on his recent calls list and dialed. The ringing seemed deafening through the car's speaker system. Tom lowered the volume just as the connection was made.

"Mr. Leblanc," Trevor said with bemusement. "What can I do for you today?"

"We have some information for you," Tom replied.

"We?" Trevor asked.

"Hi Trevor," Julie said. She tried to sound upbeat, hoping it would lessen the brutal blowback she knew was coming.

"Hello Julie," Trevor said flatly.

Julie frowned that Trevor did not sound happy to hear her voice. He normally perked up when she was on the call with Tom.

"So how are things in Providence, today?" Trevor asked.

Tom looked at Julie. She just shook her head.

"We found something," Tom continued. "And maybe someone."

"Found what? Who?"

Julie muted the phone.

"He already sounds pissed," Julie said.

Tom unmuted the call.

"Where are you right now?" Trevor asked.

"We're in Eastham," Tom said.

There was a long pause before Officer Stevens spoke.

"Cape Cod?" Trevor asked.

"Yes, but hear me out," Tom said.

"Didn't I explicitly tell you *not* to come out to the Cape?" Trevor asked. His voice was strained as he tried to reel in his anger. "So, when we spoke yesterday you were already here, weren't you?"

"Yes," Julie said.

"Why didn't you tell me yesterday?" Trevor asked.

"We ... we didn't want to upset you," Tom said.

"Trevor, you need to hear what we found," Julie added. "Please. This is important."

Trevor Stevens was at home lounging in his recliner and attempting to enjoy a relaxing day off. He had a feeling this was going to be a long phone call. He grabbed the remote from the table by his side and muted the baseball game playing on his television.

"I'm listening," Trevor said. He righted his chair, stood up, and headed to the kitchen to grab a beer.

"It started with an online search," Tom said. "I've been trying to find that FlickerWood candle we had told you about. Julie suggested I look at yard sales. We found one here."

"The same candle?" Trevor asked.

"No. We found an estate sale. The ad had a picture of a table. It looked a lot like the one that we saw in the store back in Truro."

"Hold on. You're telling me that you drove all the way out to Eastham because of a table?" Trevor asked. He cracked his beer open and took a long sip.

"It was a unique table," Julie said. "We both thought it looked like the one from the candle store."

"Go on," Trevor said. He glanced back over at his television to keep an eye on the Red Sox game he was missing.

"We go to the estate sale and this woman Susan is there. Long story short we go see the table, and it's the same as the one from the store. She told us there were only two of them and her cousin had the other one."

"Her cousin?" Trevor asked.

"We think her cousin is the woman that attacked us last December," Julie said. "The one we call Mrs. Closed."

"The one you still haven't found," Tom added.

Julie punched Tom in the shoulder again. She thought his tone was a bit too flippant and would not help them in their desire to get Trevor to help them.

"Guys," Trevor said as he rubbed his eyes. "This is such a

long shot. Why are you telling me this? What do you expect me to do?"

"We're not done yet," Julie said. "Tom, tell him the rest."

"We were getting ready to head home when I saw an old Jeep Wrangler," Tom said. "She was driving it. Mrs. Closed."

"A Wrangler?" Trevor asked. "The woman has a Cherokee, Tom. That's what we've been searching for."

"Yes, but hear me out. When it passed by me, I was convinced the driver inside was Mrs. Closed."

"You're positive?" Trevor asked.

"Jewels saw her too."

"I was in a gift shop, and I saw her watching me from outside. But when we went out there, she was gone."

Tom and Julie waited patiently for Officer Stevens to respond. Several seconds passed before he replied.

"Can you describe her?" Trevor asked.

Julie looked over at Tom and frowned. She knew this was going to be the difficult part.

"Not really," Julie said. "Her face was covered. Most of it."

"She had a hoodie on," Tom said. "But her face had marks on it like it was burned. Remember I threw that candle at her?"

"What about her other features?" Trevor asked. He was becoming aggravated with the discussion, as well as the fact that he was missing his game. "Describe her. What did you see?"

"She had blond hair," Julie said. "Now I know that doesn't really match ..."

"Let me stop you right there, Julie," Trevor said, as he sat back down in his recliner. He leaned forward and rested his elbows on his knees. "This is what I am hearing. You came out to the Cape because you found a table that you think matches the one from the store. Then you see a woman in a Jeep that isn't the same SUV as the one from last year. And then you see a woman with blond hair and no other features other than some marks on her face. Then you call me thinking you found the killer. Did I get that right?"

Tom rapidly shook his head back and forth in disagreement. He looked over at Julie for support but found her staring down at her hands.

"It's not like that," Tom snarled. "That had to be her!"

"Tom, I think you are both seeing what you want to see," Trevor said. "You see someone in a completely different vehicle from the crime that happened in December, and she has a hoodie with their face mostly obscured. Can you confirm it was a woman? Could it have been a man with long blond hair?"

Julie realized that Trevor could be right. She started to wonder if they had both gotten so wrapped up in playing detective that they were beginning to see things that weren't there. She looked over at Tom and nodded in agreement with Trevor.

"But what about the table!" Tom exclaimed. He was desperate now. He couldn't believe Trevor was dismissing everything they had told him. "It was absolutely identical to the one from the store. We are both sure of it!"

Trevor studied the replay showing on his television. He realized he was missing a good game.

"That sounds like a long shot to me," Trevor said. "But if you two are confident it was the same table, then I can go talk with the woman at that estate sale for you. Or have someone from the Eastham police swing by. See if there really is any sort of connection."

"Thank you!" Julie said with relief. Julie looked over at Tom hoping to see that he too was happy. He still looked upset.

"When?" Tom asked.

"When?" Trevor responded.

"When are you going over there?" Tom continued. "Should we meet you there?"

Julie closed her eyes and sighed. She knew that any support they may have earned with Trevor had most likely been destroyed by Tom.

"Meet me there?" Trevor asked. He stood up from his chair and took a deep breath. "You two shouldn't even be out here! Listen. Your tip about the table is worth investigating. By the police! Send me the address, and I will follow up tomorrow."

"Tomorrow?" Tom cried. "That may be too late! I know it was Mrs. Closed in the Jeep! You have to ..."

Julie hit the mute button to cut him off before he angered Trevor anymore.

"This is my day off, Tom," Trevor said. His words were short, terse, and to the point. "Look. I will happily investigate this for you. Tomorrow. The table and the house and the owner will still be there. Tomorrow. Do you hear me?"

Julie unmuted the phone.

"We hear you," Julie said.

"I want you two back on the road to Providence immediately. Don't make me get the Eastham police to escort you out of town."

"But ..." Tom said.

"But nothing, Tom. Do you know who else called me today? Your mother. She heard the news about the bodies being found. She told me you were in Hyannis and she was afraid you would head to Provincetown once you heard what was found. Hyannis! She also told me about your dad and your childhood obsession with finding his killer. We had a nice long talk about you, Tom. Do you want me to call her back and tell her where you really are, and what you are doing out here?"

Julie and Tom stared at one another in total shock.

"Listen," Trevor said as he tried to calm himself down. He took a deep breath before continuing. "I gave you both some devastating news yesterday. It's only natural for you to be very emotional about it today. Knowing that we found the bodies of Chris and Marc has to hurt. I don't doubt that you saw a shadowy figure in a window. Or in a Jeep. You didn't imagine either of those. They just weren't what you thought they were. The Jeep is the wrong model. Her hair is different. Neither of you got a good look at the person."

Tom lowered his head and let out a long sigh. His eyes began to well up as Julie reached out and took his hand.

Is he right? Tom wondered.

"Go home and get some rest," Trevor said. "Send me that address, Tom. We'll look into that tomorrow, OK? I promise. Maybe there is some connection. Give us a few days to track down her family's history. I'll call you later this week with an update. Or sooner if anything comes up."

"Thanks, Trevor," Julie said. She ended the call and glanced over at Tom. "Do you really think we are just overreacting?"

Tom wiped his eyes as tears started to flow down. He gripped the steering wheel for support and hung his head in sorrow.

"I don't know, Jewels," Tom said softly. "I mean, hearing it from his point of view I get it. Was the Jeep I saw the same? No. Was the woman you saw the same?"

"I don't know," Julie said with a heavy sigh. "I thought she was. Her jawline? Could I tell? I really didn't see that much. Maybe it was a man. Trevor has me so confused now. Was he right? Did the news of their bodies being discovered rattle us more than we realize?"

"Maybe ..." Tom said.

"Let's head home," Julie said as she squeezed Tom's knee. "Trevor will follow up on the table. Oh, speaking of which you need to send ..."

"Send what?" Tom asked. "Oh, the address for Susan."

Tom turned toward Julie to see why she had stopped talking. Her eyes were staring straight ahead. She had a look of shock across her face.

"Jewels?" Tom asked.

Julie did not move. She continued to stare out the windshield. Tom turned to see what she was looking at.

Sara Johnson had pulled her Wrangler into the parking lot that Tom and Julie were in. She had stopped several feet in front of them. The driver's side window was open. Her head was shrouded in a hoodie. She sat there and stared at Tom and Julie. Her eyes were like daggers glaring at them from beneath her cowl.

"What the hell?" Tom whispered.

Sara pulled a dagger from her pocket and pointed it at Tom and Julie. She then turned her gaze ahead, and floored the accelerator, and quickly sped out of the parking lot.

"Tom?" Julie asked.

Tom and Julie watched as the old Jeep raced away. At the next intersection, it turned down Old Orchard Road, heading toward Route 6.

"Was that ... was she ..." Tom said. He could feel his heart pounding in his chest.

"What the fuck was that?" Julie asked.

"It was her!" Tom stated. "You saw the dagger, didn't you?"

"Was it?" Julie asked. She looked to Tom for confirmation, but his focus was on the now empty Brackett Road. "I ... I couldn't really see her face again. What do we do now?"

"Fuck Providence," Tom said.

Julie grabbed the nearest handle for support as Tom slammed his Wrangler into drive and headed off to follow Mrs. Closed. He quickly made his way to Old Orchard Road. There were a few cars ahead of him, but Tom could see the old Wrangler way up ahead. He watched as it turned onto Route 6 East.

"She's going east, Jewels," Tom said.

"East. I don't want to go back there."

"I doubt she's going to P-Town."

"Should we call Trevor back?"

"And tell him we are in a high-speed chase? I don't think so. You heard how angry he was."

"You just don't want him calling your mother."

"That's not it! He won't believe us, Jewels. We ... we need evidence. Let's see if we can get close enough to get a picture of her license plate."

Once onto Route 6, Tom found himself trapped behind a large semi truck in the right lane and slow-moving traffic in the left. The old Wrangler was half a mile ahead of them and pulling away. Tom slid one lane over and began to beep his horn to try and coax the slower traffic along. All that did was anger the car in front of him and cause them to drive slower.

"Shit!" Tom yelled.

"Relax," Julie said anxiously. "The traffic will clear."

"We're coming up on Wellfleet, and the lane is going to drop from two to one once we do."

Tom watched in frustration as the old Jeep pulled further and further away from them. Eventually, he was able to slide over in front of the tractor-trailer truck just before the lanes merged together. The old Wrangler was ten cars ahead of them.

Julie felt her palms begin to sweat as they passed the town line and were greeted by a sign that said "Entering Wellfleet."

We need to be elsewhere, Julie said to herself.

"I don't suppose you can get a picture of her license plate from here?" Tom asked.

"She's too far ahead," Julie said. She was surprised at how difficult it was for her to speak. Her chest tightened with fear as they continued their return to the wrong end of the Cape. "I'm calling Trevor."

"No, Jewels!" Tom said. "He's not going to believe us. Not without proof!"

Julie ignored Tom and began to scroll through her contacts looking for Trevor's number. Tom grabbed the phone from her hands and tossed it into Ruby's back seat.

"What the fuck, Tom?" Julie yelled.

"He won't listen to us!" Tom yelled back. "I promise we will call Trevor once we get that license plate."

The two sat in silence as they plodded along for another five miles. The old Jeep was well ahead of them and often disappeared from view as they crested the various twists and turns of the road.

Sara used her rearview mirror to keep an eye on the bright red Wrangler way off in the distance. The game of cat and mouse amused her. She smiled as she turned off Route 6 and headed toward the ocean.

"She's turning!" Tom cried. He pressed down on the accelerator and pulled closer to the vehicle he was trailing. "This traffic is insane. We are going to lose her down that road."

"Relax, Tom," Julie said. Deep down Julie was perfectly fine if they did not catch up to her. Her days of playing detective were behind her. All she wanted to do was head home. "You won't do us any good if you get us into an accident."

Tom wiggled his fingers and loosened his grip on the steering wheel. He eased off the gas and slowed as they reached the exit that the old Wrangler had taken. It was a narrow two-lane road. He turned right and was disheartened to see the road ahead was empty.

"Now what?" Julie asked. She looked out through the windows as she nervously rubbed her hands together.

"We see where it leads," Tom replied.

Julie grabbed Tom's phone and pulled up the map.

"It looks like it leads directly to the ocean."

The road was narrow and barren with no signs of houses anywhere. Every now and then they would pass a driveway or dirt road that would disappear behind dense foliage.

Julie closed the map on Tom's phone and tucked it between her leg and the seat. She lowered her window and leaned her head out. The aroma of the Atlantic Ocean wafted into the Jeep. Off in the distance rang the sound of waves crashing to shore.

"We're almost at the beach," Julie said as she closed her window.

Tom slowed as the blacktop road became covered by the golden sands of the National Seashore. Several small sand dunes were nestled directly ahead of them. They entered a small parking lot. At the very end of the lot was a series of large boulders. Tom drove to the end and turned his engine off. There were no other vehicles around.

"She must have turned off at one of those narrow roads that we passed," Julie said. She looked at Tom and waited for a response. He kept his gaze ahead toward the ocean. "What do you think?"

Tom did not answer. He popped his door open and stepped out. The intensity of the wind coming in off the ocean took him by surprise. He gently released his door as a strong gust blew it shut. Tom looked back at Julie and pointed toward the beach.

"I'll be right back," Tom said. He turned and headed through one of the openings in the boulders.

"And leave me here?" Julie yelled from inside the Jeep. She quickly hopped out of the vehicle and ran to catch up to Tom.

The beach in this part of Wellfleet was wide and deep. It was also quite desolate. This was not the tourist part of town. Lifeguard chairs and snack stations were nowhere to be found.

"What do you see?" Julie asked as she reached Tom.

Tom pointed toward the ocean.

"Shit!" Julie said.

The boulders at the end of the parking lot were not meant

to prevent people from driving onto the beach. They were placed there so that people would not drive off the cliff. The beach was about fifty feet below them. A narrow path snaked its way down from the parking lot to the golden sands below.

"Now what?" Julie asked.

Tom grabbed Julie by her hand, and the two began the descent to the coastline. Julie stopped at the bottom of the path and let Tom continue ahead.

Tom walked about a dozen yards out toward the ocean before something caught his eye. He turned and faced north.

"What is it?" Julie asked nervously.

"She's here," Tom said as he pointed up the coast.

Several hundred yards away was the old Wrangler. It was parked in an opening in the cliff wall.

"Oh my God," Julie said as she ran ahead to be by Tom's side. She took a few moments to study the parked SUV. "Where is she?"

"I don't know, Jewels," Tom said with concern. "It looks like it might be abandoned."

"How did she get there?"

"There must be an opening somewhere down one of those roads that we passed."

Julie studied the sides of the sandy cliff and realized it was mostly giant sand dunes that lined the shore. A chill ran down her spine. *The bodies.*

"She's in the dunes!" Julie said as she turned to face Tom. "Is this where she hid the bodies? Didn't Trevor say they were buried in sand dunes?"

Julie felt the pounding of her heart reverberate over and over in her temples. Adrenaline coursed throughout her as she struggled to catch her breath.

"We have to get out of here, Tom. We have to call Trevor!"

Tom began to walk back toward the path that led up to the parking lot. Julie grabbed his arm and walked with him. When they got to the top Tom stopped and leaned against one of the large boulders.

"Not yet, Jewels."

"What? Why?"

"Because we still have no new evidence for him. What have

we discovered since we last called him?" Tom stared at Julie's eyes and could see the fear and confusion washed across her face He did not wait for a response. "Nothing. All we've done is follow someone that Officer Stevens told us was irrelevant."

"But it was her! She aimed that knife at us!"

"I know, Jewels. But will Trevor believe us? You heard how angry he was on the phone. He will ask us to describe the knife. Can we? Did we see the handle?"

"No," Julie muttered. "No, we didn't."

Julie turned away from Tom and glanced out at the ocean. The clouds above were thin and scattered, but far out at sea, they were thick, dark and menacing. The wind was cold and uncaring as it cut across her skin.

"We need to get closer," Tom said.

"What?" Julie asked. "Fuck no! Are you crazy?"

Tom walked past Ruby and made his way down the middle of the parking lot. Julie quickly followed his lead. He stopped at the exit and began to survey the sides of the lot. The edges were lined with shrubs and dunes.

"We get closer and get a picture of the license plate. Then we call your cop boyfriend and send it to him and ask him to look it up."

"Trevor's not my boyfriend!"

"But you wish he could be," Tom said with a chuckle.

"Stop trying to change the subject! You are only trying to distract me so I will not go into a full-blown panic."

"Is it working?"

"No!"

Tom turned and took Julie by both hands. She refused to look him in the eye.

"Look, Jewels, there is a path back there behind the dunes." Tom walked behind Julie and pointed over her shoulder. "We can take that and stay hidden from sight."

There was a tight opening on the left side of the entrance to the parking lot. Tom hadn't noticed it when they drove in. The path was very narrow. Branches from a small pine tree obscured most of the opening. Tom pointed to a fresh set of tire tracks that disappeared behind the foliage. The right side of the path was a mix of dunes and brush. The left side was denser and filled with a blend of hearty shrubs and trees. Julie folded her arms in protest.

"One picture," Tom said. "Let me get that license plate, and we are gone."

Julie felt her nose begin to run. The wind was picking up in intensity. The salt air bit at her cheeks. She rubbed her face a few times and took a deep breath.

"You're obsessing."

"No, I'm not."

"Tom, what did Trevor mean when he mentioned your dad's death? He said your mom told him all about it."

Tom looked down at his feet as he quietly considered how to respond.

"You refuse to tell me. I know it was traumatic for you. I know you obsess over it. I know that ... that you ended up in therapy."

Tom looked up at Julie.

"Who told you that?" Tom asked with surprise.

"Your mother."

"What? Is she telling everyone about my childhood? You. Trevor. Who the hell else?"

Tom stormed off toward the boulders at the edge of the cliff. Julie ran after him.

"She's just worried, Tom. She said you are going to obsess about Mrs. Closed like you did with your dad's killer. I know they never found out who did it."

The wind blowing off the ocean was cold and salty. Tom closed his eyes and allowed the scent of the sea air relax him. After a few moments, he turned to face Julie.

"Yes, I obsessed about it. In my early teens. Yes, I went to therapy for it. Am I obsessing now? Maybe. Maybe I am, Jewels. But we are close. So close to getting the evidence we need! I promise I won't take it beyond getting that picture."

"That's what you said about the estate sale. That was going to be the end of it. Then again about checking out the shops. Then the car chase. When does it end, Tom? When?"

"It ends now, Jewels. I swear. One picture."

"You promise?" Julie asked.

"We'll get the license plate. Send it to Trevor. Then we will head home."

Julie glared at Tom shaking her head. She knew there was no way to change his mind.

"Fine!"

"C'mon Detective Valley, let's wrap this case up."

Julie let out a long sigh as she followed Tom back to the hidden path at the entrance to the lot.

"Are we driving?" Julie asked.

"No. Look at those branches. I don't want Ruby getting all scraped up. She might not even make it. Who knows how rugged this trail is. That old Wrangler had some serious tires and off-road gear on it. Besides, it shouldn't be that far of a walk."

"Lead the way, Max."

Tom smiled as he started down the narrow trail. Julie stayed close behind him. The path was uneven, changing drastically in both width and elevation. Trees, shrubs, rocks, and sand dunes all collided haphazardly along the edge of the ocean. Tom felt this was to their advantage, as it gave them a lot of places they could hide if needed.

The trail zigzagged as it descended toward the shoreline. After several minutes they turned a corner and found themselves facing two large sand dunes. At the edge of one of the dunes was the old Jeep. They were less than forty feet away.

"Shit!" Julie whispered. They turned and immediately took cover behind some trees and shrubs. "Now what do we do, Detective?"

Tom's heart was racing. What seemed like a logical plan several minutes ago suddenly began to unravel. He had assumed they could just step out, take a picture, and head back. The layout of the terrain did not make his strategy easy to execute.

The Wrangler was parked nose first deep against one of the dunes. This meant the only exposed license plate was on the rear of the vehicle. Tom realized he would have to walk out onto the beach to get his evidence.

"OK, I am going to go get the picture. You stay here and cover me."

"Cover you?" Julie asked. She was completely flustered. "How? With what?"

She looked at Tom for an explanation. He just shrugged.

"You're an idiot," Julie said. "This is the part of the movie where the victims get killed because they were being fools. This is stupid, Tom. What if she is on the other side of the dune? There is no easy way to get that picture. We need to leave and call Trevor."

"No. It's too late. We're too close."

Tom stepped back out from behind the trees and began to walk toward the dunes.

"Fine!" Julie hissed. "I'm going to call Trevor. Be the fool, Tom."

Tom ignored her and got down on his hands and knees and began to crawl around the dune that was south of the Jeep. He thought it would lead far enough away that he could jump out and take a quick picture.

Julie reached into her coat pocket to grab her phone to call Trevor. Her pocket was empty. She tried a few others, including her jeans. Then it dawned on her that Tom had thrown her phone into the back seat of the car.

"Shit," Julie muttered aloud.

Julie turned to head back to the parking lot. The blow to the back of her head was both quick and severe. She blacked out as she collapsed to the ground.

Sara smiled as she looked down at her prize catch. She pocketed the small baton she'd used to knock Julie out, and quickly dragged her body deep into the woods. Julie remained unconscious as Sara began to bind her ankles and wrists together.

Once the knots were done, Sara took a moment to remove the dagger from her pocket. The wooden handle with the nickel and turquoise inlay felt good in her hand. She slowly scraped the freshly sharpened blade across Julie's throat.

"Mother is going to be so pleased," Sara said triumphantly.

Tom's shirt was filled with sand. He was finally to the other side of the dune and could see the edge of the Jeep twenty feet away. He decided it was as close as he was willing to get. He reached into his pocket for his phone. It wasn't there. Tom tried his other pocket. Nothing. He crawled back up against the dune and sat upright so he could check the rest of his pockets. Then he remembered he had given it to Julie during the car chase.

"Fuck!" Tom whispered.

Tom quickly crawled back to the path and ran behind the brush where he had left Julie. It was empty. He clenched his fists in frustration.

"Jewels!" Tom whispered. He looked around and remembered she said she was going to call Trevor. He turned south and headed back toward his Jeep. The first one hundred feet of the trail proved to be a rather steep climb up from the beach. Once he reached the top Tom paused to catch his breath. He stepped out onto the edge of the cliff to see how much further it was to the parking lot. He still had a long way to go. He turned and looked back at the bottom of the cliff where the dunes were. The old Jeep was still there.

Sara quietly emerged from the brush on the opposite side of the trail. Her right hand gripped the baton she had used on Julie. Her left hand held the family dagger. She paused several feet from Tom. *Which to use?* Sara wondered.

As much as Sara wanted to strike Tom with her dagger, she knew her mother had other plans. Sara raised her baton and smiled. *Time to pay.*

Tom turned to face the path just as Sara swung her arm down at him. The baton missed his head, brushed against his cheek, and struck the edge of his right shoulder. Sara stumbled forward and grabbed Tom to keep herself from falling to the ground. When she did, the dagger scraped against his forearm, shredding his sleeve.

"What the fuck?" Tom cried.

He grabbed Sara by the shoulders and shoved her away. Sara took a few awkward steps backward and stumbled to her knees. She stood up and glanced down at her feet, which were now dangerously close to the edge of the cliff. She glared at Tom and pointed her dagger at him.

"Mother is waiting," Sara said.

Just as Sara was about to step forward, the sand and rock beneath her feet gave way. She screamed as she slid off the side of the cliff. Sara plunged her dagger into the top edge to stop her fall. She quickly drove her baton into the sandy side wall. For one brief second, she was able to halt her descent. It did not last, as the sand and rock were too soft to hold her weight. The dagger and baton lost their grip, sending Sara tumbling down the side of the cliff.

Tom dropped to his knees and watched her roll along the edge of the hillside. The baton and dagger flew from her hands as she crashed against rocks and sand, finally coming to a halt on the beach fifty feet below.

Tom stood there for a minute, waiting to see if she would move. She did not. He looked around in a panic to see if there was anyone else around. He was alone at the top of the cliff. A sense of dread washed over him. *Where's Jewels?*

Tom continued south along the path. He was in a full sprint, anxious to make sure Julie had made it back to his Jeep unharmed. Traversing the narrow road back seemed to take forever. Tom was completely out of breath as he emerged in the parking lot.

"Jewels!" Tom called out.

Tom ran to the window of his Jeep and looked inside, but the vehicle was empty. He opened the driver's door and saw his phone sitting on the passenger's seat. He grabbed it and called Julie's number. After a brief pause, it rang through the earpiece. Then he unexpectedly heard his own voice coming from the back of his Jeep. It kept saying "Ditto on that, Jewels" over and over again.

"Shit!" Tom yelled. He reached into his back seat and retrieved Julie's phone. A sense of despair washed over him as he stared at the screen. He tossed her ringing phone onto the driver's seat and ended the call.

Tom bounded across the lot to the boulders. He ran down the narrow path until he was back on the beach. He quickly scanned his eyes along the boundary between the cliff walls and the sandy beach. The body of Mrs. Closed was nowhere to be found. He then looked further north. The old Wrangler was nowhere to be seen.

Panic quickly began to set in. Tom's breathing became much more rapid. He had no idea what to do next. He nervously looked back and forth up and down the coast, and out at sea. He felt lost. Alone.

Where is she?

Tom slowly strolled back up the path to the parking lot. Tears burned as they ran down his face. He realized he may have gotten his best friend captured. Or possibly even killed. He pulled his phone back out and wiped his cheeks dry.

Who can I call?

***

Officer Jeff Jones was reclined in his chair at the Truro Police Station. His feet were resting on the corner of his desk. The desk itself was a mess. Stacks of papers, in no structured grouping, covered most of the surface area. His fellow officers wondered how he ever got things done. He always told them not to worry, that he had a system. Jeff was easily distracted. His focus at this moment was on his current phone call.

"Tell me again why they are here?" Officer Jones asked into the receiver.

"Because they are a couple of pains in my ass!" Officer Stevens bellowed back. "I'm home trying to enjoy the Sox, and they call me with some bizarre story about seeing a woman in an old Jeep in Eastham."

"A Cherokee?"

"No! Don't even get me started on that one. Once I get the address of that estate sale, I will send it to you. I really don't want to bother the Eastham police with this one. And like I said, it's my day off."

"No problem. Where are they now?"

"If they listened to me they will be halfway back to Providence."

A beep interrupted the phone call. Officer Jones glanced at his phone but realized it was not his.

"Do you have another call?" Officer Jones asked.

Officer Trevor Stevens was reclined in his chair at home, enjoying his fifth slice of pizza and third beer. He glanced at the screen of his cell phone. "It's nothing I need to take. Any updates on the search for Mr. Sirola's truck?"

"We've come up dry," Officer Jones said with frustration. "This entire case has been nothing but dead ends. My guess is it ended up in a chop shop somewhere."

"And the woman? The one they call Mrs. Closed."

Another beep rang out through the earpiece. This time the notification was from Officer Jones' cell phone. It was a text message. He read it twice to make sure he understood it.

"I need to go," Officer Jones said. He did not wait for a reply and ended the call.

After grabbing his hat and jacket, he ran toward the back door. His Dodge police cruiser was only a few spaces from the rear exit. He jumped in, fired up the engine, turned on the lights, and headed for Route 6.

EIGHTEEN

Hunter

The storm front hanging off the east coast of the outer Cape was stalled. Forecasters were giving conflicting predictions. Some thought it would turn out to sea and drift off into the Atlantic. Others were expecting it to come barreling onto shore sometime before midnight.

Tom sat in his Jeep, staring out at the ominous black clouds. Far off in the distance, bolts of lightning would occasionally erupt, setting off a rumble of thunder. He found the light and sound show to be a calming distraction. The windows were down, allowing the ever-shifting breeze of salt air to envelop the interior of his Wrangler. He inhaled the damp sea air and tried to gather thoughts.

Tom glanced at his phone. It was just after 5:30 p.m. He had less than two hours of decent light before the sun disappeared. All of that, however, depended on what direction the storm took.

What now? He wondered.

Tom unlocked his phone and pulled up his location on the map. He switched the view to Satellite and zoomed in as tight as the app would allow. He gradually slid the image north, following the coastline of the beach. Tom could barely make out the trail he had followed earlier. The two dunes at the end of the path, however, were easy to spot.

Where did she go?

This area of Wellfleet was devoid of manmade structures. At least any that could easily be seen from the map. Trees, lakes, and ponds blanketed the terrain. The only houses that Tom could spot were well inland, only half of which were connected to easily identifiable roads. He continued to slide the map north, hoping to find some sort of road or trail that led off the beach. Tom sighed as he realized he had gone too far north.

"Fuck!"

Tom zoomed out until the map showed all of Wellfleet. He tossed his phone onto the passenger's seat and began to cry. Tom gripped the steering wheel as tears rolled down his cheeks.

Where are you?

Tom shook his head in anger. He looked at his phone on the seat beside him, resting screen side up. A pulsating circle showed his current location along the eastern coastline.

"No! She couldn't have disappeared! She has to be close by. She has to!"

Tom grabbed his phone and zoomed back to his location. He scrolled back to the two large dunes at the end of the trail. Tom panned north again, but this time instead of looking for a second trail he studied the green leafy forests that bordered the dunes and cliffs. Inch by inch, he scanned for some sign of life. Tom suddenly stopped dragging his finger.

"What are you?"

Buried deep within the lush green foliage was the corner of a building. It was barely noticeable. Tom zoomed in and out a few times to confirm it was indeed a manmade structure.

That has to be a house.

He noticed the hint of what looked to be a broken trail that ran from the building out to the ocean. It was green and overgrown, with no clear exit to the beach. The house sat far away from any roads. A small pond was situated north, midway between the house and the ocean. Tom marked the location with a pin.

"So, if that's you then how ..."

Tom scrolled and zoomed in and out a few more times.

"How the fuck do I get there?"

Tom reset the map back to his location in the parking lot near the ocean. He attempted to retrieve directions to the pin, but the app would only deposit him on the main road that was disconnected far from the house.

I can't walk in the front door.

He canceled out of the directions. Tom then pulled the image out so that he could see the lot, the twin dunes, and the hint of the trail that led to the hidden house. He glanced out his window at the jagged opening of the narrow path he and Julie had traversed earlier. The branches were thick. Several had already been snapped off. To Tom, the shrubs looked like claws. He fired up his engine and turned to face the trail.

"Sorry Ruby, but we have to save Jewels."

Tom eased off the brake to let his Jeep roll forward. He popped the transmission into neutral and slid the transfer case to 4L. Once engaged, he went back into drive. Tom nudged the throttle, inching Ruby closer to the entrance. He closed his eyes and winced as he heard the branches drag across the sides of his door.

Once through the opening, he accelerated, and cautiously followed the trail that led to the twin dunes. His Jeep easily handled the mix of rock and sand. There were only two sections that proved to be a challenge for him, resulting in a few painful sounding scrapes from beneath his SUV. He was just relieved he did not get stuck. After a few minutes, he reached the beach.

Tom stopped at the end of the trail and jumped out of his vehicle. He walked out to the beach and gazed at the tire tracks from the other Jeep. The wind had picked up, but the tracks were still somewhat visible.

"This should be easy."

Tom sighed as he walked back to his Wrangler. The passenger side had a couple of small scrapes on the front fender. The driver's door, however, had a deep gouge down the side. He shook his head as he jumped back in and fired up the engine. Tom and Ruby headed north, following the tracks in the sand.

The ease of his plan faded quickly, however, when the

tracks turned abruptly out toward the shore. Tom tried to follow them, but the tide had washed them away. He continued to crawl along, looking for any sign of them reappearing.

After a few minutes, Tom came to a halt. He pulled up his phone and looked at the map again. He had driven past the pin he had marked earlier. Tom turned south, this time driving along the edge of the dunes. The hills were few and far between here. Unlike the sharp cliffs to the north, these were mostly composed of sand and seagrass.

Tom slowed as his Jeep came into alignment with the pin on the map. He looked out the passenger window. There was no sign of an opening where the map showed the hidden trail to be. However, the top of the dune had two long indentations going over it. Tom surmised those had to be tracks made by the old Wrangler.

The grade up the hill was somewhat steep. Tom decided not to risk getting stuck in the sand. He would have to go the rest of the way on foot. He parked his Jeep in a recessed part of the dune. The back of his vehicle was filled with an assortment of bags. Tom groaned as he pulled Julie's overstuffed duffle bag up so that he could get to his backpack. As he yanked his bag free, he saw another bag buried beneath it. One he had forgotten about.

Tom removed his binoculars from his pack and hung them over his neck. He slid his arms through the straps of his backpack and adjusted it to a comfortable fit. After a slight pause, he reached into the back of his Jeep and removed his archery case.

***

The tip of the matchstick roared to life with a searing crackle. The paraffin wax gave way, exposing the underlying ammonium phosphate to the edge of the stone. Sara smiled as she stared into the bright orange glowing tip. The cradle of stones beneath the cauldron was packed with kindling. She slid the long match between the rocks and waited for the fire to roar to life.

The rusted iron hinges of the front door of the barn creaked and groaned as the massive door swung open. Zeus, the family Doberman, came running into the barn. Just as he was about to reach Sara, the dog slid to a halt. He turned his head and flared his nostrils. A low rumbling growl emerged. He walked over to the school chair sitting several feet from the cauldron and began to sniff the feet of the occupant.

Julie was seated upright, but she was unconscious. Her hands were bound behind her back, and her feet were tied to the legs of the chair. Blood dripped from her hair.

"No, Zeus," Laura commanded.

The dog huffed, reluctantly taking several steps backward.

"I just started the fire," Sara said.

Laura strolled over to the cauldron and knelt down next to her daughter. The kindling was ablaze, igniting the bigger logs within the firepit. She nodded in approval.

Zeus walked over to Laura and sat by her side. As Laura was about to stroke his neck, his ears shot up. Zeus furled his lips and began to growl.

"What is it?" Sara asked.

Zeus leaped to all fours and rushed over to the side door of the barn. He barked and growled as he waited for Sara to come over and open the door. Once she did, Zeus ran outside and bolted toward the path that led to the beach.

"You told me you weren't followed," Laura said.

Sara turned and stared at her mother, somewhat confused.

"I wasn't! That's why I lead them out to the beach. To keep them away from here. He was gone when I looked up. I covered my tracks when I made my way back along the coast. I'm sure of it!"

"You know how Zeus gets when strangers are on the property."

"It must be an animal. Or maybe the wind. There's a storm offshore."

Laura stepped out into the yard and looked around. The wind had picked up, and the tree branches above the barn were banging against one another.

"Zeus knows what the trees sound like," Laura replied.

"It's fine, Mother. Relax."

177

Laura frowned and shook her head. She knew Zeus all too well to think it was anything other than a stranger on the property.

"Zeus! Zeus!" Sara called out.

After several seconds, the dog emerged from the woods behind the barn. Sara clapped her hands, and he began to run toward her. He stopped next to Sara and sat down.

"See. He's fine Mother."

Zeus ran inside the barn. Sara followed him.

Laura remained outside, scanning the trees and shrubs. She tilted her head, listening for something. Anything out of the ordinary. After several seconds she sighed and went back inside, closing the door behind her.

Sara was at the end of the wooden table. A whetstone was in front of her, along with a machete and two knives. She pulled a dagger from her pocket and began to run it across the grinder.

"I think we should play it safe, Sara. Go get your gear."

Sara ignored her mother and continued to sharpen her blade.

"I think you are overreacting."

Laura walked up to her daughter and grabbed the dagger from her hand.

"What if that boy did follow you? These daggers and knives are only good at close range. We need to be ready."

"But Mother ..."

"Now!"

Sara pounded her fists on the table, glaring at the cutting instruments spread out across the weathered surface. She took a few cleansing breaths, smiled at her mother, and headed toward the front door.

Once her daughter had left the barn, Laura took her phone from her pocket and began to scroll through her list of contacts. She briefly held her finger over the person she intended to call. *Is now the time?* She wondered.

With an uncertain sigh, Laura initiated the call. After several rings, it went to voicemail. She waited patiently to leave her message.

"Hi. It's ... well ... you ... you know who this is. Please listen.

There may be trouble here at the house tonight. Too soon to say, really. I'm sorry. I ... I didn't want to get you involved in any of this. I know you have your hands full right now. But I'm worried things may fall apart here. If they do, well ... you may have no choice but to come. I hate to do this to you. But I need you. Sara needs you. Family bonds still matter to you, don't they? Please listen closely to what I'm about to tell you."

NINETEEN

Secrets

Susan declined the incoming call on her cell phone and placed the phone in her pocket.

"Are you sure you don't need to get that?" Dr. Beaumont asked. "I can step outside."

"No, really, it's fine. Please continue."

Susan and Dr. Beaumont were standing in her living room. He had just finished examining her mother.

"I think it's time we move Jennifer into a facility where we can take better care of her."

"Well that's always been the plan, but ..."

"I mean now, Susan. Today. You understand that my treatment options here are quite limited."

"I do. But will it really make a difference?"

Dr. Beaumont slid his glasses up to his forehead and rubbed his weary eyes.

"You know the answer to that, Susan. It's only a matter of time. She's too far gone. But with better monitoring and care we should be able to ..."

"To what? Keep her around a few more days? A week?"

Susan stared patiently at the doctor, waiting for him to respond.

"You don't really know," Susan continued. "She wants to be surrounded by her pictures and memories. If I thought that moving her somewhere else would add months to her time left, or even a full recovery, I wouldn't hesitate. If her choices are to die in a hospital in a week or die at home today, the choice is obvious. At least to me. I think it's best to abide by her wishes. Don't you?"

Dr. Beaumont smiled. He leaned forward and kissed Susan on the cheek.

"It's been my pleasure taking care of your mother all these years. Both of you. I still remember the day she brought you into my office with that knee cut wide open."

"Don't remind me," Susan said. "What was I? Seventeen years old?"

"Something like that. Your family has been through so much, Susan. I hope Jennifer finds peace in these final hours."

Susan shook Dr. Beaumont's hand and led him toward the front door.

"Thank you. For everything."

"Take care, Susan."

***

Susan leaned forward to stretch her back. The small folding chair she had placed next to her mother's bed had no padding along the back of it. The cold hard metal of the chair had brought her much discomfort. She groaned as she twisted her torso.

Susan refused to leave her mother's side. Dr. Beaumont had increased her mother's morphine to help ease any remaining pain. Jennifer's breathing had become more and more shallow with each passing minute. Susan did not want her mother to die alone.

"Mom? Are you awake?"

Susan ran her fingers across her mother's hand. She stood up and brushed Jennifer's hair back. Susan smiled as her mother blinked and opened her eyes.

"Well hello there," Susan said, her eyes filling with tears. "It's good to see you."

Jennifer tried to raise her head but could not. She looked at the door and then at her daughter. She pulled her hand away from Susan's and dragged her oxygen mask away from her mouth.

"No, Mom, you need that."

Susan reached over to put the mask back into place.

"No. Susan. Please. I ... I heard you. You and the doctor talking. I know ... I know my time here is limited."

"We don't really know ..."

"We need to talk, Susan."

Susan sat down on the edge of the bed and took her mother's hand into hers.

"I don't want you to tire yourself," Susan said. "You should rest. I told you that ..."

"Rosemary. I ... I have to tell you about rosemary."

Jennifer pushed her palms against her mattress and groaned as she willed herself to sit upright.

"Mom! Please!"

Susan reached behind her mother and pulled the pillows forward. Jennifer began to cough. Susan tried to put her mask back on, but her mother brushed it away.

"Your garden is fine, Mom. Relax."

Susan glanced out the window at the dead garden in the backyard. She felt a wave of guilt wash over her.

"I promise to take care of your herbs for you. Spring will be here soon. Rosemary. Sage. All of it will be cared for."

"You don't understand. How ... how could you? It was so long ago."

Jennifer began to cough again. This time her cough was coarse and rough. She looked over at her nightstand. There was a glass of water in front of her wedding picture. The rosemary-scented candle was tucked behind the frame. Jennifer tried to reach for the nightstand, but the IV tubes caught the edge of the drawer pull.

Susan freed the tubes and grabbed the glass of water. She held it up so her mother could take a sip from the straw. Jennifer pushed the glass away.

"It's your birthday," Jennifer said.

"My birthday? Mom, that's not until June. Please stop. I need you to rest. The doctor ..."

"I need to tell you about that day. Your birthday. The day ...

the day that you turned thirteen."

"My thirteenth birthday?" The color drained from Susan's face. "Mom, that's ... that's the day ... the ... death."

Susan stood up and took a few steps back away from her mother's bed. She clasped her hands and began to mash her palms together.

"I don't want to talk about that day, Mom. I don't!"

"You have to hear me. You don't know what happened."

Jennifer reached out toward her daughter and began to cough. Her throat burned from fluid and mucus collecting deep inside of her lungs. She started to gasp for air.

Susan ran back to the bed and slid the oxygen mask back across her mother's mouth. Jennifer took a few shallow breaths before dragging the mask back off.

"You don't know ..."

"Please, Mom. I know ... I know enough."

"You need to know the truth!" Jennifer's voice was faint and cracked. Each breath she took was a burden. "It's about your sister."

Jennifer reached up and put her hands around her daughter's head. A tear rolled down her face as she looked into Susan's eyes. She pulled her daughter toward her.

"Come here," Jennifer whispered.

Susan slid closer to her mother and moved her ear next to her mom's mouth. Jennifer smiled as she began to tell her daughter a secret that she had kept from her for over thirty years. As she told the story, she felt her guilt, despair, and anguish melt away.

Susan stared across the room at her mother's collection of family pictures. With each sentence uttered by her mother, the anguish and horror within her increased exponentially. She began to shake her head in confusion as the details of the story came to their conclusion.

When Jennifer was done, she felt as if a great weight had been lifted. Susan sat upright, staring across the room at the pictures of her and her cousins and sister. *This can't be true,* she thought to herself.

Susan stood up and walked over to the bureau and looked at the pictures that were taken on her thirteenth birthday.

"Mom, there's no way what you just told me is true. I was there. I remember what aunty and uncle told us. What *you* told us!"

Susan walked back over to the bed and looked down at her mother. She suddenly realized how quiet the room had become. Her mother's raspy breathing had subsided. Susan sat down on the bed and placed her head on her mother's chest. All was silent.

Susan began to cry. The door to the bedroom swung open. The creak of the hinges was masked by her sobbing. Moments later a hand came to rest on her shoulder. Susan jumped and turned around.

"Sorry son," Susan said. "You just missed her. Your grandmother is gone. She's gone."

Officer Jeff Jones of the Truro police sat next to his mother and put his arm around her. Susan fell forward into her son's arms and wept. Jeff stared at the body of his grandmother. In his short time on the police force, he had yet to witness death up close. He kissed his mother's head and held her close.

"Was she in pain?" Jeff asked. "In the end. Did she suffer?"

Susan sat up and wiped the tears from her face. She smiled and ran her hand across her son's scruffy red beard.

"No, she was fine. Alert, actually."

Susan turned to look at the body of her mother. She took a moment to study her face. Susan smiled. Her mother looked at peace.

"She told me the most bizarre story."

"A story?"

"Something that happened at my birthday party. Back when I turned thirteen."

Susan stood up and walked around to the other side of her mother's bed. She turned off the drips on the IV bags and pushed the IV stand and tubes aside. Susan glanced down at the wedding picture of her parents and shook her head.

"What did she say?"

Susan picked up the frame and studied the image of her mother and father. *They were so young then.* Susan retrieved the rosemary-scented candle and placed it and the picture on the bed beside her mother.

"I'm still trying to process it all. To put all of the pieces together."

She walked back over behind her son and put her arms around him, resting her chin on his shoulder. Jeff took his mother's hand and kissed it.

"If what she said is true, it turns out everything I was told about that day was a lie. Your grandmother just told me what really happened. I don't understand why she never told me the truth. Maybe she was trying to protect me? I don't really know. I'm ... I'm still in shock."

"What is it, Mom?"

"I will have to tell you about it. But not today, Jeff. Not today."

TWENTY

Marilyn

1984 Saturday 25-Jun 12:45pm

Fred stared at the small dagger in his hand. He briefly admired his handiwork in the design of the wooden handle. The nickel and turquoise inlay were perfectly aligned. He turned to his right and looked at the bale of hay wrapped in twine. With a few quick swipes from his blade, the bundle was free. He pocketed the dagger and grabbed the pitchfork that had been resting up against the middle stall.

The mindless work of spreading out the hay was a distraction that Fred found calming. Cows paced within the stalls. Fred looked up at the recently hung nameplates over each pen. He had designed and carved them for his daughter Sara to paint. It brought a slight smile to his face. He walked over to the nearest cow and ran his hand across her ears.

"Sara loves you the most, Becky," Fred said to the cow as it stared at him. "She's a good girl. A good daughter. *My* daughter."

Fred slammed the blunt end of the pitchfork's handle onto the floor of the barn. Becky shuddered and took two steps back.

"Sorry, girl. I'm just trying to calm myself down. How can she lie to me? My wife!"

Becky kept her distance at the back of the stall, silently watching Fred.

Apollo had been sleeping underneath the metal table at the other end of the barn. Fred's raised voice and the slam of the pitchfork woke him. He cautiously made his way over to his master. Fred looked down at his dog and frowned.

"Sorry. My anger is spooking all of you, isn't it?"

"You talking to the cows again, Fred?" Carl asked as he entered the barn. He was carrying two unopened beers in one hand, and an open one in the other. "Don't tell Jennie I stole a beer. I'm not supposed to have alcohol with the latest combo of meds my doc has me on. It will be our little secret, OK?"

Carl walked up to Fred and offered him a beer.

Fred glared at Carl. His eyes never looked at the drink. They stayed locked on Carl's face. He felt blood rush to his cheeks. His knuckles whitened as his hands clasped the pitchfork's handle like a vise-grip.

"Secret?" Fred asked with astonishment. "You've got some serious balls to talk about secrets, Carl."

Fred walked past Carl, slamming his shoulder against him. Carl turned and watched Fred walk over to the ladder that led to the loft. Fred slid the pitchfork between two of the rungs, securing it in place.

"What's up with you, Fred?"

Fred leaned back against the ladder, crossed his arms, and clenched his fists. His face was still flush with suppressed rage.

"Don't play stupid, Carl. Although, I know that's hard for you to avoid."

Carl walked over to Fred and stood within a few inches of his face. He was an inch shorter than Fred, but Carl had a stocky build. He was not the least bit intimidated by his brother-in-law.

"The guy that talks to cows is calling me stupid? What is up with you? You've been a grouch since we arrived. Why are you hiding out here in the barn?"

"I know, Carl, OK? I know all about the affair."

"Affair?"

Carl took a step back and looked Fred up and down. He

chugged back the last of his beer, crushed the empty can, and tossed it toward the workbench. It bounced off the top and fell to the hay covered floor. He wiped his chin and popped open a second one.

"What affair?"

Fred stepped forward and pressed his nose against Carl's.

"You and Laura."

Carl's eyes widened. He then began to laugh. Fred took a step back, somewhat confused.

"And people say that I'm the one that's overmedicated! Jesus, Fred, how much have you had to drink? Have you been popping pills that we don't know about?"

Carl laughed as he walked over to the wooden table and placed the unopened beer on it. He looked down at the whetstone and collection of daggers and knives. He picked up the one closest to him and ran his finger across the edge of the blade.

"Enough of this bullshit, Carl. I heard the phone call, OK? Stop playing stupid!"

"Fred, I have no idea what you are talking about. What call?"

Fred clenched his fists. He walked over to Carl and yanked the dagger from his hand. After a slight pause, he put the knife back on to the table with the others. Fred took a deep breath and walked to the other side of the work table. Carl followed him.

"Last night. The call between you and Laura. I was on the porch. She doesn't know that I was listening in on her conversation. But I heard it. I heard it all."

"Last night? I didn't talk to Laura last night. Did I?"

Carl put his half-empty beer on the freshly stained rosewood table. Fred glared at the can. Carl ignored him and looked back at the stalls. He closed his eyes trying to remember what he had done the night before.

"Sorry, but these new meds cloud my head. I don't ... I don't remember talking to Laura last night."

Fred walked over to the circular table, removed Carl's beer, and placed it on the large workbench. He immediately began to wipe down the ring the can had left.

"Don't pull that crap with me, Carl. Everyone is tired of you using your depression and medications as excuses. There's no excuse for you fucking my wife!"

"Fucked your ... Laura? You think I'm actually having an affair with Laura?"

Carl started to laugh again.

"Laugh all you want. I know you got her pregnant, Carl."

"Pregnant! Laura's pregnant?"

Fred grimaced as he watched Carl suddenly become concerned.

"Drop it, Carl! We both know that Marilyn is not off playing with her cousin. She's playing with her half-sister."

Carl shook his head and let out a long sigh. He walked up to Fred and jabbed his finger into his chest.

"Fred, you have seriously lost your fucking mind. I'm not having an affair with your wife. I never got her pregnant. We don't have a secret love child."

"Bullshit! I heard her on the phone talking about *your* daughter. As in the two of you. When I asked her who she was talking to she told me it was you!"

"Well, then your wife is not only a whore but a liar!"

Fred had reached his breaking point. He swung his right arm at Carl's face, but Carl was ready for it and ducked. Fred struggled to catch his balance as his fist missed its mark. Carl took advantage of Fred's imbalance and punched him in the stomach. Fred doubled over and stumbled backward.

"You need to calm the fuck down, Fred. Drop it now. I've had more than my fair share of bar fights, and I won't hesitate to beat the shit out of you."

Fred was bent over, resting his hands on his knees, gasping for air.

"If you heard Laura on the phone talking about an affair, it wasn't with me, OK?"

Fred raised his head and took a deep breath. He looked up at the loft and was stunned to see Marilyn looking down at him.

"Marilyn!" Fred said. His voice was weak and cracked as he struggled to get his breath.

Carl spun around and looked up in shock.

Marilyn was peeking through the lower banister of the loft. Her hands gripped the edge of the floor. Her hair had several pieces of golden hay stuck to it.

"What are you doing up there?" Carl asked.

"Playing."

"You shouldn't be up there. How did you get up that ladder? Stay right there! I'm coming to get you."

Marilyn crawled backward and disappeared from view.

"You are going to end this affair, Carl. End it now. Now! Do you hear me?"

Carl turned back to face his brother-in-law.

"Enough of this bullshit, Fred. The only way to settle this is to get Laura in here. If you don't believe me, maybe you will believe her. Stay here and catch your breath."

Carl grabbed his beer and walked over to the ladder.

"Marilyn, I need you to stay there. Hold on baby, I'm ..."

Fred's right fist slammed into Carl's lower back, knocking Carl against the ladder. The force of the impact made Carl drop his beer. The aluminum can gurgled as the malt liquid spilled across the hay. The blow was severe, and Carl fell to the ground.

Up in the loft, Marilyn adjusted her dress and brushed the hay from her knees. She turned to her cousin sitting against the back wall. There were dolls scattered across the floor. Her cousin, always the quiet one, picked up her favorite doll and clutched it close to her chest. Marilyn crawled over to the top of the ladder and looked down at her father and uncle.

Carl had managed to pull himself back up. He lunged at Fred, pushing him up against the large wooden table. With Fred off balance, Carl was able to land a blow against his jaw.

Apollo was upset and began barking. He growled as he circled the two men.

Fred swung at Carl, missing his head by a few inches. Carl swung back hard, hitting Fred in the stomach. Fred lunged forward and tried to grab Carl. Carl stepped to the left and struck Fred on his right shoulder. Fred stumbled to the side. He was still out of breath from the blow to his stomach. He fell to the ground and crawled behind the table.

"No fighting!" Marilyn yelled.

The two men stopped and looked up at the young girl.

"Mom said no fighting!" Marilyn repeated.

The loft was over fifteen feet above the floor of the barn. The ladder to the loft was set at a very steep angle. There were no railings. Marilyn turned around and began to descend the ladder.

"No, baby!" Carl screamed. "The pitchfork!"

Marilyn turned to see what her father was yelling about. There was a large pile of hay to the left of the ladder. She looked over her shoulder and noticed the pitchfork sticking up thru the rungs. She took another step down.

Carl looked over at the pitchfork. A sense of dread washed over him. He began to move toward the middle of the barn, only to find his progress hindered. He looked down to see Fred holding onto his foot. Carl attempted to kick Fred with his free leg, but Fred was ready and managed to yank Carl's leg harder, sending Carl crashing to the ground.

The rickety old ladder, its wooden rungs round and worn, shook as Marilyn lowered her right foot. Her new yellow shoes, yet to be broken in, trembled across the treads. Marilyn screamed as her right foot slid off the rung. She instinctively turned to catch herself. Spinning sideways, she pushed off with her left foot. Marilyn's arms flailed as she reached out for something to grab hold of, but nothing was there.

Carl kicked Fred in the head and scrambled to stand up. He lunged for his daughter with his arms stretched out, but his arrival was too late. Marilyn bounced off his left arm, her head knocking into his. Carl desperately tried to grab her by her legs, but his attempt to catch her only pushed her away. The fragile girl's screams stopped as Marilyn crashed headfirst onto the wooden table. The daggers that had been perfectly aligned rattled and shook from the impact. Two of the knives fell to the floor, along with the can of beer.

Fred watched in horror as Marilyn's head caught the edge of the wooden slab. Her body missed. It rotated, twisting her neck as she fell on the far side of the table, landing next to the small rosewood table.

Carl screamed and ran around the workbench. He fell to his knees and pulled his daughter close.

"Marilyn! Marilyn!"

Carl wiped her hair from her face and gently slapped her cheek as he desperately tried to wake her. He ran his hand down her neck to check her chest for a heartbeat.

"Wake up, baby! Wake up! You need to ..."

Carl suddenly realized that his hand was resting on the back of his daughter's dress. He stared into Marilyn's lifeless eyes and slowly released her. Carl's entire body began to tremble. Her head was facing the wrong way.

Fred sat in silence, staring at the young child. The severity of what had just happened slowly sunk in.

"Carl, I ... I don't know ... what ... what ..."

"This is your fault, Fred." Carl's voice was a raspy whisper.

"Mine? It was an accident. I ... I ..."

Carl looked over at the dagger lying next to the body of his dead daughter. He picked it up and pointed it at Fred.

"I could have reached her. I could have saved her. But you stopped me. Why? Why would you do that?"

"Carl, I ..."

Carl stood up and stared at the twisted body of his daughter. Tears and sweat ran down his face. He turned his gaze toward Fred.

"You will pay for this, Fred."

TWENTY ONE

Dinner

Julie's breathing was shallow. Her head pounded in pain. The throbbing in her temples had been rhythmic since she woke up earlier. She glanced around the dank, dusty barn, scanning the walls and doors. The cauldron bubbling away at the center of the room proved to be a big distraction for her.

Laura was seated in front of Julie. The school chair she was in was several feet away. A metal mixing bowl filled with pasta sat on the small foldable desktop. She used her fork and spoon to twirl the spaghetti, being sure to catch a piece of sausage in the process. She slid it into her mouth and smiled.

Julie stared at the old woman, with a mix of disgust and caution. Laura ignored her and continued to enjoy the pasta.

"So, what's your story?" Julie finally asked.

Laura raised her eyebrow and smiled. She took another bite of pasta and wiped her lips with a small white linen napkin.

"My story?" Laura replied. "My story, dear, is one you wouldn't' want to hear."

Laura lifted her bowl and folded the desktop to the side. She stood up and stretched her back before strolling over to Julie. She placed the bowl of pasta down in front of her.

"How's that head of yours?" Laura asked. "My daughter hit you pretty hard."

"I'm fine," Julie said sternly.

Laura walked around to the back of Julie's chair. Julie's hair was matted with blood. She ran her fingers through it, rubbing the large bump on her skull. Julie recoiled in pain.

"That lump says otherwise."

Laura dug her thumb deep into the bump. Julie howled in agony.

"That's better," Laura said. She walked back to the front of the chair and picked up the bowl of pasta. She used the spoon to pull out a piece of sausage. Laura held it in front of Julie for a moment, hoping she would take a bite. Julie refused, and Laura popped it into her mouth. "Lying is disrespectful."

Julie turned her gaze toward the back of the barn, inspecting the dark stalls under the loft.

"Is this where you took Marc and Chris?" Julie asked.

Laura smiled and walked back over to her chair. As she walked away, Julie began to wiggle her wrists to test the strength of the knots that bound her in place. The ropes were tight. Laura dragged her chair across the hay covered floor. The chair's metal legs stuttered and rattled as they caught uneven sections of the floor. A small set of tracks carved their way through the hay as the chair made its way across the barn.

"Marc and Chris?" Laura took another bite of her pasta. "You look hungry dear."

Laura twirled some pasta onto her fork and held it next to Julie's lips. Julie turned away.

"Oh, come now, you must be hungry. It's just pasta and sausage!"

"No thank you."

Laura shook her head and sighed. She stuck her fingers into the bowl and retrieved a chunk of sausage. She turned and tossed it toward Zeus, who leaped into the air, and swallowed it whole.

"See dear, it's safe. I insist. There's no reason to starve yourself. Try some."

Julie reluctantly turned back to face her. Laura smiled and collected a few strands of spaghetti along with a piece of sausage. She raised the fork to Julie's lips. Laura smiled as Julie opened her mouth and took a bite.

"There! See, that wasn't so bad."

Julie was indeed hungry. Her stomach had been growling since she woke up. Having the warm food in her stomach felt good.

"My daughter Sara told me you were the one that had lots of questions about that book of urban legends."

Julie stopped chewing and swallowed what was left in her mouth. *Sara? If Sara is Mrs. Closed. That means ... Mother!*

"There are lots of wonderful stories in that book, aren't there?" Laura asked. "Did you have a favorite? Let me guess. It had to be the one about the candles. Am I right?"

"They are just stories," Julie said dismissively. She opened her mouth to signal for another bite of pasta.

Laura chuckled as she prepared another helping. As Julie waited patiently, she began to twist her wrists back and forth. Her movements were slow and methodical. She made every effort to make sure her shoulders did not move. Julie hoped that the food and conversation would keep the woman entertained and distracted.

"They are more than stories, dear. Trust me. I have first-hand knowledge of two of them."

Julie stopped twisting her wrists. She was trying her best not to take an interest in anything the woman had to say. Deep down, however, Julie was curious to know more about the stories in that book.

"Which ones?" Julie asked.

"Obviously the candle story. Truth be told, the way it ended up in that legend is a bit of a mess. Those myths get passed down and reinterpreted. There are a few mistakes in it, that's for sure. It's best to think of it as ... a collection of candle stories merged into one."

Laura fed Julie another bite of pasta and sausage.

"The most accurate story is the one about the sausage maker."

Julie stopped chewing.

"Did you read that one dear?"

Julie and Laura stared at one another, neither of them willing to blink. Zeus fidgeted off to the side, quietly waiting for another bite of food.

"It's the one about the sausage maker in Truro. You must

remember that one. The sausage meat is made from humans! The candles are made from humans! Oh, the horrors!"

Laura chuckled and leaned closer to Julie.

"My family makes the candles. My friend in Truro makes the sausage. That, my dear, is the truth behind those stories. As for what's really in the sausage? Well ..."

Julie felt her stomach begin to churn. Blood drained from her face. She felt herself getting lightheaded.

Laura stood up and dragged her chair back to the metal table. She put her bowl of pasta on top and licked her fingers.

"Let's just say that whenever I make my candles, I always send my leftovers to Truro."

The half-eaten piece of sausage was still in Julie's mouth. She stopped twisting her wrists. Her body began to shake.

"You asked about your friends Marc and Chris. Do you miss them? You shouldn't. Not anymore. In fact, you could say you are closer to them now than you've ever been."

Julie turned her head to the side and immediately threw up. Her throat burned as she strained to expunge the contents of her stomach. Julie coughed and cried over and over again, her body shaking violently as she spewed. Panic coursed through her as she hacked and spit every ounce she could. *Marc? Chris?*

Laura laughed as she took another bite of pasta.

"No wonder you were so easy to subdue," Laura said. "You are a weak girl. The weak always falter."

Sara came into the barn. She had her bow in her right hand and a collection of arrows in her left. She looked down at the pile of puke next to Julie.

"Did she not like dinner, Mother?" Sara asked.

"I guess not. Be a dear and get the lanterns lit, will you? I want to have a walk around outside. Darkness is coming. We need to be vigilant."

Laura grabbed the last piece of sausage from her bowl and tossed it to Zeus. He snatched it from mid-air and followed her as she exited the front door.

Sara took one final look at Julie before heading over to the large white propane tank tucked away in the back corner of the barn. After turning a valve on at the base of the tank, Sara walked over to the ladder. She ascended to the loft and proceeded to light the lanterns that ran along the top edge.

Julie casually kept a watchful eye on the front door. Every few seconds she would turn her gaze toward Sara. During all the commotion over her throwing up, she had managed to free most of her right hand. Julie twisted and thrust her wrists back and forth, slowly and methodically. The knots binding her were tight, but her wrists were smooth and slippery. *Thank you, cocoa butter.*

Sara descended the ladder and walked over to Julie. Julie kept her head down. Sara knelt in front of her and forced her to look at her face. Julie couldn't help but stare at the faint burn mark that ran from her eye down the side of her face. A small smile spread across Julie's face.

Sara frowned. She flared her nostrils, pulled a dagger from her pocket, and thrust it into Julie's thigh. Julie screamed in shock and pain.

"That's for Seabreeze!" Sara hissed.

The front door let out a loud creak as Laura and Zeus returned.

"Everything seems quiet outside," Laura said. "But I'm going to want you on lookout, Sara. Just to be safe."

Julie stared at her thigh. The right leg of her faded blue jeans was stained in blood. The dark spot slowly expanded across the denim. She continued to work her wrists.

Laura walked over to Julie and inspected the fresh wound her daughter had just inflicted.

"You and your friend Tom will suffer the same fate that the other two did. You think that small cut is painful? You have no idea what's coming."

Julie exhaled as she felt her right hand finally free itself from the bindings. She looked over at Sara standing next to the table. With only one hand free she debated if now was the time to strike at the mother.

Sara leaned across the table and grabbed a candle. Julie recognized the design as the one from the store. The same one that Tom had bought last December. Sara brought the candle over to her mother. Laura held the open jar up to Julie's face.

"Smell it," Laura said.

Julie turned her head away.

"Smell it!" Sara yelled.

Julie took a sniff of the candle. It smelled like the ocean.

"Do you like that?" Sara asked. "It's scented. You like scented, don't you?"

Laura closed the jar so that Julie could see the "Seabreeze" sticker on top of the lid. Julie went pale.

"Yes dear," Laura said. "It's exactly what you think it is. This barn saw the death of your friends. It will see the death of you. And eventually your friend Tom."

Julie glared at the old woman. She tried her best not to show her shock and disgust, but her eyes filled with tears at the thought of Marc and Chris somehow being in the candle.

"Don't look so surprised, dear," Laura continued. "This barn has a long history of death."

"What scent should we turn her into, Mother?" Sara asked. "She looks Mexican. Maybe some kind of pepper?"

Laura leaned against Julie's neck and inhaled.

"No," Laura said as she pulled away. "I'm thinking ... cocoa butter."

TWENTY TWO

Precious

1984 Saturday 25-Jun 12:55pm

Rosalyn sat in silence at the back of the loft. The screams of her cousin, uncle, and father had terrified her. Tears ran down her face as she stroked the hair of her favorite doll, Suzie. The small child's rapid breathing slowed as she realized she could no longer hear her cousin.

With Suzie in tow, Rosalyn crawled to the edge of the loft. She could see the legs of her cousin sticking out from the other side of the table. She wiped the tears from her bright blue eyes, grabbed the post closest to her, and pulled herself to her feet.

Down below, Carl had Fred pinned against the edge of the wooden table. Carl's right forearm was pressed hard across Fred's neck. His left hand still had the dagger that he had picked up earlier. Fred was using both of his hands to keep the weapon away.

"Daddy!" Rosalyn cried out.

Carl relaxed the pressure he was applying and turned to look up at the loft. Fred used the distraction to slide his arm up and break free of Carl, shoving him backward.

"I'm not your daddy," Fred said as he gasped for air. "She's yours, Carl. Admit it! Admit to the affair!"

"You are crazy, Fred! I don't know what you are talking

about. All I know is you stopped me from saving Marilyn. My child is dead, and you are going to pay!"

Carl lunged at Fred and attempted to thrust the dagger into his stomach. Fred dove to the side and rolled away. As he righted himself on all fours, he noticed a machete lying on the floor under the rosewood table.

"This ends now, Fred!"

Carl raised his dagger above his head with both hands and fell to his knees in front of Fred. He had taken aim dead center to Fred's chest. Fred grabbed the machete and looked at Carl. Carl's eyes widened at the site of the long knife. He tried to halt his descent, but it was too late. He fell directly onto the machete. The newly sharpened blade plunged straight through Carl's torso.

Carl gasped as his body came to a halt against Fred's hands. He dropped his dagger and grabbed Fred by his shoulders.

"Why?" Carl asked. "It wasn't me, Fred. I never ..."

Carl began to cough up blood. Fred pulled the machete back and pushed his brother-in-law away. Carl fell backward, resting next to the body of his dead daughter.

"Uncle Carl!" Rosalyn screamed from the loft.

Fred turned around and looked up. The young girl was now standing at the edge of the ladder, holding her doll with both hands. Fred looked back at his hands. They were covered in blood. He looked over at the bodies of Carl and Marilyn, and then at the weapon in his hand.

What have I done?

Rosalyn strained to see her cousin on the other side of the table. She tucked Suzie under her arm, turned around, and began to make her way down the ladder. After descending a few steps, the doll slipped from her grasp.

"Suzie!" Rosalyn cried.

Rosalyn reached out to try to catch her doll. She immediately lost her footing and plummeted downward. Fred watched in horror as Rosalyn fell directly onto the pitchfork.

"My God! Rosalyn!"

Fred ran over to the ladder and stared at the warped arched body of the young child. Blood ran down the handle of the pitchfork and began to pool onto the floor of the barn. Tears ran down Fred's cheeks as he stared into Rosalyn's bright blue eyes.

"It was an accident," Fred said quietly. He caressed the girl's forehead. "They must all know this was an accident."

The side door of the barn opened, and Laura entered.

"Jennifer went to the pond to get the girls," Laura said. "The food is ready. What's ..."

Laura stopped and stared at her husband. It took a moment for her to realize what was on the pitchfork in the middle of the barn. Her mind raced as she inspected the white and yellow flowered dress covering the twisted body. Her eyes came to rest on the white shoes.

"Rosalyn?" Laura whispered.

Laura collapsed to her knees, covering her eyes as the tears fell mercilessly and without hesitation. She sobbed for her daughter. Laura looked up and noticed her husband was covered in blood. Her gaze focused on the oversized blood-soaked machete in his hand.

"What have you done, Fred?" Laura screamed. "What on earth have you done?"

Laura stood up and ran over to the ladder. She shoved Fred aside and kissed her daughter's face.

"My Rosalyn! My precious Rose!"

"It ... it was an accident."

Laura could not face her husband. She embraced Rosalyn and wailed, her chest heaving as she released an endless amount of grief.

"The girls were up in the loft playing," Fred continued. His nervous tone betrayed his words. "They ... they both fell. It was an accident. An accident!"

Laura stopped crying and opened her eyes. She forced herself to release her daughter and marched toward Fred.

"Both? What do you mean ..."

As Laura approached Fred, she noticed Carl lying on the ground behind the workbench. She shoved Fred aside and ran to Carl. Laura stopped when she saw her niece lying next to him.

"Marilyn!" Laura cried.

Laura fell to her knees, positioning herself between Carl

and Marilyn. She ran her hand across Carl's blood-drenched abdomen. The golden hay beneath him floated in a pool of blood. She turned to Marilyn and went to touch her face. Laura recoiled when she realized her head was twisted backward.

"My God! Mary!"

Laura took Carl's arm and held his wrist. As the seconds passed, hope faded away. She released his lifeless body and wiped her blood covered hands on her apron. She looked over at Fred. He had not left his position next to the ladder.

"He's dead," Laura cried. "They are all dead! What happened? Tell me!"

Fred walked over to the corner of the table. Each step was abbreviated. Cautious. He knelt down near Carl's legs, a few feet away from Laura.

"Marilyn was the first to fall. See, they were up there playing. The girls. And we had no idea they were up there. Marilyn came down first. So ... so Carl ran over to help her. And she ... well she ... she slipped on the ladder."

Laura moved closer toward Fred. He took a few steps back, stopping halfway between the ladder and the table. Laura looked over his shoulder at her daughter's body, impaled on the pitchfork.

"And Rose?" Laura asked. Her voice trembled as she tried not to look at the dangling corpse. She raised her right eyebrow and stared into Fred's eyes. He immediately looked away.

"She fell. She was right behind Mary."

Laura's eyes welled with tears as she fought off the pain and anguish over the death that filled the barn.

"And Carl? What ... what of Carl?"

Fred looked over at the body of his dead brother-in-law. Beads of sweat formed on his brow as he studied the machete in his hand. He could not face his wife.

"He ... he ... he was ... I was trying to help him. To help save the girls. I ... he ... he ran into it when we tried to catch Mary."

Laura grabbed Fred by the chin and forced him to look into her eyes.

"You are a horrible liar, Fred. You always have been."

Fred yanked his chin from Laura's grip. He looked over her shoulder at the bodies behind the table. He closed his eyes and turned away.

"I believe that the girls fell," Laura said. "But Carl? No. You killed him. Your hands are covered in blood, Fred. Tell me what happened. Now!"

"It started as an argument. That was it. Things escalated. He came at me with a dagger. He ... He refused to admit it. I know ... I know, Laura. I know!"

"Know what?"

Fred looked up and peered into his wife's ice blue eyes.

"I know about the affair!"

"Bobby!" Laura cried. She shoved Fred aside and ran toward the side door of the barn.

Bobby was standing in the doorway, his jaw agape, as he stared at little Rosalyn speared on the pitchfork in the middle of the barn. Laura threw herself into Bobby's arms and buried her face in his chest. He pulled her close as she began to sob.

"Marilyn?" Bobby asked.

"Our precious Rose," Laura whispered back.

Fred stared across the barn, confused by the embrace between his wife and friend. He adjusted his grip on the machete and headed over to the pair. Bobby did not release Laura as he approached.

"What the hell happened in here, Fred?" Bobby asked.

"Fred killed Carl!" Laura cried.

Fred rested his hand on Laura's shoulder, but she yanked it away.

"Don't touch me!" Laura yelled. "Murderer! You killed him! You killed them all!"

Bobby cautiously glanced down at the blood-drenched machete in Fred's hand.

"You want to explain yourself, Fred?" Bobby asked. He unfurled Laura from his embrace and stepped forward. Fred slowly backed away.

"It was an accident. The girls ... they ... they fell. I swear!"

Bobby stepped past Fred and walked over to the ladder in the center of the barn. Blood had stopped running down the handle of the pitchfork. The wooden handle was now a deep burgundy color. The rungs that held the pitchfork in place were also covered in blood. Bobby looked into the eyes of his daughter. He allowed a single tear to fall. *I will have to mourn later.*

"What about Carl?" Bobby asked. "Mary?"

Fred pointed to the table. Bobby walked to the other side of the barn and stood next to the two dead bodies. Fred followed him.

"We got into an argument. It got heated. He grabbed a dagger. It was self-defense. Honest."

"What were you arguing about?"

Fred turned around and pointed at Laura.

"Her!" Fred bellowed. "I told him I knew about the affair. And that bastard child!"

Laura took several cautious steps toward Fred and Bobby. She stopped at the ladder and looked at her daughter.

"What affair?" Laura asked. She glanced at Bobby and then at the table.

Bobby looked down at the collection of knives spread across the top of the workbench. He casually made his way past Fred until he was standing next to the daggers.

"I heard you on the phone last night, Laura," Fred continued. "I was outside on the porch. I heard you say that Rose was not mine! Do you deny that?"

Laura looked over at Bobby. He started to reach for one of the daggers. She subtly nodded "no" to him.

"Not your child?" Laura asked with confusion. "I remember you asking me who I was talking to. I ... I told you it was Carl."

Bobby withdrew his hand from the table, leaving the knives in place.

"He denied it!" Fred said angrily. "He denied the whole thing. But it's true, isn't it? Do you admit that it's true, Laura?"

Laura darted her eyes back and forth between Bobby and Fred as her mind raced to recall exactly what she and Bobby had discussed on the phone.

"Fred, what exactly do you think you heard me say?"

"You said to Carl 'our daughter' was driving you crazy! You asked if Jennie was suspicious! You said you loved him!"

Laura looked at the contorted remains of her daughter. Her

fear and panic over Fred's possible discovery of the truth about her and Bobby were suddenly replaced with anger. Rage began to churn from deep within her gut. She felt her hands clench into fists.

"You are a fool!" Laura thundered. She stormed across the barn, grabbed the machete from Fred's grip, and flung it to the ground. "All of this death because you heard wrong! You are a jealous stupid man! You heard it all wrong!"

Laura pushed Fred aside and made her way over to the other side of the wooden table. She knelt between the bodies of Marilyn and Carl and shook her head. Bobby and Fred watched with a mix of concern and confusion.

"Carl and I used to joke that Mary and Rose were twins separated at birth," Laura said. "He would sometimes make light of the fact that Mary was really mine and Rose was Jennie's. Jennie and I always dressed them the same. He said that we never knew who had which child. It was all in jest."

"That's nonsense, Laura," Fred bellowed. "That doesn't explain the affair ..."

"There was no affair!"

"You asked if Jennie knew ..."

"Jennie's birthday is next month! I was helping Carl to plan a surprise for her. That was the big secret!"

"But you ... you said that I ... I was clueless."

"Because you are!"

Laura stood up and walked over to her husband. She jammed her finger in his chest and glared into his eyes.

"I didn't want you to know what Carl and I were planning because you would have ruined the surprise for my sister! You can never keep a secret, Fred. Ever!"

Fred felt his heart begin to race. Beads of sweat started to form along his brow. His mind began to replay yesterday's phone call that he overheard. Laura's explanation had him completely confused.

"But you ... you said you loved him."

"He's my brother-in-law! Of course I love him!"

Fred looked down at the bodies of Carl and Marilyn and began to cry.

"Look around!" Laura cried. "Look what your stupid,

clueless jealousy has resulted in!"

"I ... I ... I really thought that you and Carl ... that Rose ... Rose was ..."

"I can honestly say that Rose is not Carl's daughter," Laura said. She was struggling to regain her composure and calm herself down. "Has there ever been any hint of an affair between Carl and me?"

"No," Fred replied. He sighed as he wiped the tears from his face. "That's why that call you had with him shocked me."

Laura let out a long slow exhale as she turned to face Bobby. The tension, confusion, fear, and anger were all subsiding. She felt as if a bullet had been dodged. Her secret with Bobby was still safely hidden from her husband.

Bobby stared at Laura with a mix of awe and pride. Fred was shaken and broken. Laura had utterly destroyed him. He looked down at the bodies of Mary and Carl, and then over at Rose. He realized there was a much bigger issue that had to be dealt with.

"Fred, I need you to look me in the eye and tell me the truth," Bobby said. "Did the girls die by accident."

Bobby walked over to the corpse of Rosalyn, mangled atop the pitchfork. The tines were covered in fragments of entrails and clothing. He dropped his head, took her hand, and kissed it.

"They fell," Fred said. He turned and looked back at Bobby and Laura. "I swear! I killed Carl in self-defense, but the girls ... the girls ..."

Bobby walked over to Fred and put a calming hand on his shoulder.

"It's OK, Fred. I believe you. I need you to give me a hand."

Bobby climbed up a couple of rungs and slid his arms under Rosalyn. Fred grabbed the pitchfork as Bobby took another step up and pulled her body up from the tines. Fred gently pulled the pitchfork down and out, away from her body. Bobby brought Rosalyn down from the ladder and lovingly lowered her to the floor.

"My precious Rose!" Laura cried. She ran over and fell to her knees, resting her head on her daughter's face.

"What are we going to do?" Fred asked. "I ... I have a record.

You know my past, Laura. I can't get convicted! I can't go to jail!"

"But you killed Carl, Fred!" Laura yelled. "You admitted it!"

"Laura, if I go to jail then you lose this house. You won't be able to care for the kids. You know that."

"You and your damn temper," Laura continued. "A jealous rage that had no bearing on the truth! Carl should not have died, Fred."

Bobby quickly ascended the ladder to inspect the loft. He found the dolls the girls had been playing with. He returned to the main level of the barn and picked up the doll that Rosalyn had dropped.

"I need everyone to calm down," Bobby said. His tone was calm and reassuring. "Fred is right, Laura. You have to think about your family. Fred is the only witness to what really happened in here. Laura, you are covered in blood from Carl and Rose. Your hands and fingerprints are everywhere in here, including the machete."

Laura looked down at her blood-stained apron. Anxiety began to wash over her as she noticed her fingernails were caked in blood. She began to nervously rub her hands across her apron.

"Do you really want Susan and the twins exposed to all of this?" Bobby continued. "Do you want the twins to know their dad killed their uncle? Even if it was in self-defense. They will never look at him the same way again."

Fred and Laura stared at one another, saying nothing.

"And what about Jennie?" Bobby asked. "Her and Carl have been fighting for months over his state of mind. How would she cope with this loss? None of them can know what happened here."

Bobby grabbed the pitchfork from Fred and shook it back and forth.

"Even this!" Bobby said. He walked over to Marilyn's mangled body. "Do you want them seeing Mary's contorted body? This pitchfork covered in blood?"

Fred knelt down next to Laura and attempted to console her. She pushed him away. He turned back to Bobby.

"So, what do we do, Bobby?" Fred asked.

Bobby rested the pitchfork up against the table. He looked around the walls of the barn and the posts at the stalls. Each column had a large hook protruding from the front side. Two of the hooks had large canvas tarps hanging from them.

"OK. OK. I ... I have a plan. It will only work if we all follow it. Everyone needs to focus. We don't have much time."

TWENTY THREE

Point of No Return

Tom had taken refuge behind a cluster of pine trees situated on the opposite side of the driveway, halfway between the house and the barn. A large shrub gave him additional shelter from a direct line of view from both the barn and the house. The sky had darkened with menacing black clouds. Thunder rumbled off the coastline, but the impending rain had yet to fall.

Tom polished the lenses at the end of his binoculars and sat up high enough so that he could see over the bushes. He held the goggles to his eyes and focused on the interior of the barn. The front door was partially open, allowing him to see a portion of what was inside.

He couldn't see Julie, but he saw an old woman standing talking. She was having a conversation with someone outside his field of view. He adjusted the focus ring as he scanned the rest of the space. There were two large tables separated by a giant pot, resting above a fire pit. He quickly realized that the small fire was not the only source of light in the barn. Tom refocused on the rear of the interior and noticed two gas lanterns anchored along the main beam supporting the loft.

Tom zoomed in on the lanterns. He steadied his arm as best he could to keep the image from shaking. He followed the lines connecting the lanterns, but his limited view prevented him from seeing where they led. Tom lowered his binoculars and sat down behind the safety of the trees.

Now what? Tom wondered.

A gust of wind rushed past Tom, followed by a crack of thunder off in the distance. He heard a loud creak come from the barn. The wind had forced the door to open wider. He saw Julie, tied up in a chair, facing the old woman. He was relieved to see she was still alive.

Tom's backpack was resting behind the shrub. He put his binoculars inside and pulled out his cell phone. The lock screen image of Mrs. Closed came to life.

Where are you?

Tom opened his archery case and removed one of the bows. Another blast of wind shot across his face. Tom put the bow on top of the case and took a deep breath. He closed his eyes and recalled Marc telling him that when it came to fight or flight, he had to work on his fight. Then he remembered his conversation with Julie at the restaurant when he told her what he would do if he ever saw Mrs. Closed again.

Am I a killer?

Tom opened his eyes and stared at the bow for several seconds, debating what to do next. He lowered his weapon and picked up his phone. Tom's hands trembled as he unlocked his phone and called Officer Stevens. Beads of sweat formed across his brow as he worried what the cop would think of them playing detective. After several rings, the call went to voicemail.

"Hi, it's ... it's Tom. Jewels and I did not leave town. We ended up following that Jeep. She ... she got captured. She's tied up in a barn. I'm ... I'm looking at her right now. You can scream at me later for disobeying you, but I'm afraid she is going to be killed. We need you. We need the police. I'm going to send you our location. Please hurry."

Tom ended the call. The feeling of relief that washed over him was immediately interrupted. A scream echoed from within the barn. He stood up to get a better look. The old woman was jerking Julie by her hair.

Jewels!

Tom pulled up his location on his phone. Just as he hit the

button to send it to Officer Stevens, an arrow tore through the center of his cell phone, ripping it from his hands. The blade on the arrowhead sliced through Tom's right hand, between his thumb and index finger.

Tom gasped but did not scream. He dropped to the ground and took shelter behind the pine trees. The arrow that had snatched the phone away from him landed at the base of the tree a few feet away. Tom inspected his hand that had been sliced open. The wound was not that deep. Tom took a few deep breaths to try to calm himself down. He looked back at his shattered phone pinned to the tree. The bright yellow fletchings at the end of the arrow fluttered in the wind. Tom stared at them in disbelief.

Is that the arrow from the store?

Tom followed the shaft of the arrow to the impact point in the pine tree. Half of his phone was pierced and embedded in the tree. The other half was nowhere to be seen.

Did he get my location?

Tom looked at the arrow again, taking note of the angle and trajectory. He realized the arrow had to have come from the house.

Tom glanced down at his blood covered hand, and then over to his backpack. He spread his body flat on the ground and wiggled over to his bag. Tom pulled out a roll of gauze and quickly bandaged his hand. He then retrieved his binoculars and peered through the branches of the shrubs. His target was the second floor of the old Victorian house.

The corner window was open. Tom adjusted his focus ring. He immediately caught a glimpse of Mrs. Closed holding a bow and arrow. Tom crawled back behind the pine trees for shelter.

Daylight was quickly fading. The sun would set soon, and the storm hanging off the coast had blanked the outer Cape in cloud cover. Tom looked over at his phone dangling from the side of the tree. He then looked at his archery case.

Tom pulled the case closer and did a quick inventory. There were a dozen arrows, all of which had simple bullet tips for arrowheads. He remembered his instructor Rick telling him he would need to get broadheads for hunting.

What will these do?

Tom moved to the side of the pine tree and looked over at the barn. Despite the door being wide open, he could not get a clear look inside. He was too far off center. He would need a more direct line of sight.

Fifteen feet past the shrub was another cluster of trees and bushes. Tom determined it would give him a better view into the barn, as well as shelter from the house. He zipped up his backpack and slid it over his shoulders. He tossed his gear back into his archery case and stood up.

I hope this works.

Tom flung his archery case over to the cluster of trees and shrubs. It landed exactly where he had hoped it would. He waited briefly to see if another arrow would fly, giving him time to make a run for it while she reloaded. All was quiet.

"Well, here goes nothing," Tom muttered.

Tom exploded into a sprint. After a few long strides, his left foot caught the edge of a root. He stumbled just as he dove behind the trees. It was not the most graceful landing. He spun around to inspect his legs and feet. Tom let out a sigh of relief as he realized he had not been shot. He removed his backpack and was surprised to see an arrow sticking out of the back. Tom reached inside his pack and pulled out his binoculars and turned his attention back to the inside of the barn.

***

Laura placed a copy of the book *Urban Legends of Cape Cod* on the desk in front of Julie. Julie stared at the book. The binding was cut, and there was a gash through the front cover.

"A little memento from the night Sara tried to kill you," Laura said smugly. "Maybe one day *your* story will end up in a future edition of this book."

Laura snatched the book from the desktop and walked back over to the metal table. Two tarps were resting across it. She began to spread them out across the table.

"I always keep a little something from each ... incident," Laura said. "That candle I showed you earlier. It's just one of many that we've made here in the barn."

Julie watched as the old woman took her time to unroll and stretch the tarps across the table. She looked over at the front door wondering where Sara had gone. Julie's right hand was free, but her left was still tightly bound. She could not get it to loosen up.

"Remember those candles that you and your friends broke at the store?" Laura asked. "I have a set of those as well. They are hidden away. Like so many family secrets. Speaking of which ..."

Laura turned and walked back over to Julie. She laid her hands on the desk and leaned forward.

"The legend in that book talks about the bones being wicks. You may have noticed that our candles don't have bones in them. They really don't make good wicks."

Julie clenched her fists as her heart began to pound in her chest. She looked over at the main door. All was clear. She wiggled her left hand, but it was still locked in place.

Should I strike? Julie wondered.

"So, you don't have to worry about us chopping you up to turn your bones into wicks," Laura continued. "No dear, it's your tallow I am after."

Tallow?

Laura ran her right hand across Julie's chest.

"I've never worked with this much raw material before," Laura said. "I really don't know what to expect when I cut you open. That poor Asian woman was as flat as a board. But she had some nice belly fat. And honestly, that's the best source of fat for tallow. In the end, she did make a nice sesame-scented candle. I put her husband in the ginger ones."

Laura turned and headed over to the wooden table on the other side of the cauldron.

Julie glanced over at the "Seabreeze" candle resting on the corner of the metal table. She felt her throat begin to close up. Her heart began to pound hard in her chest.

Laura reviewed the tools spread across the table and picked up a jagged tooth saw. She smiled as she walked back over to Julie.

"All of the candles we've made here have been to punish

those that disrespected us. I know that may sound cruel, but I have to protect my family. To take care of those that I love. That's why we do these candles. There is only one time that we made a candle out of love. The rest? Yours? Well ..."

Laura folded the desktop away from Julie and rested the saw across her legs.

"Time to pay."

TWENTY FOUR

Rosemary

1984 Saturday 25-Jun 1:30pm

Sweat poured down the face of Fred Johnson. The armpits of his shirt were soaked. He clenched the wheel of his Jeep Cherokee as he and Bobby pulled up to the big Victorian house. He parked next to Carl's Caprice. The wraparound porch of the dwelling was empty. The area around the barn was also deserted. Fred shut off his vehicle and turned and looked at Bobby for direction.

"Good, they still aren't here," Bobby said.

"What if they are in the barn?" Fred asked.

"So what? It won't change things. Just stick to the plan."

Bobby looked at Fred's sweat-stained shirt and frowned.

"And Fred?"

"Yes?"

"Relax. Just stick to the plan. This will all work out."

The two men exited the Cherokee and made their way to the side of the barn. Apollo came running out from the barn. Fred stuck his head inside and glanced around. He was relieved to see nobody was inside. He looked over at the ladder. The faint scent of varnish from the freshly stained rungs still hung in the air. The entire floor of the barn was covered in a fresh batch of hay, concealing the blood-stained floor. It was a temporary solution that they would rectify later.

Bobby walked behind the barn. The picnic table was covered in a flowered plastic table cloth. Bright blue plastic clothespins secured the corners, preventing the occasional gusts from blowing the covering away. Multi-colored balloons dangled and bounced from the branches of the towering trees that surrounded the barn. A banner proclaiming "Happy Birthday" hung against the back wall. Below it sat two folding tables covered with plates, cups, and other items for the cookout. Nobody was around.

"Where are they?" Fred asked as he approached Bobby. "You don't think they went to the beach, do you?"

Bobby looked over at the path that led to the beach. He felt his pulse quicken. His concern was immediately broken as Jennifer, Susan, Emma, and Sara emerged from the narrow path that led to the pond.

"Fred!" Jennifer yelled out. "Have you seen the other two?"

Fred opened his mouth, but could not respond. He felt his eyes well up with tears. He just shrugged and shoved his hands into his pockets. Bobby studied Fred for a moment and frowned. He left Fred by the barn and headed toward Jennifer.

"Bobby, have you seen them?" Jennifer asked. "They weren't at the pond. I only found these three."

"You don't listen, Mom," Susan said. "I told you they love to go exploring. They ran off with their dolls after dad took the pictures."

"I don't listen?" Jennifer abruptly turned around and jammed her finger into Susan's chest. "It was your job to watch your sister!"

"They went to the beach," Bobby said.

"The beach?" Jennifer asked as she spun around.

Bobby looked back at Fred, but he could see he was frozen in terror.

"Carl took them earlier," Bobby continued. "Laura went to get them a few minutes ago."

"Carl should know better," Jennifer replied. "The waves are way too rough today. I hope he didn't let them go swimming. Do you know if that was the plan? What did he tell you when he left?"

"Me?" Bobby asked. "He, uh, I ... I didn't see him leave."

"Well, then how do you know where he went?"

Bobby looked into Jennifer's eyes. He could see the look of concern spread across her face.

Dear God! Mary. Our Mary! Bobby thought to himself. He closed his eyes.

"Jennie ..." Bobby said.

"Jennie!" Laura screamed as she emerged from the path that led to the beach.

Bobby opened his eyes. Everyone turned toward the path. Laura was running as fast as she could. Tears ran down her cheeks. Her face was pale. Her mouth agape as she wheezed and struggled to breathe.

Jennifer began to run toward her.

"Jennie!"

Laura ran into her sister's arms and began to cry on her shoulder.

"What?" Jennifer screamed. "What is it, Laura?"

Laura gasped as she tried to catch her breath. Her lungs burned from the long run she had made from the beach. She pushed herself away from her sister and leaned forward, resting her hand on her knees.

"We need ..." Laura said. "We need to ... the girls. The beach."

Laura looked over at Fred, Bobby, and the three girls. She stood up and took a deep breath.

"Fred," Laura said. "You stay here with the girls, OK? Bobby, I need you and Jennie to come with me. Now!"

Laura did not wait for a reply. She turned and ran back down the path she had just emerged from. Bobby and Jennifer quickly followed.

"What's going on, Uncle Fred?" Susan asked.

Fred stared at the path and closed his eyes. He could not think of a single response that would not result in him bursting into tears.

***

It took a few minutes for Bobby, Jennifer, and Laura to reach the beach. They had to stop a couple of times for Laura to take a moment to catch her breath. The path ended at a pair of enormous sand dunes. All three clawed their way to the top. Once there Jennifer began to look around.

"What is it, Laura?" Jennifer asked. "What are we looking for? You wouldn't say a word on the way here. Where are the girls?"

Laura did not respond. Her shoes filled with sand as she descended the ocean side of the dune. When she got to the bottom, she pointed to an alcove against the side of the cliff just south of where she was standing.

Jennifer stared at the body reclined against the gritty hardened wall. The wind blew sand across her face, blurring her vision.

"Who is that?" Jennifer asked as she flicked her eyelashes to clear them. Her eyes scanned the figure again. "Carl?"

Jennifer ran toward Carl. She stopped several feet from the cliff and fell to her knees. She began to scream.

Carl was impaled into the side of the cliff, with a machete sticking out from his abdomen. The nickel and turquoise embedded in the handle glistened in the afternoon light.

Bobby knelt next to Jennifer and put his arm around her.

"What happened?" Jennifer asked. "I ... I ... I don't understand."

Laura stood behind her sister and stared at Carl's body. She ran her hand across the top of Jennifer's head and walked around to be in front of her sister. Laura sat down in front of her, blocking her view of Carl's body. She gently took her hand.

"Jennie," Laura said. "It's not just Carl. There's ... there's more."

"More?" Jennifer asked as she wiped the tears from her cheeks.

Laura nodded toward the sea.

Jennifer turned and looked back at the rumbling waves of the Atlantic. The sky was crystal blue. The wind was strong and covered her face in salt and sand. Her eyes slowly scanned the shoreline, until they came to rest on two small piles at the edge of the sea. Her heart sank.

"What ... what is that?" Jennifer asked. Her voice trembled as she struggled to contain her sobbing. "Is ... is ... that? No. No!"

Jennifer pushed Laura and Bobby away and ran toward the sea. Each step brought her closer to a terror she could never have imagined. She collapsed in front of the two bodies lying in the sand and began to wail.

Rosalyn had been sliced in half. The little girl's eyes were closed, and her hair was caked with sand. Jennifer knew it was Rosalyn because of the white shoes she was wearing. The other body, with the yellow shoes, had no head attached to it. Both children were missing their hands.

Laura knelt down next to Jennifer, and the two sisters embraced and sobbed. Bobby walked past them and approached the shore. The waves were rough today. He searched the shoreline until he found what he was looking for, roughly fifty feet away. He headed north, to retrieve Marilyn's head.

***

Laura stood at the entrance to Bobby's house, staring at the doorbell. She raised her finger to the buzzer, but then lowered it. Her thoughts were a jumble.

What do I say?

The door suddenly swung open.

"Laura!" Bobby said. He stepped forward and threw his arms around her. "It's been weeks since the funeral. I thought I would never see you again."

Laura did not return the embrace. She slid her hands into her pockets and waited for Bobby to release her. Bobby kissed the top of her head and tried to tilt her head up, but she resisted.

"Please come inside," Bobby said.

Laura took a few steps in and turned around.

"I've held off from driving over," Bobby continued. He closed the door and walked over to Laura. "Why ..."

Laura slapped Bobby across the face.

"How could you?" Laura screamed.

"What?"

"Those bodies! What you did to those bodies! Marilyn. Rosalyn. Our precious Rose! You butchered them!"

Laura burst into tears. Bobby tried to pull her close, but she pounded her fists against his chest. He stood there, silently taking the blows.

"Did you forget our plan?" Bobby asked.

Laura stopped hitting him and looked up. Her face was wet with tears.

"Our plan did not include you mutilating those bodies!"

Laura pushed Bobby away. She turned and walked over to the sofa in the living room, collapsing on the far end. Bobby quietly sat down next to her and took her hand in his.

"Laura, the plan was to make it look like Carl killed the children and then committed suicide."

Laura wiped the tears from her face and stared at Bobby. She felt her defenses weaken as she looked into his dark brown eyes.

"We both know how the children died. I had to cover all of that up. I removed Marilyn's head to get rid of the fact that her neck had been twisted and snapped. And Rosalyn ... our ... our precious Rose. Cutting her in half got rid of the punctures from the pitchfork. Her spine had been pierced. I had to hide the truth."

Bobby stood up and walked to the other side of the room.

"Do you think I enjoyed doing that to those kids?" Bobby continued. "I had to smash Mary's head against a rock to mask the impact her skull made to the table!"

Bobby began to sob. Laura ran over to him and threw her arms around him.

"I'm so sorry, Bobby. I didn't know. I didn't ... I didn't understand."

"What kind of a monster do you take me for?"

Laura took Bobby's hands in hers and led him back to the couch. Bobby put his arm around Laura, and the two sank back against the cushions. Laura kissed his hand and wrapped her arms around his waist.

"I have a question, Bobby. Why ... why didn't you let Fred

take the fall? There was a moment. A brief moment in the barn after you came in and saw what happened. If we'd just turned him over to the cops, we'd be together. We'd finally be together!"

"Because he was right, Laura. If he went to jail, you would end up losing that home. You could never afford it on your salary as a substitute teacher. His future pension and inheritance matter. That income is too important for your future. For *our* future. If he went to jail or divorced you, you would be penniless. This little two-bedroom home of mine is nowhere for us to raise a family."

"I suppose. I guess I hadn't really thought it through."

"Besides, can you imagine the emotional toll on the twins if their dad was arrested for murder? Or your relationship with your sister? She's already a wreck because of Carl."

Laura ran her hand across Bobby's chest and allowed herself to enjoy his scent. They had not been this close in a very long time. She forgot how much she missed his touch.

"Jennie has been beside herself with the loss of Mary and Carl. I've been over there almost daily to check on her and Susan."

"Now imagine she knew the truth. That Fred killed her husband. Not only would she disown you, but she'd have no one but Susan to care for her. You are family. What we did will keep that family bond together. As best it can. We all lost so much in that barn."

Laura leaned up and kissed Bobby on the cheek.

"I'm sorry I doubted you, Bobby. I've been so confused. I just love you so much."

"I love you too, Angel."

Laura pulled herself to the edge of the couch, propped her elbows on her knees, and rested her chin in her hands.

"What is it?" Bobby asked.

"Our precious Rose. She's gone. Gone forever."

Bobby sat up and put his arm around Laura and kissed the top of her head.

"Not forever."

"I know. She'll always be in our hearts and memories."

Bobby stood up and took Laura by her hands.

"Not just that, Laura. I have something I want to share with you. Come with me."

Bobby and Laura made their way through the kitchen and exited the back door. They crossed a small fenced in yard and approached a dilapidated work shed in the back corner of the property. Laura stopped a few feet from the entrance.

"Isn't this where you make your sausage? You've never let me in there."

"It's fine. Please."

Bobby opened the door and allowed Laura to enter first. The stench of rancid meat gave her pause as she stepped into the disheveled workspace. There was a small window above a tool rack a few feet from her. She walked over and opened it to get a breath of fresh air. A goat briefly stuck its head in through the window, before sauntering away.

"Sorry about the mess," Bobby said. "I wish I had as much room as that big barn of yours. Someday."

Bobby turned and pulled a glass candle off the shelf closest to him. He put it down on the table next to Laura.

"I made these," Bobby said. "To honor our girls. There are three of them."

Laura picked up the small mason jar candle.

"Three?"

"Yes. One for you, another for me, and the last one for Jennifer. Go ahead. Open it."

Laura grabbed the metal wire tab with her thumb and released the seal. She freed the tab from the clip and flipped the lid open.

"Take a whiff," Bobby said quietly.

Laura raised the candle to her nose and inhaled.

"Rosemary? Where did you ..."

"I went to see your sister the day after everything happened. She's not well, Laura. She blames herself for Carl's apparent suicide."

"I know. It's horrible. I keep trying to tell her it's not her fault."

"Apparently they had been fighting that morning. I did my best to calm her down. I took the rosemary from their herb garden out back. That's where I got the scent from. Carl loved that garden as much as Jennifer."

"It's lovely." Laura slid the candle closer to her nose and inhaled again. "This is indeed very special, Bobby. Rose and Mary. So sweet. Thank you for this."

Laura returned the candle to the table and leaned into Bobby's embrace. He kissed the top of her head.

"There's one more thing, Laura. You can't burn these candles, OK."

"Oh, I would never want to. Well, maybe once or twice a year. Perhaps their birthdays?"

"No, Laura. I'm sorry, but you don't understand. You can't burn them because they won't burn. It's the wicks, Laura. The wicks are special. This may upset you, but I wanted these candles to really honor the children. Let's ... let's sit down."

There was a small bench under the table in the middle of the shed. Bobby dragged it out and dusted the top off. He put his arm around Laura, and the two sat next to each other. Bobby grabbed the candle from behind him and set it on his lap.

"I make the candle wax using tallow and a few other things. It's a family recipe that's been handed down over the years. Tallow is basically animal fat. In addition to the wax, you need to make the wicks. Our family recipe is a special one. This isn't something you would do for just any candle. It's for a candle for ... well ... for remembrance."

"Bobby, I'm not following. I thought Jennie's herbs were what made these special. The scent. The names. I'm not ..."

"The rosemary was for that. Yes. The family recipe includes something else. More."

"More?"

"It includes a part of the person you want to remember."

"A part? Bobby, what are you saying?"

"The wicks, Laura. I made the wicks from the bones of Rose and Mary."

Laura pried the candle from Bobby's hands. She held it close to her face and stared into the candle jar. Two pointy wicks were jutting through the sage green wax. They stood less than an eighth of an inch high. Laura held the jar up to the light so she could get a better look.

"They don't look like bones."

"Trust me, they are in there. I used finger bones. There are two wicks in each candle. Each candle has one from each child."

Laura inhaled the fragrant scent of rosemary one more time before sealing the jar shut.

"I ... I don't know what to say, Bobby."

"One more thing, Angel. Each candle also has just a bit of fat blended in as well."

"Fat? Fat from where?"

"The tallow, Laura. When I make candle wax I use the fat from my goats. For these candles, I also made sure to include a tiny bit of fat that I took from each of the girls."

Laura stared at the candle jar and then back to Bobby.

"Where ... how ..."

Bobby took the candle from Laura and ran his finger across the edge of the lid.

"Like I said, this process has been handed down from generation to generation in my family. We've used it anytime a family elder has passed away. That candle on the mantle over the fireplace is one."

"The one next to the picture of your grandfather?"

"Yes."

"You mean he's?"

"Yes."

"My God. I ... I had no idea."

Laura took the candle from Bobby and opened the cover again. The twin wicks and the sage green wax suddenly looked wholly different to her. She could not stop staring at it.

"And Carl?" Laura asked. "Is he ..."

"Just the girls."

"This is truly beautiful."

Bobby watched as Laura's ice-blue eyes studied the small glass mason jar.

"Would you like to learn the recipe?"

TWENTY FIVE

Bullseye

Tom grabbed an arrow from his case. The bandage wrapped around the palm of his right hand was soaked in blood. He attempted to make a fist, but the pain was too severe. He wiggled the fingers of his injured hand and looked over at the barn. Tom estimated the entrance to be roughly 40 meters away.

But how far in do I have to go? He wondered.

Tom removed his binoculars from his pack and focused on the interior of the barn. He was shocked to see the old woman holding a saw in front of Julie.

Jewels!

Tom tossed his binoculars to the ground and leaned back against the tree behind him. The wind from the offshore storm rushed by, rattling the leaves and branches of the shrubs.

Tom knelt beside the cluster of trees, making sure he was still out of view from the house. He nocked his arrow onto the bow and took aim at the barn. The shrubs were a few feet tall. Tom attempted to shoot through the branches but quickly realized this was not an option. He would have to risk exposing himself to the second floor of the house.

Tom stood up and stood as close as possible to the large pine tree by his side. He closed his eyes. He tried to picture himself back on the practice field, with Rick coaching him.

Rotate your bow elbow out. You only want the tips of the fingers on the bow. Keep your body in a T shape.

Tom opened his eyes and focused on the old woman standing over Julie.

Are you a hunter?

Tom adjusted his aim a few inches and to the side, to compensate for the wind.

Am I a killer?

Tom lowered his weapon as he struggled to answer the questions that were swirling in his head. He knew he had to act. Time was running out. His heart pounded in his chest like a caged animal. Tom jumped as an arrow raced past his right arm. The yellow fletchings were a blur as the projectile disappeared into the forest beside him.

Tom shook it off and quickly took aim once more. His right hand screamed in pain as he pulled back on the bow. He felt the cut in his skin rip open. Blood began to run down his wrist. His hand began to shake as he struggled to keep tension on the string. The rustling of the branches and leaves quieted down as the wind subsided. Tom took direct aim at the old woman's head, tilted his weapon higher, and released his arrow.

Tom exhaled as he lowered his blood-soaked hand. The red and white fletchings fluttered as the arrow blasted its way into the barn. Traveling at 150mph, it barely made a sound as it flew past Julie and the old woman. The arrow's journey ended as it crashed into the lantern centered on the beam of the loft.

Bullseye!

Tom collapsed to the ground and took refuge behind the cluster of pine trees. He grabbed another role of gauze from his pack and began to wrap his bleeding hand.

The arrow had not only shattered the lantern, but also the valve assembly at the end of the hose. The twisted remnants of the old lamp had become a miniature flame thrower. The beam with the lanterns anchored to it began to burn.

Laura screamed at the sound of the exploding lantern. She ran to the back of the barn and tossed the saw onto the table. As Laura looked up at the fire, the remains of the arrow fell to the ground. She picked it up and studied the blue shaft with the red and white fletchings.

"What is this?" Laura cried in bewilderment. "This isn't Sara's!"

Julie looked over at the arrow and immediately recognized the colors and construction. A wave of hope washed over her. She slid her right hand free and began to untie her right foot.

Without warning, a second arrow ripped through the barn. It flew high above the loft, embedding itself in a pile of hay. Seconds later another arrow whistled through the air, shattering as it struck the beam. Laura looked around, bewildered and confused.

The hose attached to the lantern suddenly tore itself loose as a fourth arrow impacted the clamp that was holding it against the beam. The gas line was now free and began lashing around in circles, shooting flames across the rest of the loft.

"Sara!" Laura screamed. "Sara! Hurry!"

Laura did not wait for her daughter to return. She ran to the back corner of the barn to turn off the main valve that fed the lanterns.

Julie now had both legs free. She stood up and ran around to the backside of her chair and began to untie her left wrist. The flames were starting to spread across the ceiling of the barn. The entire loft was ablaze. Julie glanced over at the lone cow that was in a stall beneath the loft. The animal was in a panic.

Laura ran over to Daisy and opened the pen. Daisy ran past her, knocking her to the ground. The cow ran out the side door, lowing in fear and confusion.

Sara came running into the barn carrying her bow and a handful of arrows. The site of the fire roaring overhead forced her to slide to a halt. The loft and large sections of the ceiling were covered in flames. The air inside the barn was filled with the odor of burning hay. Sara looked down at her mother lying on the ground in front of the stalls. She ran over to help her, tossing her weapon to the ground.

"Mother!" Sara cried.

Laura sat up as Sara fell to the ground by her side. The roar of the flames from above grew louder as the heat began to build up in the barn. Beads of sweat began to form on Laura's forehead. She wiped them away as she looked up at the blaze above her head.

"I'm fine, Sara. It was Daisy. I ... I had to free her."

"We have to get out of here!" Sara yelled.

"Wait."

Laura raised her arm and pointed toward the corner of the barn. Sara turned to see what she was looking at.

Julie was standing next to her chair, rubbing her newly freed left wrist. Small pieces of hay began to waft their way down from the overhead rafters.

"No loose ends," Laura said.

Sara looked at her bow lying a few feet from Julie at the other end of the barn. She stood up and attempted to take a deep breath, but coughed from the soot and smoke that was beginning to surround her. Sara walked over to the table next to her and grabbed a dagger. The blade shimmered from the fire blazing across the ceiling.

"Where do you think you're going?" Sara asked Julie. "Your friend is dead. I shot him in the back."

Julie turned and looked at the exit. Her thigh throbbed from the knife wound. The roar of the fire reverberated in her head as her mind raced through her options. Julie paused, turned, and glared across the barn at her two jailers.

Julie clenched her fists and took a couple of steps toward the metal table in front of her. She closed her eyes and recalled her last conversation with Julio. *I am strong. I am confident. I believe.*

"There's nowhere you can run," Sara said as she made her way toward Julie.

Julie looked at the bow and arrow resting beside her feet. She briefly considered picking it up, but knew it would be useless. Burning chunks of the roof began to fall to the ground between the two women. The crackle and roar of the burning ceiling had become deafening. Sara continued her march toward Julie. She pointed her dagger in front of her as she passed the cauldron.

"Time to pay," Sara said.

Julie kept her fists clenched. Her entire body felt like it had become one with the floor. She kept her eyes on the dagger as it got closer and closer. At the last moment, Julie leaned back and kicked her right leg forward. Her foot landed dead center into Sara's stomach.

Sara dropped the dagger as she stumbled backward. She gasped for air as she tried to catch her breath, but her lungs only filled with soot. The knife was resting on the floor halfway between her and Julie. Sara coughed as she grabbed the metal bowl from the table and flung it at Julie. Julie quickly knocked it away. The bowl tumbled across the ground, stopping beside the stainless-steel table.

"This is for Tom!" Julie yelled.

Julie took a few steps forward until she was only a couple of feet from Sara. Her injured leg wobbled briefly until she locked it to the ground. She leaned back at the last second and thrust her leg into Sara's gut, knocking her away.

Julie watched as Sara's arms flailed as she fell backward, landing directly against the cauldron. Sara screamed from the searing pain from the hot iron pot and fell to the ground. She tried to use her legs to push herself away from the firepit but ended up knocking two of the base keystones loose. The pile of rocks shifted, and the cauldron started to tip sideways.

"No!" Laura screamed from the back of the barn. "Sara!"

The weight of the massive pot was too much, and the rocks completely gave way, sending the cauldron tumbling to the ground. Sara cried out as the molten tallow gushed across the floor, engulfing her legs. Julie took several steps backward and leaped onto the chair. Sara used her arms to drag her body forward. She cried out in pain as she glared at Julie.

Sara paused as bits of burning straw fell to the ground in front of her. The flickering bits of hay reminded her of the fireflies that danced across Flicker Wood Pond. Her memory vanished as embers from the firepit rolled onto Sara's body, igniting her clothes. Her hands inched their way toward Julie. Sara's screams subsided as her body came to a halt. Bubbling tallow wrapped itself around her melting burning body.

"Jewels!" Tom yelled.

Julie spun around to see Tom standing in the front doorway. She could barely hear him over the thunderous roar of flames that had engulfed the ceiling. Her eye burned from the ashes that were swirling around her. She turned and looked back at the body of Sara as it continued to melt into the floor.

"Jewels! Hurry!"

Julie looked at the back of the barn and saw the old woman crawling toward her daughter. The fire had punched several small holes through the roof, but it was not enough to clear the air. Black smoke filled the upper half of the interior of the barn. The support beams began to crack and moan from the intense heat and fire. The sound of splintering wood and roaring flames was overpowering.

Laura came to a halt a couple of feet from the body of her daughter. The tallow was still liquified due to the extreme heat inside the barn. Sara's clothing was still on fire. Laura reached out to her daughter, but the tallow prevented her from getting close to her. Tears ran down Laura's face as she looked up at Julie.

"You will both pay for this!" Laura cried.

Julie jumped off the chair, landing just on the other side of the puddle of tallow. She stumbled and fell as her feet hit the ground. Julie looked up at the ceiling. The blinding orange flames began to fade from view as black smoke began to descend and fill the barn. She knew there was no way she could stand up without being consumed by the smoke.

"Mark my words, this is not over!" Laura yelled.

Julie turned and looked at Tom. She was now on her hands and knees, scrambling to get to the door. The exit was only twenty feet away, but Julie felt like it was a mile away. She began to cough and gasp as soot entered her lungs. Tom crouched down below the smoke and ran inside. He pulled Julie to her to her feet and threw her arm around his neck.

The scorching heat had become unbearable. Tom turned back and began to lead them to the door. The exit was barely visible through the smoke. Julie was limping from her injured leg, but Tom forced her to run. The fire bellowed and growled as it continued to consume the barn. She pressed her head against Tom's shoulder and covered her other ear with her hand to try and drown out the noise. Tears ran down her face as she gasped for air. They sprinted through the door just as one of the support beams surrendered to the inferno and crashed to the ground.

Julie tried to slow down once they got a few feet from the barn, but Tom would not stop. He adjusted his arm around Julie and pulled her up, forcing her to run faster. The deafening roar of the fire had subsided, but they could still hear the beams snapping and breaking. Tom guided her across the driveway until they were behind the shrubs and pine trees where he had left his gear.

Tom sat Julie up against the cluster of trees and held her upright as she coughed and gasped for fresh air. Burnt pieces of hay clung to her hair and clothing.

"Are you OK?" Tom asked.

"She said you were dead!" Julie cried. "I saw your arrows. I knew you were here. But then she said she had killed you!"

Julie began to shake and cry. Tom pulled her close and kissed her on the head.

"I'm fine, Jewels."

Julie grabbed Tom's hand with the blood-soaked bandage. "Fine? What's this?"

"It's just a cut. You don't have to worry."

"She said she shot you in the back. Are you really OK?"

Tom pointed to the shrubs next to them. His backpack was resting on the ground, with the arrow still sticking out of it. Julie managed a slight chuckle.

"That fucking bag really is a lifesaver, isn't it?" Julie asked.

"I think it hit one of the stainless-steel mugs. Like I said, Jewels, I'm OK."

The barn let out a groan as the remaining support beams struggled to keep the walls in place. Black smoke billowed into the sky. The wind rushed in from the coast, pushing the smoke toward Tom and Julie.

"She's still in there," Julie said.

"Who?"

"The mother. Didn't you hear her? She said ..."

The support posts could no longer take the ever-shifting weight of the burning roof. One by one the beams gave way, each cracking loudly as they shattered. The sound of the wood beams snapping echoed against the trees as the barn collapsed onto itself. The ground shuddered from the impact. Smoke, embers, and dirt blasted across the land for hundreds of feet.

Tom and Julie dove deeper behind the trees to take shelter. Julie buried her face in Tom's chest as she waited for the air to clear. Tom closed his eyes and covered his nose and mouth with his bandaged hand.

Several seconds passed as they waited for the dust to settle. The barn was still ablaze, but it was now a hulking pile of searing timber. The wind continued to blow in off the ocean, keeping the flames from spreading to the house. The sky became black from the mix of clouds and smoke.

"We need to get out of here," Tom said softly.

Julie stood up and looked over at the burning barn. The cow that had run off earlier was several dozen yards away staring at the burning structure. The dog was nowhere to be found.

"We need to call the cops," Julie said.

Tom pointed to the tree with the arrow in it. Julie walked over and picked up the remnants of his phone resting at the base of the tree. She glanced back at the Victorian home.

"Maybe we use the phone in that house?" Julie asked. "I bet if we wait here long enough someone somewhere will call the fire department."

"No. We can't be here when they show up. As you so often like to say, Jewels, we need to be elsewhere."

Tom walked over and snatched the arrow from the tree, along with the chunks of his phone. He then grabbed the lone arrow that had strayed off into the woods. Tom put all of it into his archery case.

"Your leg," Tom said as pointed to her blood-soaked thigh. "What happened?"

"Sara did that to me. It's not that bad."

"Who?"

"Mrs. Closed."

"We both need to get to a hospital. Besides, your phone is back in Ruby. At the beach. It's a long walk. Can you make it?"

Julie looked over at the burning barn. Faint drops of rain began to blow against her cheeks. She walked out past the shrubs and looked up at the sky. The rainfall started to intensify. She smiled as the water began to run down her face.

"You don't happen to have an umbrella in that bag, do you?"

Tom picked up his archery case and backpack and walked over to Julie. He handed her his pack.

"What do you think, Jewels?"

Julie reached into Tom's bag and pulled out a small black umbrella. Tom tossed his backpack over his shoulder. Julie opened the umbrella and put her arm around Tom. The rain intensified as the two made their way around the burning barn, and headed to the path the led to the beach.

TWENTY SIX

Closure

The smell of roasted chicken filled Tom's kitchen. Max was laying in the hallway staring into the room. A small puddle of drool had pooled beneath his chin. Julie was standing at the island opening a bottle of Malbec.

"Oh my God, that smells amazing."

"It's really not that hard to make, Jewels. I can teach you."

"Why bother when it's easier for me to just come here?"

Tom chuckled as he selected a pair of wine glasses from the back cabinet.

"Right as always, Jewels."

Tom slid the glasses over to Julie, and she began to pour the wine. He then opened the oven and removed the pan with their dinner. He placed it on a hot mat in the middle of the island. Max stood up and licked his lips.

Julie smiled as she looked at the dinner that Tom had prepared. The roasting pan was filled with potatoes, onion, and broccoli, along with the fully baked chicken. Julie leaned over and took a whiff of the meal.

"Is that ... rosemary?" Julie asked.

"Yes. I grow it fresh."

Tom pointed to the window on the opposite side of the kitchen. He had three small pots with a variety of herbs in them. Julie stared at his makeshift garden and frowned.

"Why?" Tom asked.

"Like I have to ask?"

Tom began to remove the vegetables from the pan to place them into a large bowl. His right hand was bandaged, resulting in his fingers having a limited range of motion. Julie reached over to help him.

"I've got it, Jewels."

Julie grabbed their glasses of wine and set them on the table. She waited and watched as Tom struggled to carve the chicken.

"Have you heard from Trevor today?"

"No. He's been pretty quiet all week."

"It's been two weeks. You'd think he'd have answers by now."

Tom carried two plates over to the table. One had half of the chicken carved up, while the other was filled with the vegetables. Max walked into the kitchen and took a strategic position just behind Julie.

"Do *not* feed him, Jewels."

"I know the rules, Tom."

Tom sat down across from Julie. She immediately began to fill her plate.

"Tom, do you think we made a mistake when we left Wellfleet?"

"We've been through this already."

"We didn't tell the police the truth."

"Of course we did."

Julie took a sip of wine and studied Tom's face.

"We never told them you shot out the lantern. You told them nothing about the arrow fight."

"It wasn't a lie, Jewels. It was an omission."

Tom filled his plate and took a bite of chicken. He frowned and grabbed the salt and pepper to season it.

"What did you do with them?" Julie asked.

"With what?"

"The arrows. Your old phone."

"Oh, it's long gone. I dumped them in a trash bin behind the pharmacy up the road. Including my personal set of arrows."

Tom took a big sip of wine and looked over at Julie. She had stopped eating.

"Relax, Jewels. It's fine. Everything will be fine."

"It just doesn't feel right."

"Do I need to remind you that you also left a few key pieces out of your story?"

Julie looked down at her plate of food and sighed. She suddenly had no appetite.

"That was different."

"We did the right thing, Jewels. Listen. If you'd told the cops that you kicked that woman into the firepit, they could have charged you with murder."

"But it was self-defense."

"Excuse me, Miss Paralegal, do you know what you would have gone through if you had played the self-defense card?"

Julie took another sip of wine and nodded.

"I know. It's just that I ... I ... I don't know, Tom. It doesn't feel right."

"All they needed to know was what we told them. You were abducted against your will and tied up. Trevor has my voice message to back all of that up. After that, it's just our word. That giant makeshift firepit in the middle of the barn fell apart, starting the fire. It was a shitty old barn. You ran out in the commotion just as the building collapsed on itself. I was there hiding and waiting for Trevor to arrive. End of story."

Tom tossed a chunk of potato into his mouth and raised his eyebrows as he waited for Julie's reaction.

"I agree with you, Tom. I just don't have to like it. I mean you took evidence with you, and then destroyed it."

"Oh shit," Tom added. "That reminds me."

Tom excused himself and walked into his bedroom. Max watched him until he was out of sight. The dog then turned his attention back to Julie.

"Those killers are dead, Jewels," Tom called out from the other room. "At the end of the day, that's all that matters."

Julie looked down at Max. He raised his head and flipped his ears forward. Julie quickly tossed him a chunk of chicken. He snatched it from the air.

Tom returned, carrying a small plastic bag and handed it to

Julie.

"We don't need to get implicated in any of this," Tom continued. "They kidnapped you and tried to kill you. They also killed Marc and Chris. The Seabreeze candle you told me about? I can't even imagine ... Look, we were the victim. Those bastards got what they deserved."

"What's this?"

"Open it."

Julie reached in and pulled out a pair of sunglasses. The frame was bent, and the lenses were missing. Julie's eyes widened as she inspected the coloring of the frame.

"Are these ... Tom! These are Chris' glasses!"

"I found them in front of the shrubs by the house. They were crushed in the ground. I tossed them in my pack and then forgot about them. I found them last night when I was restocking some supplies for it."

Bits of sand fell from the cracks in the frame. Julie ran her hands across one of the temples.

"Tom, this is another piece of evidence! Why would you take this?"

"Honestly, Jewels, I forgot all about it. I can ship it to Trevor this weekend. Unless ... unless you want to keep it."

Julie stared at the mangled frames. A chill ran down her spine as she tried to wonder what happened to Chris and Marc in front of the house. Or inside of the barn. Her thoughts were interrupted by the ring of Tom's phone.

Tom pulled the phone from his pocket and smiled. He accepted the call and put it on speakerphone.

"Hello Officer Stevens," Tom said.

"How are you this evening?" Officer Stevens asked.

"Just fine."

"Hey Trevor," Julie said.

"Miss Perez. Why am I not surprised to find you are there with Tom? Am I interrupting?"

"Not at all," Tom replied.

"We have the results back from what we found at the barn. We've identified two victims from the fire."

Tom smiled and took a sip of wine. Julie felt her heart race as she stared at the phone.

"The first is Sara Johnson. Julie, that's the woman that you identified as having attacked you at the Seabreeze condo complex last December, as well as abducting you the other week. Her body was partially recovered."

Julie looked over at Tom and exhaled a long, loud sigh.

"The other was her mother," Officer Stevens continued. "Laura Johnson. She owned the house, and her daughter lived with her. We got a positive ID on the mother from her dentures."

"Dentures?" Tom asked.

"They were found under a crushed metal bowl. We were able to get a match."

"What ... what about her body?" Julie asked.

"Nothing positive yet. There weren't many bones in all of that rubble. The fire was very intense. Half of Sara's remains were mostly ash. We have to assume that the other bone fragments are from the mother."

Tom and Julie stared at one another for a few moments, silently taking in the news.

"What about Marc's truck?" Tom finally asked.

"For all we know it ended up in some chop shop somewhere. Listen, Tom, you and Julie need to let this go, OK? The remains of your friends have been found. The two that did it are dead. You are both safe. Celebrate that, OK?"

"You're right, Trevor," Julie said. "I promise you we are done. If Tom gets out of hand, I will just call his mom."

Trevor burst into laughter. Tom glared at Julie.

"Thank you," Julie continued. "Thank you for everything you've done for us."

"Just doing my job. You two take care. If you have questions, you can call me. The formal statement on our findings has already been issued. Enjoy your weekend."

The call ended. Tom returned the phone to his pocket.

"Wow," Julie finally said. "Is it really over?"

Tom walked over to the island and grabbed the bottle of red wine. He brought it back to the table and refilled their glasses.

"I think it finally is, Jewels."

Tom sat down and took a sip of wine. Julie had a blank expression on her face as she cut into her chicken.

"Are you OK?" Tom asked.

"I ... I think so. It's just all ... all so surreal. Still."

"What is?"

"The events at the barn. I ... I have to ask you. Do you? Did you?"

"What?"

"Did you mean to kill her?"

"Who?"

"The mother. When you shot out the lantern. I never really asked you. Were you aiming for the lantern? Or ... or her?"

Tom turned and looked out the kitchen window. The sun had set, and the sky was a deep cobalt blue. A handful of stars shimmered across the evening sky.

"For a very brief moment, Jewels, I ... I almost killed her. I mean, I had her in my sights, you know? I just ... I just couldn't. I don't know why."

"Because you are a sweet man, Tom. It's who you are."

Tom sighed as he took another sip of wine.

"That was a compliment!" Julie said with a slight chuckle.

"I know, Jewels. There was a small fraction of a moment where I almost did. I just couldn't. So I aimed for the lantern instead. Trust me, I was shocked I hit my mark. Twice! But what about you?"

"Me?"

"You and Sara. Did you ..."

"I already told you it was an accident! All I was trying to do was kick her away from me. I never meant to ..."

"Detective Valley has some bad-ass moves, doesn't she?"

Tom grinned as he raised his glass and held it across the table.

"As do you, Detective Wood," Julie replied with a wink. She held her glass up and clinked it against Tom's. They both took a sip.

"In the end Jewels, the only thing that matters is they are dead. We didn't intend to kill them. All I was trying to do was save you. And you were saving yourself. They killed our friends. This nightmare is over. It's finally over."

"Speaking of nightmares, I haven't had any since we got back."

"See. We can finally move on with our lives. We can finally move forward. Have fun. Like we talked about in Eastham."

"And we're never going back there, Tom. Ever. I'm done with the Cape. We need to vacation elsewhere next time."

"Ditto on that, Jewels."

TWENTY SEVEN

Reflections

The Subaru Outback Sport slowed as it approached the old Victorian home. The remnants of the barn sat in a pile of charred timber and ashen gray soot. Bright yellow police tape surrounded both the debris and the house. The vehicle crawled along the driveway until it came to a stop in front of the main entrance to the home.

The driver emerged from the chunky green hatchback. Enshrouded in a black hoodie, the figure glanced around the vast property. The stench of burnt wood was still present, despite the fire having been extinguished weeks ago.

Zeus emerged from the path that led to the beach. He was thin. Weak. His rib cage pressed against his skin. The dog growled. He was intent on protecting his property. He approached the figure with caution.

The figure knelt down and waited. Zeus began to whimper and quickly ran to the person, wiggling his bum with joy. After giving the dog a brief pat on the head, the pair made their way toward the front porch. Zeus bounded to the doorway and began to scratch his paws against the frame. The figure slipped under the yellow tape and cautiously ascended the stairs.

Zeus' new friend pulled out a key and unlocked the front door. The dog pushed the door open with his nose and ran down the hallway to the kitchen. The stranger followed. Once in the kitchen, Zeus was quickly rewarded with a bowl of water and an even larger bowl of kibbles.

As Zeus consumed his meal, the person walked over to a doorway off the kitchen and opened the door. The stairway to the basement was pitch black. A faint light at the bottom of the stairs illuminated the floor. A flick of the light switch at the top of the stairs confirmed there was no power in the house. Zeus stayed in the kitchen as the hooded figure descended the staircase.

The basement was vast and made up of several large rooms. A handful of narrow windows cast a small amount of light into the area. It was a dank, dusty space. The figure maneuvered through three of the rooms, stopping at a workbench in the far corner of the basement.

The wall had two narrow wooden shelves perched above a dust-covered workbench. They had a handful of glass candle jars spread out across them. Beneath the table sat several heavy wooden boxes pushed back against the wall. After dragging them out of the way, the stranger began to feel along the back wall, searching for the small recessed latch.

There it is.

It took a few tugs before the narrow doorway swung open. The stranger stood up and grabbed a candle and book of matches. Once the candle was ablaze, the figure entered the hidden passageway.

After crawling for several feet, the tunnel widened, and the stranger was able to stand up. A string of lights hung from the top of the tunnel, suspended from a wooden ceiling. The unlit bulbs and wiring were covered in soot. The walls and floor were composed of cement and caked in patches of mold and fungus.

After a dozen yards, the path came to a fork. The tunnel to the right reeked of ash and feces. The channel to the left was long and had a faint unsteady light at the end. A dull droning howl could be heard in the distance. The figure turned and proceeded down the corridor toward the light.

The stranger paused just outside the entrance to the room at the end of the passageway. All was quiet, but for the sound of the wind and a plinking noise. The hooded figure stepped into the room and looked around. The howl was coming from an air vent in the ceiling at the back of the room. A shelf along the side wall contained rows of canned beans and vegetables. A faucet was attached to a pipe sticking out of another wall. It dripped into a metal bucket, half filled with water.

There were other shelves with a variety of daggers and knives. The uppermost sill had several mason jar candles across the top. None of them were lit. A large round coffee table sat in the middle of the room. It was filled with a variety of candles in different shapes and sizes. All were ablaze. The figure turned and looked at the sofa at the far end of the room.

Laura Johnson sat quietly on the couch, enjoying a can of beans. She motioned to the chair across from her. The figure walked over to the chair and sat down. Laura leaned forward and smiled as the stranger lowered her hood.

"Emma!" Laura said, exposing her toothless grin.

***

Emma Johnson ran her hands across the back of Zeus' neck. The kitchen floor was littered with droplets of water and several uneaten bits of dog food. The dog had consumed two bowls of water and three servings of kibble. He was now sitting by her side, resting his weary head on her thigh. Her focus was not on Zeus, however. It was on the sage green candle sitting in the middle of the table. The stairs at the top of the hallway staircase let out a loud creak.

"This should be fun," Emma said sarcastically.

After a few moments, Laura Johnson entered the kitchen.

"All refreshed?" Emma asked.

"As fresh as one can be with no hot water. I wonder if the tank in the barn can be salvaged. It's under all that rubble somewhere. Maybe Bobby can get it running again."

"Bobby? So, he's still in the picture?"

Laura glanced around the kitchen.

"Thank you for putting this back together for me," Laura said. "The cops really made a mess of this place."

Laura pulled out the chair opposite her daughter and joined

her at the kitchen table. She smiled as she reached out and took her by the hand.

"It's so good to see you," Laura said. She ran her fingers across Emma's face, brushing her bangs away from her eyes. "I like your hair short like this. You look good, Emma. Fit. Sara had really let herself go."

"How are the teeth?"

Laura slid her index finger into her mouth and ran it across the side of her gums.

"These old dentures fit poorly. They never fit right after cracking that back tooth. That's why I had replaced them last year. But they will have to do for now."

"For now? Mother ... you ... you do know that everyone thinks you're dead. You and ... and Sara."

"Yes, dear. You told me when we were in the bunker."

"Well, you won't be getting new dentures anytime soon. Or a working propane tank. I honestly don't know what you have planned. What? Will you miraculously come back to life?"

"Why? Did you already have my funeral?"

"No, I didn't have a funeral. But ... but ... the funeral."

Emma lowered her head and rubbed her fingers across her eyes. She looked up and frowned.

"What about it?" Laura asked with amusement. That amusement turned to concern as she noticed a look of worry cascade across her daughter's face. "What is it?"

"The funeral. You missed it. I just realized that you ... you don't know."

"Funeral? What? Not ... not ... Jennie?"

Emma nodded as she stood up and walked over to her mother. She put her arms around her and pulled her close. Laura's face became flush as she buried her head into her daughter's chest.

"When? How long ago?"

"It was the day of the fire. The day that you called me from the barn."

Emma kissed the top of her mother's head and rubbed her back. Laura released her embrace and motioned for her daughter to sit back down.

"I knew she was ill. Susan told me she didn't have much

time left. Did you know that Sara and I had stopped in the night before?"

"I did. Susan told me."

Laura glanced over at the mason candle jar sitting between her and Emma. A single tear made its way down her cheek as she thought of little Rose and Jennie's family and what might have been.

"We both lost our sisters that night," Laura said solemnly.

Emma lowered her head and quietly nodded in agreement. The past weeks had been filled with a lot of drama for Emma. She'd had so little time to consider that both her aunt and sister had died on the same day.

"I waited too long to reconcile with her, Emma."

"You tried, Mother. Aunty Jen was the stubborn one. Just like Sara was with me."

"That's still no excuse," Laura said. She began to sob. "If I've learned anything these past weeks trapped in that bunker, it's that the bonds of family should never be broken. I never should have walked away from my sister. I never ... I never should have let you run away."

"Well, I'm here now, Mother. We'll figure this out, OK?"

Laura nodded as she wiped the tears from her cheeks. She looked up at her daughter and smiled.

"We will get through this," Laura said. "Together. We are family, Emma. It doesn't matter how long we've been apart. Our bond. Our blood. We must stick together. Now, more than ever."

Emma stood up and walked over to the porch door. She glanced out at the pile of wood and ash that used to be her family barn. After a few moments, she turned back to face her mother.

"Then let's start with the truth," Emma said. "I want to know what happened out there."

"The truth?"

"I've seen the police reports ... the news ... They say that you and Sara tortured a girl out there. They say that ..."

"And they are wrong!"

Laura stood up and joined Emma by the door. She pressed her hand to the glass and looked out across the yard. Even with the doors and windows closed she could still smell the charred remains of the family barn.

"You only know half the story. I promise I will explain it all to you at some point, Emma. Just not today, OK? I'm a bit tired after all that time in the bunker."

Emma sighed as she studied her mother's face. She looked old and frail. Weeks of living on canned food and water had taken their toll.

"I know we have a lot of history to get past," Laura said with sorrow. "So many things to tell you. I have to earn your trust back. I do."

Emma led her mother back to the kitchen table. Laura's gate was slow. She still had not recovered from her fall in the barn. The bruises still ached. She held her daughter for support as they sat beside one another.

"What next, Mother? Do you want me to call Jeff?"

"Jeff? No. We can't pull the police into this yet."

"But he's family."

"He may be family, but I don't know where his loyalties are."

"Loyalties? Mother, we need ..."

"We need to be discreet, Emma. At least for now. At least until this is finished."

"Finished? What else is there? I don't understand ..."

Laura squeezed her daughter's hands and smiled.

"I know you don't. There is a lot to explain. I just can't right now. You ... you aren't ready. I'm not ready."

"Ready for what?"

"To hear the truth, Emma."

Emma let go of her mother's touch and shoved her hands into her pockets.

"Why is everything such a big secret in this family? Aunty Jen was just like you! It drove Susan and me crazy. Anytime we'd ask questions about events from our childhood we'd get these half answers or obvious lies. If you want my help, Mother, you are going to need to be honest with me."

"And I will be, Emma. Let's just take this day by day for now, OK? Let me earn your trust. Let me tell you what really happened in that barn. Everything those horrible kids did."

"What *they* did?"

Laura paused, unsure of how much to tell her daughter. She knew she had to proceed with caution if she was going to regain her trust.

"To your sister. You weren't there. The police weren't there. I was. I watched it all happen before my eyes."

Laura pulled the hem of her dress up above her knee, exposing a wide purple bruise on her thigh.

"I was on the ground. Injured. The barn was already on fire. Sara tried to save me. Those kids killed her, Emma. Knocked her right into the fire. That girl did. Burned her alive. Right in front of me. I watched your sister burn to death!"

Emma stared at her mother, studying her eyes. Searching for a hint of truth. Looking for a potential lie. She did not know what to say. What to believe.

"When you know the whole story, you will know I'm being honest. No more secrets, Emma. Once you know everything, you can decide what happens next. If you want to call Jeff and the police we can do that. But right now ... right now I need to rest. Should we stay here or at your place?"

Emma studied the lines on her mother's wrinkled face. Her ice blue eyes looked hollow. Empty.

"My place? The world thinks you're dead. How can I hide you there? I know you don't trust Jeff, but he's family, and I think ..."

"Enough, Emma! I don't have the energy for this. I look in your eyes, and I see Sara. But your words ... your words are not hers. Please stop arguing with me. Sara would understand. Sara would support me. I wish you would as well."

"I'm sorry to be such a disappointment. I'm only trying to be realistic."

Laura sighed with frustration.

"I'm sorry, Emma. That was unfair of me. It's foolish of me to expect you to be like Sara. You honestly never were. She was the short-tempered one. You were the thinker."

"That's what I'm trying to do, Mother. Think this through."

"I know you are. So alike. So different. I'm ... I'm sorry you never got to say goodbye."

Emma lowered her head as she thought about the decades

that had passed, the missed adventures she could have had with her sister, and of a future that would never be.

"I was fortunate enough to make peace with my sister," Laura continued. "I got to say goodbye. Jennie forgave me on her death bed. I think in that moment she realized we never should have stayed apart. Unfortunately, you never got that chance. I'm so sorry you got dragged into all of this."

"Don't apologize. For what it's worth, I'm ... I'm glad you survived."

"I just ... I just miss Sara right now. Seeing her die that way. I ... I can't think clearly. I'm sorry. I can't argue with you when you don't know the full story. The truth. And I'm too tired to explain it all. If Sara were here right now she ... she would ... Well, she would know what to do."

"What to do?" Emma asked. Her tone was soft as her eyes wandered toward the window overlooking the rubble.

"She was always there for me when I needed her to be. Don't get me wrong. Sara and I fought all of the time. But in the end, she wouldn't question me. It's sort of funny. Sara was always the fighter, and you were the peacemaker. And here you are arguing with me. Being the opposite."

"Opposite?" Emma stared at her mother, lost in her thoughts.

"Why the confused look?" Laura said with concern. "I'm not judging you. All I meant is there is a lot of Sara inside of you, despite your differences. She was your sister. Your twin. Flesh and blood. That's a special bond, Emma. A family bond that you will carry forever."

Emma looked back to the window, past the pile of gray rubble to the path that led to Flicker Wood Pond. She closed her eyes and recalled her childhood adventures and dreams she had shared with her sister. Their bond. Their blood bond.

"Excuse me," Emma said.

Tears ran down Emma's face as she made her way to the small bathroom in the hallway. She instinctively flicked the light switch. She sighed realizing there was no power. She grabbed a few tissues and wiped her face dry. Emma looked at her reflection in the mirror. The ambient light in the hallway cast a faint glow across the right side of her face, leaving the rest shadowed in darkness.

Emma placed her hand against the mirror.

"Sara ..."

Emma ran her index finger against the mirror, drawing a circle around her face. She recited the poem from her youth.

> If I'm unsure and feeling blue,
> It only takes a look from you.
> Do I see me?
> No, I see ... I see ... we.
> Your eyes will tell me what ... what ... to do.

Emma felt her heart begin to pound hard in her chest. Her cheeks became flush with pulsing blood. She realized she would never be able to recite this poem with her sister again.

Emma let out a roar as she smashed her fists against the mirror. The glass shattered into a dozen pieces. As her scream died down, she looked at her hands. She was surprised they were not bleeding. She looked at her fractured reflection in the shards scattered across the inside of the sink and began to cry.

"I don't know what to do, Sara. What should I do? What ... what would *you* do?"

Laura appeared in the doorway and looked at the broken mirror over the vanity. Emma was still staring into the sink.

"I heard the glass break," Laura said with confusion. "What happened? Are you hurt?"

Emma spent a few moments studying her shattered reflection before she answered.

"She's gone. Forever."

Laura put her arm around her daughter. She pulled her close and kissed Emma on the cheek. Emma began to sob on her mother's shoulder.

"Let it out," Laura said. She took Emma by her hand and led her toward the kitchen. "I didn't mean to upset you. It's wrong of me to expect you to suddenly trust me the way Sara did. You've been away from home for so long."

Emma shook as the tears ran down her face. She held her mother for support as they entered the kitchen and sat next to one another at the table.

"Give me time to earn your trust, Laura said as she wiped the tears from Emma's cheeks. "You have doubts. I understand why. There is so much to tell you. I promise you there will be no more secrets. No more lies. Just the truth."

Laura reached across the table and pushed the sage green candle toward her daughter. The mason lid top was sealed shut. It was still covered in dust from years of storage.

"Why did you bring that up from the bunker?" Emma asked. Her eyes had finally dried, and the tears had stopped.

"Do you recognize it?"

Emma leaned forward and carefully picked up the candle. She turned it around in her hands a few times to inspect it.

"I've seen this before."

"Open it, Emma."

Emma pried the metal tab up, releasing the seal on the mason jar. She flipped the top back and took a moment to study the two small wicks that were barely protruding from the surface of the leathery wax top. Ever so slowly, she raised it to her nose and inhaled.

"Rosemary," Emma said softly. She took a longer deeper breath and smiled. "Aunty Jen had a candle just like this. It was always in her bedroom."

"What did she tell you about it?"

"Nothing. It was one of those family secrets she refused to share. She said it was very special, and that Susan and I could never light it. We never understood why."

"She never told you where the candle came from?"

"No."

Emma placed the candle on the table and closed the top.

"I noticed the bunker had several of these candles down there. They were all different colors."

"So observant," Laura said proudly. "Those candles are all part of our family history. Part of the secrets that were kept from you."

"What makes it so special? I remember ... Didn't? I thought Aunty Jen said it was made for her. Who made it?"

Laura smiled as she cleared the dust from the top of the mason jar. She opened the lid and stared longingly at the green wax. *My precious Rose.*

"It's not so much who made it, Emma. It has more to do with how it was made."

"How? What's in it that's so special?"

"It's an old family recipe. I promised you no more secrets. No more lies. I think it's best that we start at the beginning. With the candles."

Emma took possession of the candle from her mother, raised it to her face, and inhaled.

"Aunty Jen had an herb garden. Is the rosemary from her garden? Is that what's in it?"

Laura leaned forward and wrapped her palms around the back of her daughter's fingers so that all four hands encircled the candle jar.

"The recipe is a family secret, Emma. I have a lot to tell you. We have to rebuild our trust, first. Our bonds. Then, and only then, will you be ready."

"Ready for what?"

"To learn the recipe."

EPILOGUE

Never underestimate the bonds of blood and family. Their power can be both caring and ruthless. The seeds of vengeance are not planted by hate. They are sowed with love and warmth. Family cares. Family loves. Often at all costs.

Urban Legends of Cape Cod

Author – Unknown

ACKNOWLEDGEMENTS

I have learned so much since publishing my first novel. I truly feel that *Rosemary* is a huge leap beyond *Urban Legend*. As I have stated before, Urban Legend underwent a heavy rewrite for the Second Edition. This was based on knowledge gained from a seminar that I attended, as well as feedback from my new editor. That direction gave me fresh insight into story construction and telling. At this point in my life, Rosemary was already 80% completed. That didn't stop me from going back and doing many changes to update the story.

I feel *Rosemary* would not be possible without the support from my family, especially my mom and my sister Lori. Lori was the first person to read my completed draft. Her insight into my early drafts has always been spot on. I highly value her encouragement and feedback.

For *Rosemary*, I took grammar checking into my own hands leveraging some new software. It found items missed by human proof-reading, as well as helped me to refine my writing style.

I'm very excited about the next – and final – book in the Tallow Series. That novel has been in outline form for almost a year. Unlike *Rosemary*, I will be starting the manuscript with a fresh perspective. There really won't be much rework needed. I have no idea if the story will surpass *Rosemary*, but I am going to do my best to make it a killer of an ending.

ABOUT THE AUTHOR

MJ Howson was born and raised in Providence, Rhode Island. He spent many summers enjoying Cape Cod as well as the local state beaches of his home state.

Ever since college, MJ always thought he would write a book. There is a saying: "Life is what happens when you are busy making plans." After a successful career in IT, MJ finally decided to commit the time and dedication to write his first book. That novel, *Tallow – An Urban Legend*, quickly turned into the first in a series of books. Originally planned as a standalone story, once completed MJ realized he could not let go of the characters or mythology he had created. Prior to releasing his first book, he immediately set about planning the final two stories. *Tallow – Rosemary*, is the middle child in what he hopes will be a thrilling trilogy.

MJ adopted the tag line "The Terror is Real" as the focus for the Tallow Series. Escapist, paranormal, and supernatural stories are always good for a scare. The tales that run the risk of being able to come true, however, are the ones that can really haunt you.

You can connect with MJ via his website. From there you will find links to his different social media accounts.

www.mjhowson.com